OUTSTANDING PRAISE FOR
KOLYMSKY HEIGHTS:

"Davidson writes with the icy freshness of his Siberian setting. Everyone will be staying up past bedtime to discover the next sharp turn in the snow." —*People*

"The best spy thriller in years." —*Houston Post*

"Written with the panache of a master and with the wide-eyed exhilaration of an adventurer in the grip of discovery. Mr. Davidson has not only rescued one of the most familiar narrative forms of the era, the spy thriller, he has also renewed it."
—*The New York Times Book Review*

"Storytelling at its very best . . . Stunningly written . . . Thoroughly researched." —*Boston Globe*

"As good an adventure story as you will find this year."
—*Wall Street Journal*

"Shameless, wonderful, riveting entertainment."
—*Publishers Weekly*

"Davidson has created one of the most riveting characters in recent fiction. His presence keeps this taut thriller moving toward its satisfying conclusion."
—*Library Journal*

St. Martin's Paperbacks titles
by Lionel Davidson

KOLYMSKY HEIGHTS

THE MENORAH MEN

THE ROSE OF TIBET
(COMING IN APRIL 1996)

NIGHT OF WENCESLAS
(COMING IN JULY 1996)

LIONEL DAVIDSON

THE MENORAH MEN

St. Martin's Paperbacks

THE MENORAH MEN

Copyright © 1966 by Lionel Davidson.

Library of Congress Catalog Card Number: 66-21717

ISBN: 0-312-95815-3

Printed in the United States of America

Harper & Row edition published in 1966
St. Martin's Paperbacks edition/ January 1996

10 9 8 7 6 5 4 3 2 1

To Fay

Prologue

DECLARING THE END FROM THE BEGINNING

The things that are not yet done.
—Isaiah 46:10

I CAME OUT by the north, it has to be understood, and turned north, myself, ten men and twenty pack animals, with thirty days' rations.

We ate frugally, each man hoping to return with his surplus, no doubt bearing in mind that former occasion when even birds' dung had to be sold for food—at ten pieces a quarter, as history records and as we understand it.

We traveled by night, the consignment as follows: in plain terms, each beast one hundred kilograms; the total two thousand kilograms, all ingot, private ingot.

For the rest, the sergeants carried the OEED and the corporals its equipment. The private soldiers carried the implements, shovels, picks and crowbars.

In one hundred and five kilometers, as understood, we reached the area and buried the OEED. For the highest security, the private soldiers and myself only were parties to this operation. It was not witnessed. It is here: at a depth in plain terms of two meters, well-bound, covered with a layer of crushed marble, blue marble, and protected by slabs; the disposition according to the separate list.

The ingot is elsewhere, without such security, in several situations, the dispositions according to the separate lists.

After all the work we returned, more plainly myself, two officers, two sergeants, two corporals, four men. At the first halt the sergeants and corporals called aside the men in pairs and strangled them.

At the second halt, when the animals were foddered, each corporal was set to work separately, and as he worked was strangled, by the sergeants, working together; all this work with cords, and to the letter; all buried with appropriate rites.

At night in our camp, the two sergeants also, as they slept, by the officers, working together; this work by knife; all to the letter, with burial and rites.

The two officers are sworn men. No blame attaches to them.

Immediately the work was finished, we struck camp and proceeded, but about midnight were challenged in the dark and forced to halt while a mounted party drew up, a strong party. Their leader—a captain, identified by our own officers—was plainly of Northern Command, I repeat it, of Northern Command, and showed signed orders requiring us to accompany him to his command headquarters.

If I acted wrongly, it was to protect security and because of insufficient information. No one informed me Northern Command was concerned in this operation. I could think of no reason why this Command should be concerned. The young officer could give no reason. Further, the terms of his orders required our whole operation, the consignment and the men, to be turned over to Northern Command, which was no longer possible; although all was done legally and to the letter.

I therefore refused to recognize his authority and was

immediately placed under arrest, and so we proceeded till two o'clock, when we reached a bivouac position amid rocks, and camped.

The young officer acted punctiliously throughout, and no blame attaches to him. He did not require me to sleep with the men, although he posted guards over me. The guards likewise showed all respect and allowed me, during the night, to go behind a rock with the animals to fulfill a need of nature; whereupon I mounted and escaped.

The alarm was immediately raised, and I was pursued; but in this difficult terrain my more intimate knowledge allowed me to elude them, and in the dark I practiced a simple stratagem, dismounting and sending the animal in one direction and myself in another.

The pursuit was properly conducted and no blame attaches. I watched it for several hours, from a height, until it was called off about midday and they returned and struck camp and left.

I had no food or water.

I waited till night before moving.

I was weakened by my exertions, and fell and broke my arm. The bone protruded.

I was in a fever and my condition deteriorated. I could not see my way to returning so I went in the direction of the watering place where the people knew me.

I descended in a feeble state, afraid of violence. They keep pickets watching. They fear guerrillas.

I lay till it was safe and entered the village secretly, and made toward a light, and saw to my joy it was the old perfumery. The watchman was tending the boiler.

He knew me from old times, a good man, not unlettered, and he is suitable. I swore him and he took me in. If my actions are illegal, no blame attaches to him.

He said to write down the day he died so they will know. It was four days after he come, the 22nd March he died. He said he tell me what to do when I bury him but he never, he was raving, so I took him at night in the flower basket and bury him up behind the spring.

I said peace on his soul and God be merciful, he is a good man, a priest.

He wouldn't let me get any help when his arm stank, he wouldn't let me tell anybody, but I told the priest who come for flower oil and he said I said right when I bury him, which I hope, but he is not a real priest, they keep a different date.

I wrote twice that he wrote, I did my best. He said to say where I put it. I put one in The Curtains, high, two hundred meters, the Curtain you cannot see from here, turned away. It is in the first hole, you get down from the top. I put another farther on, down low, the bottom of the cliff, beyond as you go.

One

ALTOGETHER BRUTISH AND FOOLISH

The stock is a doctrine of vanities.
—Jeremiah 10:8

1

THERE WAS NOBODY there when I arrived, nobody except Birkett and his wife, that is, which was a special penance. He was eating raisins and a stick of celery, and he didn't stop when he saw me, just nodded and continued masticating his mouthful, very slowly and thoughtfully. He was wearing his black rolltop sweater in some thin, probably nylon, material, which, together with his eyes, set rather too close together, one a little larger than the other, and his high daemonic cheekbones, gave him the appearance of a mad, elderly ballet dancer.

His wife had been engaged with a similar plate at the same small oak table, but she picked hers up and said, "Excuse me a moment," and went out with it. He continued chewing, nodding to show it would soon be over, and then finished. He didn't finish his meal; he just finished the mouthful, and seemed to go into neutral.

I said, "I'm afraid I've come too early."

He didn't say I hadn't. He just looked at me in his

earnest deranged way and said, "It will give us an opportunity to talk."

"We have to congratulate you," his wife said, returning with her thin grim smile.

"Naturally," Birkett said sincerely. "I've been wanting to for some time."

"Dr. Laing is a difficult young man to get hold of. Finish your meal, dear. You'll have a drink, Dr. Laing."

It was a statement rather than a question, and seemed to imply, in her curiously insinuating way, knowledge of some special range of characteristics of mine, such as dissoluteness, greed, opportunism.

I leaned back, already enervated. I'd caught her looking at my boots. The suede boots had seemed about right for the way-out lot to be expected here tonight. I'd put on a woolen checked shirt and an old tweed jacket, too; no-nonsense Laing. The effect couldn't, I saw, have been farther out if I'd appeared in a top hat and tails. Their own brand of no-nonsense was grotesque to such a degree that any other, any other involving suede boots, looked like racy affectation. Below the table I could see Birkett's small neat feet planted side by side in some no doubt relaxed yoga position, in black plimsolls. Above them his legs were in a pair of bleached jeans. His wife wore a gym slip with brown stockings and sandals. The enormous creature quartered the room in this getup, getting me a drink, and managing to imply at the same time some medical-type urgency for one who couldn't do without the stuff.

She gave me a glass with about a quarter of a pint of whisky in it, no water or soda, just the bare commodity; she really was a rather loathsome woman.

"I hope this is the way you like it."

"Thank you."

"I think I remember that you smoke, too. The cigarettes may be rather stale. We have no use for them." She'd sprung back from a cupboard with a china box.

"They'll have a bit of go in them, then."

"A bit of go," she said, and sat down, smiling grimly and obscurely, feeling the joke all over for spring traps and double meanings. I lit the cigarette and decided not to make any more. It was dangerous to make jokes here. It was dangerous to say anything. I took a sip of whisky and felt my teeth go on edge again; head still booming faintly from the morning's hangover.

"You're having a very busy time, Dr. Laing."

"Well. People are being amiable."

"They are always amiable to success."

"I'm sure you're right," I said. It was as well to be sure of that round here.

"A most richly deserved one," she said strongly. "That goes without saying. It's a surprising thing, all the same, for a man of your age to be given his chair."

"It's a narrow field."

"Perhaps," she said carefully. "And perhaps one that is also enjoying a certain fashionable interest at the moment, together with apparently almost unlimited funds. To say all this doesn't detract from the achievement, of course."

It did, of course. She'd seen where my guard had wavered and had come through in a flash; a skilled and experienced performer. She was good, this cow. The mindless euphoria of weeks dispersed in a moment. I took another sip of whisky and felt it go.

She sat smiling, hands in her lap, well limbered up now. She tried for another round.

"I expect it'll be a bit of a wrench, all the same."

"Well. After three years."

"Leaving the accepted disciplines of an old university for something quite—new?"

"Oh, of course. Certainly."

Nothing doing there, and she saw it. She moved on hungrily. "We have at last read a copy of your paper in support of Professor Gordon of Brandeis."

"The Eteocretans, you mean."

"Most brilliantly argued and individual." (*Flashy, rabble-fodder.*) "As I understand it, you take the position that the Cretan and Hellenic cultures share a common stock with that of the Northern Semites."

"Well, Gordon does. I was just able to wing in with a few thoughts on my chosen people."

"Your chosen people?"

"The Northern Semites."

"Ah, yes. They are Jews, are they?"

"Jews, pre-Jews, Syrians, Phoenicians. That lot."

She said, "That lot," smile well-diluted. "Yes. I must say I was much more able to understand your racy and amusing exposition" (*Clown. Popularizer!*) "than Professor Gordon's more taxing work. Although as I understand it, the position is not generally accepted."

"No. Well. The readings are all fairly tentative. The daftness has to come out early, you know. Apprentices like me are expected to fly about and make wild suppositions. Every now and again one of them might turn out to be right."

This modesty was both pleasing and aggravating to her in roughly equal proportions. Her hands moved restlessly in her lap. She was ready for a workout and all I was showing her was the shoulder, a small target, kept well in, moving fast.

She said, "Perhaps we'd better not discuss it now. I know Birkett wants to talk to you about it."

Birkett wasn't talking to anybody at the moment; unless, possibly, himself. I'd been watching with fascination a certain rabbity movement of his upper lip, not quite in phase with his chewing, that could have been a few obligatory sutras of the Bhagavad-Gita or simply some metabolism-controlling procedure. If he'd heard anything of the preceding rigmarole, which was doubtful, its essential malice had certainly escaped him. An odd bird, paralyzingly barmy, with his own unique facial blend reminiscent of an overwrought John Stuart Mill and a deathbed Picasso; a man courteous, mild and modest in all but his opinions, by which of course he had to make a living. He hadn't yet made the Chair in English Literature his wife lusted after. He wasn't ever likely to. A decidedly odd bird, and with a decidedly odd-bird coterie; for whom my boots, shirt and jacket tonight.

He finished eating and drank a glass of water and went out, gravely clearing his throat, and began to have a piddle next door. He had it apparently immediately behind my chair, apparently in the very center of the bowl, at immoderate length. We sat and listened, no trace of expression crossing his wife's face, all evidently in good and wholesome order.

"And what exactly," she asked at length, "are you supposed to be doing now?"

I told her what I was supposed to be doing.

"Oh, yes. I'd heard you'd run into difficulties."

"Expected ones. A lot of the stuff is out of print and I have to find it."

The uproar behind me continued unabated. I began to worry that the amazing little devil might through sheer absence of mind be piddling himself away entirely.

"When is it you take up residence at Beds?"

"At the end of January."

"But that's—what?—two months' time."

"Yes. I shan't be here all the time. I'm having a little jaunt around the private libraries."

Behind me, to my relief, Birkett came to a tentative melodic conclusion, and a few moments later, a final one.

"That will be your last little jaunt for some time, I suppose?"

"I suppose it will."

"I imagine in one sense you will regret that. A man of your temperament likes to be out in the field."

"Well. You can't do everything."

"Certainly not. Not without making a botch, and you mustn't risk that. I imagine you'll want to give yourself three or four years to get the department established."

"That kind of period."

"I'm sure your flair will survive it," she said.

You couldn't really keep her off. A consistent scorer, always picking up points for aggression, very good inside, and with a dig in both fists; class. Once she'd opened you up, your only hope was to smother her as she came in. She came in now, hooking accurately.

"I remember reading somewhere there are two distinct types in your discipline, the intuitive and the deductive, the one becoming activated early and somewhat spasmodically, and the other much later at some critical stage of knowledge-accretion. Rather like a nuclear pile," she said, humorously.

"Or a compost heap." I smiled back, to show how unconcerned our earlier type could be at this question of flair, its periodicity and duration. She'd certainly been reading somebody, the cow; probably me.

The tap had been whistling as Birkett washed his hands, and he came in after a moment—in no way noticeably diminished, I noted with surprise. His wife got up and went—as I thought, with alarm and rapidly changing my seat, for a celebratory piddle herself. But it wasn't that. The sounds indicated presently that she was getting glasses for her expected guests, and shortly after, at nine, and not the eight-thirty I had supposed, they began to drift in.

2

By ten, having managed to dilute and recharge the mixture, the hair of the dog had done its restorative work and the persona was genial, modest or informative as the situation required; all as normal this bewildering month. This was not by any means the expected crew. With rare consideration, the Birketts had actually invited people I liked or might want to meet, who seemed at the same time to like or to want to meet me; a conjunction not so common. A reputation as a whizz-kid carries its own hazards. This lot seemed rather a jolly lot. None of them was being unduly objectionable. The air was pleasantly charged with commendation. I turned and took stock of the situation; and found a creamy young blonde, properly proportioned, taking stock of me.

"Well, Professor Laing, and how are we?"

"Well, Lady Liz, very well. I'm not professing anything

just at the moment." A pang of something, chagrin, ancient lust, had gone through me.

"Still on your feet, anyway, I'm glad to see. I heard they got you pissed last night."

She had a knack, something to do with a late labial, more specifically a fricative, convulsion, of throwing her voice as far as your ear and no farther.

"They tried to."

"Nobody invited me."

"Nobody invited anybody. They were just a few people who'd worked under me at one time or another."

She noted that one with a faint lengthening of the eyelid. Nothing in the qualifications as stated had disbarred her.

She said, "I expect you're too proud for me now." This had been a private word, too, as her eyelid again indicated.

I said, "You could always find out."

"I'd have to transfer to Bedford, wouldn't I?"

"Very bucolic."

"Very crowded, I hear."

"I expect we could squeeze in a willing body."

"I expect I'd have to compete."

We'd had relations, this randy young noblewoman and I, enjoyable ones, until an observant dog-faced girl-friend of hers had pointed out the impropriety, as between instructor and instructed. She had promptly switched courses—as I'd believed to enable us to continue. This was a couple of terms ago and I hadn't seen her since. Something in her last words made me wonder if the reason might not lie with her dog-faced friend; if this unpleasant friend might not have been keeping an eye on me.

I said, "What are you doing here?"

"I'm one of Birkett's students."

"Working hard, I hope."

"Leading a balanced life."

"I thought you might be."

"I'd heard you were, too."

Almost certainly Dog-face had told her. Chagrin filtered out, leaving only honest lust.

I said, "Are you busy on Sunday?"

"Yes."

"Very busy?"

"Pretty busy."

"That sounds relative."

"We must always try and relate the relative, Professor."

"Might you be in if I rang about four?"

"I might."

"Caspar!"

I spun round. It happens to be my given name. Only one person can make it sound like an oriental bazaar; a person quite capable of making an urbane threesome of what was rapidly becoming a fairly ripe twosome.

I said, "Hello, Uri," without enthusiasm.

"Hello, love."

He'd slipped in late, but had managed to get himself a glass on the way. He had it in his tight shiny glove and his melancholic smile was irradiating slightly, facial scar becomingly prominent.

"Here on business?"

"Just to pay my respects."

"Who to?" He hadn't taken his eye off the girl.

"To you. Naturally." He was very dark brown in the voice, and his features had the assured immobility of the tragic clown; a very international, very well-tailored tragic clown, hair en brosse, faintly lotioned. "I'm an old student of Birkett's. He knows how I respect you."

"Yes, love. Elizabeth, this is Uri Namir, warrior, bibliophile and bore."

"Charming," Uri said impartially.

"Uri is a hero. Of the War of Independence. The Israeli War of Independence. He is an Israeli."

"Hello."

"And this is Elizabeth Longrigg."

"Wonderful!"

"*Lady* Elizabeth Longrigg."

"Marvelous!" His interest, if possible, notched up a fraction. "Are you really? A Lady?"

"Always," Elizabeth said. She was looking, with frank interest, at his glove. This girl began to overstimulate me all over again. I recalled her way of looking with frank interest at anything that happened to frankly interest her.

I said, briskly, "Well, Uri, we must have a word before you go."

"You know," Uri said, "you're the first Lady I ever met —the first Lady with a capital L. Extraordinary, isn't it? After all, I've been here now some years. People abroad think England is populated entirely by lords and ladies. I try to tell them you never meet any. And now I have."

"What do you do in London, Mr. Namir?"

"I am attached to the Embassy."

I said, "He touts for books for another well-known warrior, bibliophile and bore."

"Oh, that. It was only on one occasion. Don't listen to him, Lady Longlegs." He'd have got her name accurately first time; he had this knack, the bastard, of shoving the conversation on two frequencies at once to indicate a certain interest in something that wasn't the ostensible subject of it.

"What occasion was that?" She was smiling at him.

"Oh, I was given once the task of rounding up some books for our then prime minister, Mr. Ben-Gurion, a great book collector. He was here on a flying visit."

I said, "Isn't that what you're supposed to be doing now?"

He'd been going to say something else and he paused fractionally and said instead, "Yes. That's right. Which reminds me, Caspar. I want to talk to you."

"Okay, I've got to pop off just now," Elizabeth said.

I said, "Look, don't go—"

"I have to. Just for a minute."

"I want to see you."

"Right."

I watched her wend off.

"She's crazy for you," Uri said.

"You know, you are getting to be an abnormally ubiquitous bastard."

"She's crazy for something," Uri said.

Elizabeth was just going out of the door and being rather animated with a philosophy don who'd draped himself round it.

"I envy you up here," Uri said. "It's a wonderful relationship. As a professor, my God—you'll have whole herds of the young creatures at your disposal. When do you go?"

I told him.

"And what's your schedule?"

I told him that, too.

"You don't have anybody looking out the stuff for you?"

"I've written off to tell them what I'm looking for. If staff is available, I suppose they'll help."

"I mean professionally."

"The funds won't stretch to that."

"What exactly is it you want?"

He had a fair working knowledge of the literature, so I told him. I must have drunk a bit over the past few days. I heard my own voice echoing.

"And which libraries do you expect to do best at?"

It occurred to me as I talked that it wasn't my voice echoing. It was just that I'd told him it all before. I'd told him it—when?—on Monday. Today was Thursday. I'd told him it at another gathering. He'd told *me* that he was sniffing out more books for Ben-Gurion. It was the reason I'd asked him tonight if he was here on business. He was looking at me gravely, the large en-brossed head clocking it up; all as before. He observed, exactly when it happened, my moment of recall.

I said, "Uri, haven't we been here before?"

"I have something very interesting for you, Caspar."

"Books?"

"I would like very much if you could keep Sunday free. This Sunday."

"I'm afraid I'm busy."

"Do you have to be, Caspar?"

"I simply am."

"Free enough to make dates with Lady Lulu?"

The extraordinary bastard had been listening.

He said, "Caspar, *don't* make any arrangements for Sunday. Please leave it free. I'll call you. I'll call you come time during the day."

"You do that," I said, and looked round.

"She went," Uri said.

"What?"

"She went a few minutes ago. She waved. She saw you were busy."

He went himself a few minutes later; and within half an hour most of the others had gone, too.

I stayed on, hooked by Birkett, and talked, of Greek and Hebrew hells.

3

The following morning, early, found me regarding a couple of Alka-Seltzers fizzing in a glass. I regarded them from a seated position. I felt unwell. This followed. I had drunk too much. I had drunk too much too many nights. I had drunk more than anyone, both last night and other nights. There was a reason for this, I thought, watching the tablets spit and bob and writhe.

The unseemly behemoth had not been wrong last night. There were indeed two types in my discipline. The whizz-kids had to watch out. The thing comes and goes, in flashes. It had flashed first at Jericho, with Kathleen Kenyon, which had started the notoriety; again at Megiddo. It isn't a matter of learning, although you need that, too, a prodigious amount of it, libraries full of it, enormous atom-smashing assemblies of it, to open the withered shell and in the withered fruit to see the living orchard. More, much more; and at the same time ridiculously less: the sudden moment of rapport, across the millennia, between you and *him*, who had written the thing that had been found; the flickering in the imagination, the metaphysical twilight in which, without formal process of thought, a relation is made between the found object that had been lost, and its lost user now, in this revelatory moment, found.

Something to do with the boutons, of course, those nodes of association in the brain; and there was no telling about them. Either they lit up or they didn't; erratic wiring. When it happened, as the cow had rightly said, it happened early. It behooved one to try to keep it happening. How?

Fortunate Michael Ventris, who had deciphered Linear B at twenty-eight, and died at thirty. At thirty I was taking up a university chair.

A ragged spume-like precipitate had gathered at the top of the glass. I shook it to make it settle and drew my dressing gown more closely. I was seated on the toilet in the arctic chill of the bathroom.

Further clouds of disaffection had come to trouble my pillow in the night and they gathered round the toilet this morning. Was I or was I not in tune with this educational kick at all? It was a question, a big and untimely one. To be a good educationist one had to have, presumably, an urge of some kind. One had to want to tell somebody something; preferably everybody everything. I had no urge of this kind. My urge was of quite another kind. If I learned something, my reaction was to keep quiet about it. If I uncovered something, my reaction was to put it back, exactly as it was.

It was an initial reaction, of course, and was followed by others. Perhaps, in some obscure quest for grace, I even overcompensated; thus calling into being what the female Minotaur had described as my "racy and amusing exposition." But the initial urge was there. It was not an educational one.

Not that, I thought, moving numbly and with a sense of

disturbance on the plastic seat, I was a *bad* educationist. They'd offered me, after all, a *chair*. This undoubtedly was something. My lectures always drew an appreciative hand, the classes were well attended. Too well attended. Since the frigging young Arab had failed to keep his frigging fingers off the Isaiah scroll at Qumran, everyone wanted to get in the act. I had incipient priests, advertising agents, debutantes; budding social pests of all kinds. What had the obliquities of Talmud, Mishnah, Targum and Zohar to do with them? Why should they want to know about the way of life illustrated by the Damascene and Alexandrian texts? In what possible ways could the ancient anguish, business and religious, of the peoples who had used the Akkadian, Syriac, Ugaritic, Hebrew and Aramaic tongues, enrich them? And if it did, should it be allowed to? The thing was an affront, and could become a public mischief. Already a literature of upwards of two thousand volumes had been called into being by the grotesque flowering of interest in scrollery. There was even a Home University Teach Yourself the Dead Sea Scrolls!

Far too much knowledge was going here, and undoubtedly it would get worse. The summons to the University of Bedfordshire was only a further indication of it. Develop an expert interest in any specialized branch of the academic syllabus and inevitably you found yourself in some pedagogic posture, instructing others. The thing proliferated. It was an absurdity. What did they *want* with all this information? What did they plan to do with it? It was a vanity, and I was being put in the position of pandering to it, pillaging old privacies, touting old attractions. They would all of them be much better off learning to serve the more fundamental needs of their own society; a thought that led, by a process of easy ratiocination, to some fundamental needs of my own, of the old Adam.

Why had the frigging girl gone without seeing me last night?

She'd said she'd come back and see me. Hadn't she said that? She'd waved at least, so Uri had said; a gesture intended presumably for me rather than him. What could this gesture imply?

The tablets were dissolved, the precipitate settled. I drank, pondering.

It might, or might not, imply a wish to start associating with me again out of the public gaze. But she was tricky; you couldn't tell. She hadn't, for instance, said she would be available at four on Sunday; only that she might be. Was I here being offered a fair crack of the whip or simply an explosive cigar? The old Adam, torpid now but a tyrant in his hour, would force me to find out. The prospect held no comfort. Nothing today held any comfort.

I finished my transactions and rose, unsteadily. Too much old cobblers of this gloomy kind had been afflicting the professor of late. It was no use brooding over what might be. You had to play it by ear. Four o'clock Sunday, heh? Four o'clock Sunday, then.

4

Friday and Saturday passed, bringing on Sunday. At eleven I was sitting over the breakfast debris, writing and smoking, when the phone went.

"Hello."

"Caspar?"

"I could run and see if he's gone," I said, slipping easily into the eager tones of a neighbor along the landing. "I heard him going downstairs."

"It doesn't matter."

He hung up before I did.

A knowing bastard. What could this knowing bastard have on his mind? Any number of things; most probably Jordanian. It annoyed the Israelis intensely to have so much of their old literature lying around in Jordan, beyond reach and almost, for an unaffluent state, beyond price. They couldn't buy directly, of course. Every now and again they managed to get their hands on a bit via some international agency; even so, unless donated, it worked out pricy, upwards of thirty shillings a square centimeter. They had to know what they were buying, and what else might be available. People like Uri had to keep tuned in to the international grapevine. Let him do it, I thought, at some more convenient time.

I had a lunch date at half past one, and popped out for a drink first at one. By three I was back again, somewhat restless. I had a look in the book to see if anyone had called.

1:10 P.M. For Dr. Laing. A gentleman called.
1:15 P.M. For Dr. Laing. A lady called.

What lady? What gentleman? What messages? Why no further details? A twinge of yellowing temper stirred my liver. The handwriting of Mrs. Lewin! A continuing battle this. Frigging Mrs. Lewin, who never took messages, would by now be enjoying her frigging afternoon nap. I went in search of her.

"Mrs. Lewin!"

"Eh? What—? What is it?"

I abated my thunderous hammering.

"I hope I'm not disturbing you, Mrs. Lewin?"

"Eh? No—Just a minute."

Creakings and frowsty rustling. Forked lightning leapt, not unpleasantly, from my liver.

"Only I see there were a couple of calls for me."

"Yes. I'm coming."

"And I can't seem to find the messages."

"Just a moment. I'll be with—"

"So I wondered naturally where you'd put them."

The door opened. Mrs. Lewin, teeth slipping into place, ashen jowls still quivering, peered gruesomely out.

"There weren't any!" she said.

"No messages?"

"None. I asked! He said it didn't matter. He was a foreign—"

"And the lady?"

"Her neither! She wouldn't!" She was yelping; alarm, self-pity, fury, all warring as she supported a breast with a shaking hand.

"Did you get her name?"

"No! She wouldn't give it!"

Not if you didn't ask, you cow; mind too fixed on your flaming kip.

"Maybe you recognized her voice?"

"I didn't! It was none of the usual—"

Elizabeth, then. Almost certainly Elizabeth.

"Well, I'm sorry to have bothered you, Mrs. Lewin. It's just that I'm expecting an urgent—"

"Knocking like that! I thought the place had caught fire. I just this minute dropped off—"

I heard her door slam as I went up again.

Elizabeth. What had Elizabeth been ringing me about at one-fifteen? Perhaps I'd better ring her myself. I did so. No answer.

H'm. Imminent frustration here; the old Adam soon to be at his most surly and clamorous. But at least the girl had left no message. This meant, presumably, she would call again. When would she call again? Presumably she would call again before four, the trysting hour. It was now a quarter past three.

I picked up the *Observer* and read it very carefully. It seemed to be a long report about fencing. The phone rang. I nearly fell off the seat getting at it.

"Hello."

"Caspar?"

I breathed heavily. "You are being a very persistent bastard today."

"That's my old friend. How are you?"

"Very ill."

"What's the trouble?"

"A broken leg."

"I'll come and cheer you up."

"I'm just going out. Dancing."

"Look, love," Uri said, still genial, but with a clear suggestion that the joke was over. "You'll be in at four."

"I won't be in at four."

"You haven't got a date with Lady Lulu."

"I have got a date with Lady Lulu."

"You haven't," Uri said.

"What?"

"I called her. She had to go out. If she hasn't done so already, she will be calling you."

I said, "What the hell—"

"Caspar. Old friend," Uri said, voice descending a full

old-friendly octave. "Unless it was of the utmost urgency would I do this to you? Be intelligent. And also be in—at four o'clock. I am speaking now from a telephone box. I will call for you with a car. I will take you in the car to London. I will bring you back in the car. You can be back by nine o'clock if you want. You will lose nothing. You might gain very much. I am now being quite serious."

I thought, when rage allowed, that he'd better be.

"Caspar," he said after a moment.

"Yes."

"I'm sorry, Caspar. To coin a phrase, this thing is bigger than both of us. You'll see."

"All right."

"I'll make it up to you. You'll tell me what I can do."

"I can tell you now. You can get stuffed."

"Yes, love. Stay where you are. Till four o'clock."

Two

SUBTILTY TO THE SIMPLE

To the young man knowledge and discretion.
—Proverbs 1:4

1

THE ISRAELI EMBASSY is in Palace Green, at one end of
Kensington Palace Gardens, that private and brooding
avenue, almost entirely extraterritorial, which lies between Kensington and Bayswater. It was after six and
dark when we got there, which didn't seem to be un-
planned, and we bowled into it from the Kensington end,
similarly not by chance.

"The neighbors farther along are nosy," Uri said, turning into the drive.

The neighbors farther along were the embassies of Jordan, Lebanon and Saudi Arabia; no soul from any of
them, however, stirring now. Nothing whatever seemed
to be stirring in the street. Uri's whimsy-shrouded se-
crecy, strenuously maintained throughout the journey,
had already brought on a severe attack of the habdabs, in
no way lessened now by the masterful way with which he
opened the embassy door and whipped me inside.

The Israeli Embassy is a nice embassy, very snug.
There is a democratic air about the place, of rolled

sleeves and glasses of tea. A girl was crossing the hall *with* a glass of tea as we went in, and Uri exchanged shouted *Shaloms* and *bevakashars* with her as we mounted the staircase. We went through a large room into a smaller one. Four or five men were sitting about in it, talking; one of them, I saw, Agrot. I'd never actually met him, but his face was familiar enough from book jackets and papers. He was spooning yoghurt from a bottle, and he rose with it still in his hand, a big chap, mustached, nose a bit out of true, not unlike Hunt the logistician of Everest.

He said, "Shalom," smiling, grip very hefty.

"Shalom."

"I wanted to meet you a long time."

"I didn't know you were here."

"I just arrived. Excuse this," he said. "I couldn't eat on the plane. I liked your Eteocretan work."

"I liked your Bar-Kochbah."

"Compliments!"

We sat down and swapped a few more. He continued spooning his yoghurt. Some time during the course of it someone got me a drink. I began to feel that vague uneasiness that comes with hearing a newly arrived foreigner speak your language as well as his own and exhibiting in it a lively awareness of a range of affairs you'd supposed to be purely local. The rest of the characters drifted off after a bit, leaving just Agrot, Uri and myself. It seemed to be time for business.

I said conversationally, "And what brings you here just at the moment, Professor Agrot?"

He said, "Yes," and licked a spot of yoghurt off his thumb and reached into his breast pocket and drew something out.

It was a little print, about five by three, evidently of a text fragment, square Hebrew letter, very badly done.

"What do you make of this?" he said.

Apart from the fact that some of the words were suspiciously long as if the writer had forgotten to leave spaces between, I didn't make anything of it. Certain Hebrew letters, M and T, for instance, are not dissimilar—about as similar, say, as O and D in our own alphabet. Just as the English word ODD, badly written, could come out as DDD, OΘO, DOO, ODO, so a word in scroll Hebrew using M and T could produce its own stock of permutations. In addition, scroll Hebrew uses no vowels. A group of three letters, say MTR, could therefore be read as MATTER, MOTOR, TUMOR, TOTTER or possibly some proper name, or just as possibly some word common enough a couple of thousand years ago and not encountered since.

Most often, because of the root structure of the Semitic languages, you can have a general stab at the thought implied in the word; and if there are enough of them place it reasonably in context. There weren't enough of them here, and I couldn't pick out any recognizable root.

I said, "The scribe seems to have had his wrong boots on that day."

"He was rather ill at the time."

"It's not Hebrew or Aramaic, anyway."

"How's your Greek?"

I studied it again.

"Better than his. It's not Greek."

"Try it backwards."

I tried it backwards. The consonantal clusters began to assume vaguely familiar associations.

"Here," Agrot said. "A rough reading in English of the portion you have."

The rough reading went:

> Here of the place [in the area] by the hand of the lowest and he who testifies alone [the private soldiers and myself only] so that they should not have it in their mouths [without witnesses] the OEED in darkness [is buried].

"Interesting?" Agrot said.

"Very."

"What strikes you particularly?"

"About this invalid who thought backwards in Greek?"

"He didn't think that way naturally. He was making a prearranged report to an authority who would understand."

"I see." From his confident assertion he obviously had a great deal more of the stuff.

"Anything else?" he said.

"This OEED, you mean."

"What do you think it means?"

I looked at it again. Anything with a code name usually telegraphed some piece of priestly property. From the juxtaposition with "darkness" it could indicate "light."

"Light?" I said.

"We're thinking alike."

"In that case," I said, "you'd expect a sacred article, a Book of the Law or the Prophets—anything with light-shedding properties in a religious context."

"This one needed four men to carry it."

"Ah."

"Together with its auxiliary equipment."

"H'm."

"Any further ideas?"

"Not on one drink. You don't get performance and economy."

Uri got up and poured me another.

"Why has the light got to be metaphorical?" Agrot said.

"How do you mean?"

"What sheds light physically?"

"A lamp?"

"Bravo."

I looked at him. "You're not supposing, I hope," I said slowly, *"the* lamp?"

"Well. It would be quite a turn, wouldn't it?"

"Quite a turn." He seemed perfectly serious about it. I said, "Have you got a date for this?"

"A very accurate one. March of 67."

"Then the lamp couldn't have remained in darkness very long, could it?"

"Oh, yes," Agrot said. "Tell me why."

He was leaning back, nose a little to the east, smiling gently.

He didn't need me to tell him why. He would know why, rather better than I. *The* lamp, the great seven-branched lamp, the Menorah, has been the symbol of Judaism for some thousands of years; of his own state, Israel, since its foundation. The Roman conqueror Titus took the lamp when he destroyed the Temple in August of 70. A representation of it is still to be seen on his Triumphal Arch in Rome; a group of Romans carry the massive gold object through the Roman streets in the triumphal procession. The procession was witnessed by the historian Flavius Josephus who recorded it in the finest detail. If Agrot had a date of 67 for *the* lamp, and

Titus took it in 70, then it couldn't, as I said, have remained in darkness very long.

"Because Titus took it," I said.

"We wonder if he did."

"He took *the* lamp."

"He certainly took *a* lamp," Agrot said.

I said, "Ah. H'm," and lit a cigarette.

Apart possibly from the True Cross and the True Shroud, the True Menorah has attracted a larger corpus of fairy tale and legend than any other artifact in history. Its design and dimensions were of course as specified by God to Moses—in history's earliest as-told-to, the Pentateuch—and as subsequently installed in the Temple by Solomon. With such sponsors, the devout have always accorded it magical properties, including inviolability. I'd never heard that Agrot was particularly devout, and he didn't strike me as much of a one for fairy tales. I looked at him through the cigarette smoke. He was still smiling gently.

"What's bothering you?" he said.

"What you'd expect to be bothering me."

"All right, look at it this way. Given the idea that a copy *might* have been made at some time—and after all, it's a very old idea, much older than Titus—you'd expect somebody to have had a try at making one then. The times were very dangerous."

"Right."

"And therefore for someone to bury the original."

"And therefore for someone else to whip it as soon as they found where it was."

"Ah," Agrot said. "I see what's bothering you. Quite so. The point here is that we don't think anybody ever did find where it was. We think there is a good possibility it is still where it was put."

"Why?"

"Well. There are reasons," Agrot said. "But to find out, you'll have to come to Israel."

It suddenly occurred to me that if I hadn't been brought here to listen to this load of fable-type cock I might by now be in bed with Lady Longlegs. Would the chance ever recur?

"You look worried," Agrot said.

"He has a number of problems," Uri said.

I said, "Yes. You see, Professor Agrot, although of course I'd like to—"

"I hear that you are now a professor yourself."

"Quite. And I have to get this department going. It's a new university and I have to get—"

"Dr. Silberstein will get the books," Uri said.

"Eh?"

"Dr. Silberstein. The doyen of all book-getters. Dr. Silberstein will get the books." He said it very confidently.

I drew in a lungful of smoke and looked at him. Dr. Silberstein was indeed the doyen of all book-getters. If there was a book to be got, Dr. Silberstein could get it. I'd used him before. I'd have used him this time, except that a Silberstein book came out a bit pricy. It wouldn't, however, have page 64 missing, and it would have all relevant errata slips gummed in, even if Dr. Silberstein had to lay hands on six separate copies distributed over six separate countries to ensure it.

I said, "How will Dr. Silberstein get the books?"

"How will Dr. Silberstein get *books?*" Uri said, opening his eyes very wide.

"How will he get my books? How does he come to be in the act at all?"

"I have brought him into the act," Uri said. "I have told him everything you told me. With regard to books, you have nothing further to worry about."

It occurred to me that this bastard was being not only unusually knowing and unusually persistent but also unusually intrusive.

"Who asked you to?" I said.

Uri respectfully inclined his head.

"I did," Agrot said. "Of course with the approval of the Department of Antiquities of the Ministry of Education and Culture."

"I see."

"No, love. You don't," Uri said. "I'm afraid it all had to happen in a hurry. But everything was strangely—the religious might even say divinely—propitious. The suggestion is that while Dr. Silberstein does a job for you, you do this job for us, we paying both fees. You're needed, you see."

"Urgently," Agrot said.

It took a moment for this to settle.

I said, "What's up with your own Semiticists?"

"Nothing," Agrot said. "Only I've been rereading your work at Jericho and Megiddo. It shows unusual qualities of flair. You have good hunches. They work. We need them."

"How do you know they'll work now?"

"I don't," Agrot said. "Do you?"

He was still smiling his gentle smile; a student of human nature.

I said, "What's the urgency?"

"Our copy, unfortunately, isn't the only one. And it's

certainly not the best one. The readings are, so to say, obscure. We have good reason to believe our neighbors have a better copy. You haven't been approached by them, I suppose?"

"No."

"No. I don't know if you saw this." He'd taken a booklet out of his pocket. "I've marked the page."

It was the *Revue de Qumran,* Editions Letousey et Ane, Paris, by way of being one of our trade papers. The marked page was a correspondence page. A letter signed Khalil Sidqui from Amman, Jordan, had been ringed. I began to read it, with a vague recollection of having read it before. Apropos some doings at Qumran, Sidqui had reason to believe documents had been found elsewhere that cast light on first-century place names in Northern Palestine. Scholars had a duty to publish such valuable material. It was unscholarly to allow politics . . .

The usual kind of sniping carried out by both sides to see if the other has turned up something new.

I said, "Yes, I read it."

"Do you know Sidqui?"

"Yes." I'd met him in Jordan, a little elderly worrier; not very top class.

"There's no question it's our thing he's talking about. We have other evidence. Someone put Sidqui up to this."

"A funny choice. Does he bother you?"

"Not Sidqui *qua* Sidqui," Agrot said. "Just the implications. They must have had their copy some time."

"When did he write this?"

"Before last December, anyway. He died then."

"Did he? I didn't hear about it."

"No. Nor did I till last week."

"What was up with him?"

"He was a sick man. Bilharzia. Some other things. However," Agrot said briskly, "the point is we know they have it, and that they are being very busy with it. I understand you leave your present post next week. If Silberstein takes on this thing for you, I'd be glad if you could come out then."

Would you? Everything moving a bit too fast here. Too many wheels turning too audibly.

I said, "Well, I'd have to have a word with my principal, of course—"

"No," Agrot said.

"What?"

"No."

A certain silence fell on the room.

I said, "How do you mean?"

Agrot looked at Uri. Uri said, somewhat wheedlingly, "Because there's no *need.* I mentioned everything was working out very propitiously. And so it is. Next week you leave on your library travels. So Dr. Silberstein or one of his assistants will do it for you. Any place they happen to go, you happen to be somewhere else. Who needs to know where?"

"Why shouldn't they know?" I said.

"Because," Agrot said, somewhat reluctantly, "we don't want it to get back to our neighbors that you are involved. It could very easily. It's better they don't know —and of course I rely on you not to mention any of this. The fact is, some of the background to this business is classified. Don't ask me why now. I'll tell you in Israel, together with a lot of other interesting things. But don't expect me to go on my knees. If you want to come, come. If not, we'll have to manage without. It's been known before."

He said it very soberly, very reasonably, with a built-in annoyance factor peculiarly Israeli.

I said, "Let me think about it."

"Who has to let you?"

"When do you go back?"

"In the morning. I came only to see you."

"Well. I'll have to let you know, then."

"Good. Shalom."

"Shalom."

"Just a minute," Uri said, somewhat bewildered at the rapid turn of events. I was a bit bewildered myself. "I have Dr. Silberstein below. Don't you want to see him?"

"Not now."

"But he came specially. He's waiting to see you. He's sitting with a glass of tea."

"Then we hope he enjoys it," Agrot said calmly, still pumping my hand. "Shalom. Shalom."

He shook Uri's hand, too. I thought he had a quiet word with him as I went to the door.

Just a few minutes later we were on the road again.

On the North Circular, these fantasies reverting to proportion, more prosaic matters came to mind. I said, "How did you come to get her number?"

"Lady Lulu? From Birkett. I rang and asked him."

Of course.

"Was she really going out?"

"I don't know. I told her I wanted to see you at four."

"Was she surprised at your calling her?"

"Yes. Startled," Uri said.

Better. A clearer picture emerged. All was not lost.

I said more cheerfully, "So what's your trouble, buggarlugs? You're morose."

"Just thoughtful."

"Are you disappointed in me?"

"I can't tell you what assignments to accept."

"It's fantasy, Uri. The thing can't exist."

"Okay."

"Besides, I'm in the knowledge business, love—a very international business. We're supposed to publish things, not hide them."

"Do me a favor," Uri said, "and keep that crap for your students. I don't see the Arabs hurrying to publish."

"Maybe that's why they got stuck with Sidqui."

"Maybe."

Silence. A long silence.

I said, "Also, it's a serious step taking on a thing like this without telling the principal."

"Don't take serious steps."

"It's not a thing I could decide on the spur of the moment. I don't even know if I'm capable of it now."

"Am I arguing?" Uri said. "The decision is yours. Who wants challenges? You've earned yourself reputation and position. Nobody says you have to keep testing yourself."

Agrot had certainly had a word with him; some other, subtler kind of hustle going on here. They're kind, the Israelis, and hard-working, and accommodating, and conscientious; all these things. Also frigging bright.

I relapsed into silence myself.

2

"Where is it you're going exactly?"

"Nottingham, Shrewsbury, Liverpool. Places like that."

"Alluring."

"Isn't it?"

"So there won't be much more of this."

"Alas."

"Alas indeed. Something new's got into you."

"So long as it doesn't into you while I'm away."

"Vulgar as well as vain, Professor."

"Vulgar, vain, virile, vital."

"Violent. Vulpine."

"Voluptuary. Vulvic-violationary."

"Vastly visible. Anyway," she said.

"Yes. Want to do anything about it?"

"Yes."

All going well here; assignments of the right kind, challenges of the right kind. Who wanted others?

3

"Hello," he said cautiously.

"Hello."

"Caspar?"

"Right."

"Hello, Caspar."

"Hello, you old bastard."

"That's my old friend," he said with relief. And a couple of days later I landed at Lod.

Three

A SPOIL OF GOLD

There is none end of the store.
—Nahum 2:9

1

I LANDED after dark with a Boeing load of Zionist zealots, so a reception committee was waiting: balconies crowded, crash barriers packed, arms, flags, hats semaphoring welcome. Various kinds of bedlam were still going on as I came through Customs, enormous family groups demonstrating in Hebrew, Yiddish, German and American. One group, of bearded ancients, not apparently having come to meet anyone but only to regard another aspect of the Creation, was simply demonstrating in favor of the Almighty, reciting with enthusiasm the newly composed prayer for air travel. ("If I take the wings of the morning and dwell in the uttermost parts of the sea, even *there* . . .")

A mysterious people. How had it really begun for them, their affair with the invisible lover and with The Land? And why had it persisted in such lovesick detail over the centuries, when he had requited them so ill? Fidelity: a fine thing.

"Dr. Leng?" A little chap, built like a monkey, had

sprung from a big Plymouth parked in the warm darkness.

"Yes."

"Shalom. Give me your bag. For the King David, right?"

"Right."

"What's this—overcoats? You think it snows in Israel?"

It does, of course, if infrequently, but I adjusted to the patter. There would be more of it. You have to love The Land, and fairly volubly, when you're in it.

Mercifully, the driver's passion for his land was equaled by a desire to show what the Plymouth could do in it. Just forty minutes and thirty-seven miles later we were in Jerusalem, bowling down the Jaffa Road to King David Street. He pulled up in the hotel forecourt.

"So. How was it, Caspar?"

"Very fast, Chaim." The relationship had blossomed.

"Good roads, eh?"

"The best."

"It's been a real pleasure," he said, and I thought was going to add "to do business with you." Any transaction in Israel, with a shoeshine, a matchseller, assumes the character of a deal, the sense of value very strong. But he was reaching for a card. "Here. Any time you need me."

"How much is it this time?"

"Nothing. All paid."

The deal had been done. We shook hands. I went in.

The King David Hotel, famed in film and story, was also jumping. I made my way to the reception desk, but hadn't quite reached it when a character detached himself from a group and came over to me.

He looked younger, more relaxed in his own background, mustache less military, twisted nose more genial.

He said, "Shalom," smiling, pumping my hand. "It's good to see you. I knew you'd come, my friend."

A clear case of second sight, if so, because I hadn't. All through this long and boring day, I hadn't known why I was doing it. But I'd done it now.

2

"There's no gin left. Only this," Tanya Agrot said, and looked dubiously at the bottle. "What the hell is it?"

"Arrack," Agrot said. "Ah, put it away. We've drunk enough. Who wants arrack?"

"I do," I said. "Maybe it will stimulate the understanding."

We were in his flat in the Rehavia district of Jerusalem, very select. His wife had run up to meet us from Barot. Both of them would have been at Barot, digging, if the new scroll hadn't blown up suddenly. After an attentive hour and two socking gins my understanding was as yet so unstimulated that I hadn't the faintest idea why it had blown up at all. I sipped the arrack cautiously now, not wishing to miss a trick.

So far as I could follow, the scroll had been found last November, a full year ago. It had been found by the Agrots at Ein Gedi on the Dead Sea where they had been working at the time. Somehow between that November and this one it had become suddenly hot. How? Agrot hadn't said yet. He'd been filling me in on the background.

The scroll, it seemed, purported to be the documentation of a consignment of money and valuables removed from the Temple Treasury in March 67, and deposited in Galilee. Numerous such consignments would have been on the move then—as they were from London and Paris in situations of comparable danger during the war.

The Temple, as he pointed out, was a place of enormous wealth, the Bank of England or Fort Knox of its day. It was used *as* a bank, both by business houses and by individuals whose deposits in the form of bullion were stored in private vaults. But the institution had its own reserves—immense ones. Then as now the bulk of Jews lived abroad, six or seven million of them in all in the Roman Empire and several million more in the Parthian. Each one of them, if male and above the age of twenty, made an annual donation to the Temple.

Nobody has ever been able to compute the size of this treasure, but it was certainly vast; enough anyway, when the Romans finally broke in and took it, for the price of gold to slump by a half on the Syrian market. By that time, of course, a good deal of it had already been dispersed—and Agrot's document shed light on the dispersal method.

The procedure, it seemed, was to prepare the documents in triplicate. Two would be hidden, while a third (which detailed where they were hidden) would go to Jerusalem. This copy, after its essential information had been abstracted and transferred to some master register, would then be destroyed.

Agrot's reason for believing that the Menorah was still "where it was put" was that his copy showed where the other two were hidden, and it had manifestly not been destroyed. It was the copy, he believed, intended for Jerusalem, and it had evidently never got there. And he was equally sure that nobody else had found it in between: a small hoard of coins found with it, none minted later than 66, gave fairly adequate proof of that.

I said, "Where did the Jordanians find their copy?"

"At Murabba'at, a little farther up the Dead Sea, just south of Qumran."

"When?"

"Within a few weeks of ours. We found this out only in the past week."

"So why the excitement now?"

Agrot reached for a manila envelope. "I expect you want to go to bed now, Tanya," he said.

"You expect wrong," Tanya said. "I don't."

Agrot looked at her over his reading glasses.

"We have come now to a classified area," he said. "I don't want you to be involved in it."

"Then why discuss it now? Why have you always got to do everything at once?"

"Because I have planned to discuss it now," he said patiently. "Also I wish to return to Barot sometime. You haven't forgotten Teitleman?"

"For tonight I have," Tanya said. "Gladly."

Teitleman, a baron of building (whose iniquities were known to me), had large works going forward in the Barot area. The Agrots had managed to pull a 42-day standstill order on him while they excavated the biblical tel before his bulldozers disturbed the surrounding ground. The forty-two days was going to be just enough, without interruptions, which was another reason why Agrot had called me in.

He remained looking patiently at her and she remained looking angrily back at him. She was a handsome woman, about thirty-five, with an agreeable American accent, very tanned and lookable-at in her slacks and Sloppy Joe. The flat was done up evidently to her taste: plain but stylish, with a few good pieces, amphorae, tiles, a gilt pomegranate; and a big spotlit picture, a Mané Katz, on a blank white wall. I looked round it while the silent marital duel continued, and presently, a bit put out, she got up.

"Don't make it long, then," she said. "I've got an early start tomorrow."

"All right," Agrot said, and waited till the door had closed. Then he took a few papers out of the envelope and sorted them out. "You know," he said, "I expect this is going to be one of the most unintelligent things you ever heard."

"To do with Sidqui?" I said.

"To do with Sidqui. He came here, you know. He slipped across the border."

He'd slipped across it at a place called Gesher, a few miles below Lake Tiberias, on a miserable moonless night the previous December. With a companion he'd forded the Jordan River, gone through the grounds of Kibbutz Gesher, a collective settlement, and cut across the main Tiberias road for the hill country between there and Mount Tabor.

As it happened, Kibbutz Gesher had recently been burgled and a team of night watchers was on duty. They'd spotted Sidqui and his friend but had let them quietly through while one of the observers telephoned the Border Police post at Ashdot Ya'acov four miles away.

Six policemen and a couple of trackers from Ashdot Ya'acov had got on to the infiltrators an hour or so later. They'd followed them for the next three days and nights.

Standard procedure for the Border Police in Israel is not to challenge or alarm infiltrators, unless detected in the commission of a crime, but to shadow them to see if they have business with local Arabs.

Sidqui and his friend didn't seem to have any business with local Arabs. The police couldn't make out what their business was at all. At first they'd supposed it to be a bit of sabotage in connection with the National Water Carrier from Lake Tiberias to the south, but it was soon obvious the men weren't interested in that. They were digging holes in the ground and occasionally letting off a small well-blanketed explosion. Suspecting that they might be caching arms or signaling devices, the police had carefully examined the holes. They found nothing in them.

The men were sleeping in undergrowth by day and traveling by night. On the third night, when they were nearing the heavily populated areas of Nazareth and Afula, the police decided to pull them in. Sidqui's companion produced a pistol when challenged, but dropped it as a warning burst chattered over his head. Sidqui himself remained in a patch of undergrowth, and despite two further challenges would not emerge. A corporal and two men were sent to get him.

The corporal saw Sidqui crouching with what he took to be a rifle in his hands, and accordingly put a burst over his head. Unfortunately, Sidqui had been rising at the time, and he got the burst in the chest, dying instantly. The reason for his nonemergence then became clear. He had been squatting with his trousers down. And what the corporal saw as a rifle was a length of steel piping three feet long. Three other pieces were nearby.

At Nazareth police station, Sidqui's companion was

quickly identified. He had already served a couple of terms for illegal entry and robbery. But Sidqui remained a problem. There was no clue to his identity in his clothes, his papers or his fingerprints, and his companion refused to say anything.

He was still refusing to say anything when he left to stand trial at Haifa seventeen days later on a charge of illegal entry and possession of explosives.

Between the road and the entrance to the courthouse at Haifa there is a stretch of pavement one hundred feet wide. The infiltrator was being escorted across this, hand-cuffed, when he was shot in the head and killed by a rifle bullet fired from the flat roof of a cinema on the corner. By the time the firing point had been identified and the building cordoned off, the gunman had escaped. He was never found.

In due course the file on the case went to Nazareth police station, with copies to Border Police HQ at Beit Shean. And there the matter rested.

It rested for ten months—until three weeks ago—when purely by chance a former student of Agrot's, a specialist in Arabic who had been one of the team working on the Ein Gedi scroll, entered the Border Police service and was posted to Northern Area HQ at Beit Shean. There, to familiarize himself with the work, he was told to spend a week or two in the file room. It hadn't taken him too long to come on the file of the two infiltrators, or to recognize in the posthumous photo of one of them the features, familiar enough to him from his specialized reading, of Khalil Sidqui. Just about three days later he had a pretty good idea what Sidqui had been up to.

In that time he'd retraced the steps of the infiltrators, found the holes in the ground, and identified the steel pipes as a contraption for collecting geological core samples. But while returning to Beit Shean in the dusk this young man had run into a booby-trap: a rope stretched across the road. He'd been found still on his motor-bike but with his neck broken, lying at the bottom of a steep hill off the road. His notes at Beit Shean had been very explicit, however, and they'd gone to Agrot; who after some researches of his own, had set in motion the devious machinery that had brought me to sit opposite him in the Rehavia flat, arrack in hand.

It was Israeli arrack, rather too refined and without the coarse oily kick of the Arabic, but with the same tendency to get you bowlegged after a couple. I'd now had three.

"Any comments so far?" Agrot said.

The one that immediately occurred was that funny things seemed to happen to people in the area where I was expected to work. He didn't seem to be inviting that kind of comment. I said, "What was this with the core samples?"

"The Menorah is supposed to be buried under a layer of blue marble chips. There isn't any marble in Galilee. The presumption is they were looking for it."

"That sounds a cockeyed way of going about things."

"Very cockeyed. And very Sidqui. But not without a grain of sense," Agrot said. "At least nobody tumbled to what these pipes were for a long time."

"So the idea was to find the marble, dig up the Menorah, and take it back across the Jordan?"

"No, no," Agrot said. "It would be far too heavy for them. The idea would be to locate it, so it could be picked up later."

"By whom?"

"Exactly," Agrot said. He looked around. There were double doors between the sitting room and the bedroom and Tanya had left one open. He got up and closed it. "By a military group," he said. "At least, a paramilitary group. There's always a bit of trouble of one kind or another going on up there, you know—raids, counter-raids. Where you get a full-blown military operation, a number of objectives have got to be decided for it in advance. I think the idea here would be to get the Menorah included as an objective. They'd go for it under the umbrella of whatever else was going on. And there's a certain amount of evidence to support this. For instance, we know now there must have been at least two other attempts to find the Menorah, since Sidqui's—they left core pipes behind. And after each one, about a month after, there was a fairly heavy raid. The supposition is that the infiltrators knew the raids were being planned. It now looks as if we can expect another."

"I see."

"And there are some disturbing aspects. For one thing, the last mob were very cocky. They weren't spotted coming in, but they put up a fight going out—which is unusual. And for another, they had a mine detector with them. They threw it in the river, and we recovered it. The reasoning is they wouldn't have lumbered themselves with it unless somebody, earlier, had got a fix on the marble."

"In the area that Sidqui had worked?"

"I don't know. I told you, they weren't spotted till they were going back over the border. But it looks as if they've located it. Of course, there are two things we can do. We can let them lead us to it, and jump them. But we don't want any fighting going on with the Menorah. For one thing, the bastards could blow it up—we want it more than they do. Or we can find it first."

"In how long?"

"I would say three weeks."

I finished off my arrack. "I suppose it is the Menorah they want?"

"No question of it."

"Why not the gold?"

"No, no."

"Why not?"

"Isn't anybody for Christ's sake," came an unladylike snarl through two sets of doors, "ever getting to bed round here tonight?"

Agrot rose hurriedly. "There are good reasons," he said, "which we can go into. But not now. It's late now."

It was. It was after two. Back to the hotel and to bed I went, reeling slightly.

3

We went to Ein Gedi next day. We went via Barot, with Tanya in a second jeep. "It won't put much on our time," Agrot said, "and there's some trouble up there I have to deal with."

"What is it—a war?" I said. The jeeps came with army drivers, each formidably armed.

"Not at all. Teitleman has the lower road closed for blasting and we have to take an upper track that runs near the border. Do the weapons alarm you?"

"Yes," I said. They did. The dull gunmetal and the hard scarred butts looked dangerously efficient.

"Forget it," Agrot said. His eyes were sparkling, wan-

dering nose taking in the chill morning air with relish.
"You'll soon get used to it. It's second nature to us."

I went to sleep. He was in the mood for a chat and I
seemed to have been hearing a lot of his voice lately.

I woke briefly at Beersheba (where Tanya had to pick
up stores), to find the unseemly mess of a couple of years
before but more of it; and found that Agrot was disposed
to enlarge on its growth problems, and so went to sleep
again.

When I finally came to we were chugging up a steep
incline in the rightly named Judean wilderness and the
sun was striking hard off the lion-colored rock. A hot
breeze blew. I took my jacket off and lit a cigarette and
looked around. A place of jackals and prophets, very old,
very dry, very dead. On all sides the jagged peaks and
castle-like rock formations stood in the canyons; silent
petrified cities under the blue sky. I looked at my watch.
Half past ten. A couple of hundred yards behind, the
other jeep labored in a cloud of dust out of the gulch
from which we'd just, apparently, emerged.

Agrot, beside me, seemed to have gone into a slight
trance, hands clasped in his lap, eyes narrowed.

I said, "Good morning."

"I like this place," he said softly, not looking at me.

"Yes."

"I could live here."

"That would be carrying enthusiasm too far."

"I mean it," he said in the same tone of trance. "I truly
love it. I could live here in a cave and be happy."

"Drinking the mountain dew."

"Pooh, there's water here. There's water all under
here."

"How do you get at it?"

"Drill for it. There's everything here—phosphates, minerals of all kinds, oil probably. Seek and ye shall find."

"Would you still like it when everybody'd sought and found?"

He blinked and came out of his trance and lit himself a cigarette. "Yes," he said, "that's the problem, of course. Wait till you see what Teitleman has done at Barot. He found water there. He finds everything, that bastard. There's a great lake of it miles under the rock. Tahal, the water people, said there wasn't. He said there was. He got together money and he found it. Now nobody can do enough for him. He sends water down to the Nafta gas-fields at Zohar, they send him back gas. With the gas he has free power for his generators. He's building every-thing, including a hotel with a lagoon—a lagoon in Bedouin country."

"Very convenient for the Bedouin."

"They need Teitleman's lagoon, of course," Agrot said, drawing quickly at his cigarette, "like a hole in the head. You know the Bedouin."

"Nice people."

"Beautiful people, wonderful people. Give a Bedu his camel for milk and an onion to eat—and he lives. He can live on nothing. A magnificent, hard, enduring creature. What does he care if he's in Israel, Jordan? He has the rock, the sky—this. He wants nothing more. He is my brother, the Bedu."

Just then we saw one, a rather old one, sitting in a dry wadi with a camel and actually eating an onion. Agrot nodded to his brother. The Bedu nodded back. We ground slowly past. No word and no smile accompanied the communication but both seemed satisfied. I'd seen it before, this affinity for the starker qualities of land and person in the Agrots of Israel. Arabism isn't confined to elderly romantics in the British Foreign Office; but it certainly seemed a bit more natural here. And the contemplation of it, fortunately, kept Agrot quiet. He remained quiet till we reached Barot.

You can't, I suppose, as a private capitalist, make much of a show in a couple of years against a wilderness of rock that's been quietly petrifying for several million; but Teitleman, as Agrot had indicated, was certainly doing his best. An unpleasing array of aluminum workers' huts marked the limit of his industrial operations. In a largish shallow excavation several bulldozers were noisily at work around the almost completed structure of a rock-crushing plant. An aerial railway had been erected to carry the phosphatic ore from a nearby mountain of it, and on the ground a train of wedge-shaped trucks stood on a turntable under a chute to collect the finished product. A small section of double-track rail connected the turntable with a loading point for motorized carriers, which in turn was connected with the road. It was this road, in its lower section, that Teitleman had closed. He was building a new fork from it to connect with his further operations that extended for the next couple of miles to the east.

Agrot pointed them out as we hit the new road and cruised smoothly along it. There was a fertilizer plant; a number of prepared sites for a small chemical complex; a number of unprepared sites allocated, Agrot said, for an extravagant dream of Teitleman's, a factory garden city, no less; a housing estate in process of construction; and then—the fount from which all this stemmed—Teitleman's well.

Wells do not have to be big to have significance in a wilderness. Teitleman's well was not big, but it was quite awesome in its significance. A small bathhouse or temple housed its mysteries in multicolored marble; and this Teitleman had surrounded, as a kind of oblation or testimonial to its potency, with a border of shrubs, well-watered and growing with maniacal fury. In a large paved compound an intricate assembly of pipes and pumping apparatus directed the water to its various destinations, south to the Zohar gasfields and the National Water Carrier, west to his industrial operations, and east to his greatest pride and joy—the Hotel Camphire and the Camphire Lagoon.

"Why Camphire?" I said as we brought in view the astonishing edifice. It towered eighteen stories high, a slender column of glass and unpolished marble sprouting from a broader bulbous base like an enormous fertility symbol.

"Teitleman had a song in his heart," Agrot said. "The Song of Songs. You'll remember the poet speaks of 'pleasant fruits; camphire . . . a fountain of gardens, a well of living waters.' Teitleman is providing it to the last item. Over there on both sides of the tel is the site of his garden with fountains. And here we have the living waters—it's to be an aerated lagoon. The hotel is actually in the middle of it. He's got a hydro in there and a Turkish bath, even a mikveh—a ritual bath for women. Also a bowling alley, a cinema, an observatory, four restaurants, two ballrooms and a synagogue. And from his Hanging Gardens on the roof you'll be able to see the Dead Sea together with the Mountains of Moab on the other side.

He believes in making the desert bloom, does Teitleman. What can you do with such a man?"

The question admitted of ready answer for at that moment Teitleman himself materialized, like some pantomime fairy on cue—and was almost done to death. He seemed to spring out of a crevice at the side of the road, missing the braking jeep by an inch. The crevice turned out to be a section of the lagoon, as yet dry, the walls of which Teitleman had been inspecting with a brigade of architects and foremen.

"Ah, Agrot!" he said, and came forward, no whit disturbed by his close escape, one cotton-gloved hand extended.

The inspirer of these constructional marvels was not himself designed on the grand scale. He was a small man, very small, and his bow tie and glasses were very big; but there was an over-all neatness and completeness about his specification that made up for the lack of inches. A certain stony grayness about the face told of a stoical quality, of vicissitudes endlessly endured. Among his sweat-streaked and begrimed entourage Teitleman in his gray city suit did not look a dude. He looked a dangerous little bastard.

"You didn't need to come—we could have done it on the phone. Never mind, I'll show you," he said to Agrot, and in a trice, uninvited, had sprung into the jeep.

"Almost I didn't bother you at all," he said, turning in his seat. "I could have fixed it with your beautiful wife— how is she? Ah. All right. I see. Very good. Hello," he said, and made tiny flapping motions with his cotton-gloved hand at the following jeep, mouth opening suddenly in a doglike grin to reveal a double row of unexpectedly powerful-looking teeth.

"So what's the trouble?" Agrot said.

"No trouble." The grin went as suddenly as it had come. "Readjustments. They're just now held up here so they want to do a tryout for the fountains. The same supply is serving the lagoon and the mikveh, for which the water has to be pure. It's simply a matter of running power and water lines through from the filtration beds at the other side of the fountain site."

"That would be under my tel," Agrot said.

"Under that part of it you finished last season."

"Mr. Teitleman," Agrot said mildly, "I have an order, as you know, that applies to all of the tel."

"And, Professor Agrot, as *you* know," Teitleman said, his little mouth hardening slightly, "I can go in a case of emergency to any court in the land who will tell you what to do with your order."

"It would have to be a funny court that saw a delay to your mikveh as a national emergency."

"So we won't argue about it," Teitleman said, the stoical quality stealing more grayly about his face as he strove to retain a degree of amiability.

The tel was long, shaped like a hog's back and rounded with the rubbish of three and a half thousand years. The soft detritus, as the open workings showed, went down to a depth of thirty feet or so. At the bottom, the first level of human habitation, a pattern of worked stones showed the crude outlines of the ancient settlement, built on the same hard limestone and marble as the rest of the plateau.

Because of its length, the tel had been divided into three sections, and because of Teitleman the Agrots had dealt with the two westerly ones first. Both of these had been opened up the previous season, and now the whole expedition was engaged on the third. Several dozen young men and women with some Bedouin day laborers were swarming on the far slope, their camp visible at the foot of it.

"We want to run pipes through here," Teitleman said. It was a narrow section of the tel some fifty yards from the tip.

Tanya got out of her jeep and joined us. "Those are very old stones down there, Mr. Teitleman," she said. "They have to be photographed and numbered and taken away."

"Everything will be done the way you want it," Teitleman said. "Under your supervision."

"But we can't spare the people just now."

"I'll get you people. As many as you want. A busload, today."

"You'll need to move some earth here, surely," Agrot said.

"A very little."

"But the contour isn't level down there. There are outcrops of rock. You'll have to do some boring or blasting."

"So maybe we'll do a little," Teitleman said, his gray patience shifting slightly. "As little as possible. You'll feel nothing at all."

"Mr. Teitleman," Agrot said, sorrowfully shaking his head, "I'm afraid that would shake the site. There are open workings here, very ancient workings. The slightest tremor will disturb them."

"What tremor?" Teitleman said, and suddenly lost his temper completely. "The bleddy rock is like iron. It needs a bleddy atom bomb to get a tremor. I spent five bleddy weeks blasting that bleddy lagoon and you could have rested a bleddy egg on top. I *promise* you there'll be no disturbance. You can sleep on top. *I'll* sleep on top. What other guarantees do you want?"

"Only that you respect the terms of the order. In five weeks you can have the whole tel."

"And leave a hundred men and machines to stand idle?"

"If it's simply a tryout, run your water and power from another point."

"And double my costs when I can run it from *this* point, where it's *supposed* to run from?"

"In five weeks' time," Agrot said.

Teitleman's teeth snapped with an audible click and he turned and practically shied down the slope. "Just ask some favors from me in the future," he said, holding up one cotton-gloved finger at the bottom. "Just do that!"

"Take the jeep," Agrot called after him.

Teitleman didn't take the jeep.

"That means no more water from him," Tanya said.

"So you'll send the truck down to Arad," Agrot said. "Give that man an inch and he'll take a mile. He doesn't need any tryout. He just wants to go ahead with the whole works. And he knows that I know. You've really got to admire such a bastard. . . . So how is it going here while I've been away?"

We went and had a look at how it was going. Agrot's face was dark and moody as we turned back to the jeep.

"They need me back here," he said.

"Perhaps they'll have you soon."

"So let's get on with it. To the Ein Gedi canyon," he said to the driver. "Along the top."

* * *

It's eight miles "along the top" of the plateau from the tel to the Ein Gedi canyon, and it took us forty-five boulder-dodging minutes in first gear.

Then we got out and climbed down the slit in the world, to the very bottom.

4

Either you like deserts, wildernesses, the hot rock still-nesses of the world, or you don't. If you do, you like the Dead Sea. There is a deathly, an infernal romanticism about the place that no amount of familiarity can stale. Suddenly from the high craggy wastes of the plateau a fantastic panorama opens half a mile below, the dead livid plain of the 'Arava, flickering in a haze of heat and salt evaporation. The Great Rift runs here, from Turkey to Tanzania, and finds its deepest depression between the crusted walls of Judea and Moab. And in the very center, still as a pool of pus, lies the salt lake, forty-eight miles long and eleven wide; the pit of the world.

Six and a half million tons of water enter it daily from the Jordan and other sources, and find no outlet. The stuff simply evaporates in the bakehouse heat.

Great waves of heat wafted up out of the canyon as we clambered down into it. Half a mile below on the floor the trim kibbutz of Ein Gedi swam with its date palms in the dizzy currents. A thin slash of green foliage in the cliffs farther along marked the kibbutz's lifeline and its *raison d'être*—the biblical spring and the waterfall.

We came down behind the kibbutz, three-quarters of a mile behind, in a narrow part of the canyon, and then had to climb again, up the opposite wall. Thirty feet up, under an overhang, there was a narrow shelf.

"Here," Agrot said.

It was a little hole, scarcely big enough for a man to crawl into. But someone had crawled into it, nineteen hundred years ago, and left a scroll and his money there, and never gone back for them.

I sat and mopped myself, slightly addled with the heat and the effort, while Agrot enlarged on it. He enlarged on the gold, too, and why he didn't expect any of it still to be around. Sweat poured down my body as I sat and listened. We stayed about a quarter of an hour and then climbed back.

It isn't difficult or dangerous climbing in the Ein Gedi canyon; just laborious and also, as it happens, unnecessary. A perfectly good road runs to Ein Gedi along the shore. Agrot hadn't taken it because the detour would have knocked the timetable out by an hour or so.

I was too tired to eat when we got back to Barot, slept all the way back to Jerusalem, and then went to the hotel and slept again.

Agrot woke me on the phone about nine.

"Well. There's a lot to do," he said. "You want to come out for a meal?"

"No."

"You want I should come round there for a meal?"

"No."

"What do you want?"

I told him what I wanted and hung up and got on with it. Carry on his way, I thought, drifting off again, and the man would have me nackered in no time. Tomorrow had better go my way.

Four

PRECEPT UPON PRECEPT

Here a little, and there a little.
—Isaiah 28:10

1

THE NEXT DAY went my way. I rose late, told them not to put calls through, bathed and breakfasted at leisure, and made my own way to the university by bus. A peaceful but diligent day followed, marred only by a couple of incidents, the first with Agrot, who wanted to know too abruptly where the hell I'd been, and the second with Dr. Hilde Himmelwasser, expert on photographic emulsions. This pest, on loan from the Faculty of Science, had set up a high-security photo lab in Agrot's scrollery, one of her tasks being to try to make readable some parts of the scroll that were unreadable. She had notably not succeeded.

"Any good having a go with American Kodak infrared plates?" I said helpfully.

"No, Dr. Lenk, I think not."

"Not worth a try even?"

"If I thought so, Dr. Lenk, I would surely have tried."

She was a tall sinewy type with a face not unlike General de Gaulle's and a pair of very thin legs. She stood quite still on them, hands in the pockets of her white lab coat, and regarded me with grave attention as if I were some sort of natural curiosity. Her annoying habit of replying to my perfect Hebrew with her zis and zat type English had already put me in a state of twitch.

I said, "I know Nejid Albina got excellent results in Jordan."

"That is interesting."

"And Isaac Isaacs here, at Megiddo."

"Indeed."

"They both used Linhoff cameras," I said, and was suddenly driven nearly mad by a slow supercilious smile that crossed her face. "With a number three red filter!" I cried. "And developed in ID2, and printed on soft bromide. The stuff came up like yesterday's newspaper!"

"But we are not here dealing with yesterday's newspaper," she said, still smiling and shaking her head at this foolishness. "It is an old skin, Dr. Lenk, almost totally blackened. I think it's best to stick to our own fields. I cannot tell you anything about philology and I don't think you have much to tell me about emulsions. The emulsion used here is one I made myself. To improve the quality I will perhaps make adaptations of the emulsion."

"Fine. Only it isn't quality we're after, Dr. Himmelwasser," I told her earnestly. "We only want to try to read what's on it. And time is pressing."

"So. Then if you will excuse me, I will continue."

"Don't for God's sake antagonize *her*," Agrot said anxiously as we went down the corridor. "She's a big noise in her department and they give us a lot of help. It's going to take a miracle to get anything off that skin anyway."

"I think Ike Isaacs would do better."

"Well, he can't," Agrot said shortly. "This is a security operation. And she's done quite a lot already."

She'd done a bit. The scroll was composed of three skins, wrapped around each other. The best preserved was the inner one, evidently written by a priest. The second was an addendum or postscript, written by a semiliterate, and on this one Himmelwasser had brought up several words otherwise unreadable. It was the third skin, the totally unreadable outer one, that was now in her laboratory, and this one—which is the way these things go—that apparently contained the details of where the consignment and the OEED were buried.

Apart from the latter disability, the skins were in spanking condition, the finest I'd ever seen. Jordanian scrolls tend to turn up in the form of confetti these days. The Ta'amireh Arabs, who illegally search for and sell them, rarely like to sell a scroll in one piece. They prefer to crumble it into a few hundred pieces, and to mix the pieces judiciously with those of other scrolls, and then sell the resulting assortment as lucky packets. The maddened experts whose lifework it is to put these jigsaws together again are left with a lot of holes, of course—which makes them keen customers for further lucky packets.

The two inner documents, humidified and castor-oiled, were now under glass in the scrollery. As usual, the writing was on the treated hair side of the skin, the letters hanging down from the inscribed lines (and not footing on to them as in Western practice). Every kind of scientific test had been carried out to determine the composition and age of the materials, and a considerable literature of manuscript notes had already grown up round them. There were literal, vernacular and modern readings of every sentence in a dozen different versions, and a number of elaborate papers on grammatical analysis.

The priest's document, though in a Hebrew letter, was in the Greek language, and hadn't engaged the team so ardently. It was with the second, written in a loose Aramaic, that they'd gone to town. Examples of Aramaic vernacular are not thick on the ground, and the scholars had extended themselves, chasing roots through Syriac, Hebrew and South Arabic to a hundred different sources. There were still, in both documents, some thirty-odd words either completely unknown or with readings so disputed that Agrot had classified them as unknown.

I spent all morning studying them, had lunch with Agrot in the canteen, and continued in the afternoon. About half past six we knocked off.

Agrot carefully double-locked the scrollery.

"Would you like to have dinner with me tonight?" he said.

"No, thanks. I want to do a bit of brooding. And I'd better make a few notes."

"All right. I'll call you later in the evening to fix arrangements for tomorrow."

"You're still set against Ike Isaacs, are you?"

"It's a matter of security—and etiquette. The laboratory belongs to the Faculty of Science. I can't let him in there."

"I could—on the quiet."

"I'm afraid that's not possible."

"You couldn't let the stuff out to him, then?"

"You know I can't. Look, let her continue for a bit. She is, after all, a world expert."

"All right. Let's keep the issue alive, though."

I went back to the hotel and to bed, brooding. At eight o'clock I got up and went out for a walk, still brooding. It was cooler out—Jerusalem is high, two and a half thousand feet up in its Judean hills—but still balmy after England. I turned left and wandered, and presently found myself by the wall and the mount, Zion, with the moon coming up behind me, and the old magic beginning to work.

It's not much of a town, Israeli Jerusalem, when everything's said: a strung-out untidy place not half the size of Wandsworth, and built on a series of bald red hills so that cars and lorries are forever chugging up in low gear. It's hard to think of it, when you're in it, as particularly holy or as particularly anything else. Most of it, the Israeli part, has been built since 1860.

Its whole purpose, of course, is the mount, and with that split, the place is curiously blind and without a center. Around the demarcation line, small boys kick balls and run and shout in a rubble-strewn slum; and in the town itself small shops line somewhat purposeless avenues and streets. A provincial place, and it nearly always has been; poor agriculturally; pointless commercially; on the road to practically nowhere. A fortress; a geographical location; an idea.

The remnants of all the people who have tried to destroy the idea are still around, of course, a factor of considerable attraction from my own business point of view. And, too, it's a nice place to live: pleasant suburbs, dotted cypresses, a decent university, good air. Also, the Israelis have done their bit with a few stately buildings and by-laws forbidding new construction unless in the beige Jerusalem marble; so that a certain stony homogeneity is present. All the same, and for the visitor expecting something special, a letdown.

And yet—it's Jerusalem, an affair of the heart, an old affair of mankind's. And every now and again the magic will work—as now, in moonlight, by the wall; not a provincial town any more; all geographical location and all idea. Here, built upon Zion indeed, the wall of the city of the great king, and there his tomb; and above it the room where his descendant, a thousand years later, ate his Last Supper. An old place; Genesis old; the rock of our Western ethos, for what it is.

It was quiet here, just a few mournful howls coming from the dogs' home on the hill. The place has developed higgledy-piggledy over the centuries; churches, animal shelters, hospices, elbowing each other for their bits of holy land. All about, the round hills were outlined with lights; one had the feeling of being enclosed in a circle, a rather special circle, very elevated. And all of a sudden I started thinking again of what Agrot had told me, of the gold, and of what had happened here all the years before. I was still thinking about it in Fink's Bar and Restaurant, where I drank and restaurated, and all the way back up the Jaffa Road; treading history, as they say, every foot of the way.

2

The war of 66 that threw the Jews out of their land and onto the world grew, as its historian Flavius Josephus notes, out of a background of troubles. It was an apocalyptical period. The End of Days was thought to be at hand. The Messiah was expected. In the past few decades a number of candidates had duly presented themselves—and had been dealt with as rapidly as possible by the civil and religious authorities.

The basis of the apocalyptical position was that it was perfectly proper for even the smallest force of the godly to oppose even the largest of the ungodly since God would redress the balance. This was not a point of view shared by the authorities, whose day-to-day dealings with the occupying power had given them a rather better insight into the kind of forces available to him. Their position had been perfectly expressed by one of the messianic candidates: "Render therefore unto Caesar the things which are Caesar's; and unto God the things that are God's."

Skillful political work had already annexed to God a rather larger number of things than were available to any other non-Roman body in the empire. His True Faith, Judaism, had been declared a permitted religion, a privilege from which numerous auxiliary benefits flowed. No Jew had to participate in or pay for any of the pagan rites obligatory elsewhere in the empire. No Jew had to perform military service, since its exigencies might lead him to violate the permitted religion. And the established Jewish authority, because of the social nature of the religion, was allowed an unheard-of degree of autonomy. These rights—and this was the most singular privilege of all—applied not only to nationals of Judea but to all their relations in every corner of the empire: a concept of nationality that baffled local military governors and enraged surrounding populations, who thus vied to become history's first anti-Semites.

These privileges had to be paid for, and the price was law and order in Judea. The establishment did its best.

Minority groups and apocalyptical enthusiasts were kept on a tight rein, and their various messiahs speedily attended to. But for years the situation remained tricky; and a succession of bloody-minded military governors hadn't helped.

Judea wasn't an important province—a mere sub-province of Syria—and the kind of people sent out to govern it weren't important people. Not overendowed, mentally or financially, most set out to improve the latter situation at least almost on landing. Accepted practice was to set local communities at loggerheads and then accept bribes from each for intervening; or to wash the hands of important decisions, and then be persuaded to unwash them. Many ended their careers in disgrace; including that most celebrated handwasher of all, Pontius Pilate, who, recalled after nine years as a result of an incident involving the Jews' detested neighbors the Samaritans, committed suicide.

The establishment's difficulties were not eased one Passover when the military governor of the time thought it an idea to garrison Jerusalem with these same hated Samaritans and posted a detachment of them up on the roof of the Temple cloisters. The city was crowded at the time, some thousands of Galileans, those cup-tie Yorkshiremen of old Judea, having traveled up for the festival. Trouble was bound to come, and come it did, on the fourth day of the festival when, as Josephus recalls, "One of the soldiers pulled back his garment and, cowering down after an indecent manner, turned his breech to the Jews and delivered such an utterance as you might expect from such a posture."

Pandemonium followed. The cavalry were called out. Hundreds were killed in the crush in the narrow streets.

The Jewish authorities, concerned with the well-being of their coreligionists throughout the empire, tried to take a long view. Rome must not be troubled: this was the basis of all policy. It was Rome they were dealing with and not its mischievous minions. God, undeniably, had given Rome the power to govern them. He had, also undeniably, promised that better times were around the corner. This was essentially a period to be lived through.

Alas, the minority groups, kept so long under control, could be kept under control no longer. One group, the Zealots, formed a terrorist wing called the Dagger Men, or Sicarii, with assassination as its political method. By the year 66 the daggers were found to be insufficient. Herod, a hundred years before, had stored arms for ten thousand men at his rock fortress at Massada on the Dead Sea. The terrorist wing made a surprise attack, slaughtered the Roman garrison and took the arms back to Jerusalem, where revolution had already broken out. The garrison was killed, public buildings were burned and the ecclesiastical authorities were murdered.

The Roman commander in chief in Syria acted quickly. With a strong force he raced through the country killing and destroying; but it was late autumn by the time he got to Jerusalem. Not desiring a winter campaign against armed irregulars in mountains, he decided to withdraw temporarily. But unwisely, disregarding the first rule of mountain warfare, he omitted to post pickets to cover his retreat. Formations of guerrillas began to strafe his huge column. They strafed it night and day. The retreat turned into a rout. Six thousand infantry and the entire supply train, complete with siege and ballistic equipment, fell to the guerrillas before the Roman force managed to escape.

The victory was so colossal it alarmed not only the peace party in Jerusalem but the rebels themselves. Retribution was bound to come, and when it did it was best met by a united country. The country was divided into six administrative districts or commands, and the commands allotted on a nonsectarian basis. That of the Northern District, which would bear the first brunt of the expected Roman attack, went to the scion of an old priestly family, Joseph ben Matthias.

This young man, not quite thirty, wealthy, gifted and amusing, was one of the lights of Jerusalem. He had just had a splendid year in Rome, where he had gone to plead the cause of some friends who had run into political trouble. In Rome, as a friend of the Jewish comic actor Aliturus, the Danny Kaye of his day, he had gained entry to the swinging circle of Poppaea, Caesar's wife, and had been made welcome. He found himself now in a quandary. No revolutionary, and certainly no Rome-hater, it seemed to him absurd to opt out of the empire because of the excesses of the oafs sent out as governors. But he took up his appointment, dutifully enough, some time during the winter and early spring of 67.

At just about the same time the first consignments went prudently out of the Treasury, into hiding.

Also at the same time, retribution approached.

The news of the Jewish revolt had reached the young emperor Nero in Greece, where he had been enjoying a season of Games. He had been not only watching but participating in the Games, as charioteer and singer, and this reminder of the cares of empire annoyed him. But he saw a way of canceling out one annoyance with another. Among his entourage was a dull retired general who showed a tendency to nod off to sleep while his emperor sang. It seemed to the emperor that this general would be better occupied doing a bit of fighting. He promptly told him to go off and settle the hash in Judea.

The general, a dull man indeed, was Flavius Vespasian, fifty-seven years old. Undistinguished in birth (his father had ended his days a moneylender in Switzerland) as in his military career, the highlight of which had been the capture of the Isle of Wight, he had now settled to civilian life as a horse coper.

Vespasian set about his small task very seriously. He assembled an enormous army. He marched with his army through Turkey, collecting more men as he went. He took his son with him, a jolly young man of twenty-seven called Titus, well-liked by everyone and equally proficient as an athlete, poet, soldier and barrister. They reached their first objective, Galilee, in late spring.

Ben Matthias, the commander of this district, had now been in it for a few months, uneasily. His appointment had not been approved by all, and particularly not by a somewhat intense revolutionary called John ben Levi, who had now come up to Galilee to keep an eye on him. Both ben Levi and ben Matthias operated their own intelligence services; and within weeks of taking over his command, ben Matthias was aware that disturbing rumors about him were circulating in Jerusalem.

A very curious incident now occurred. The junta in Jerusalem sent an order for the recall of the governor of the Northern Command. They went further. A force of 2,500 men was sent to bring him back. "If he came quietly," as the historian Flavius Josephus records in Chapter 21, Book Two, of his *Work,* "they were to let him give an account of himself. If he insisted on remaining they must treat him as an enemy. But the reason was not explained."

Whatever the reason, ben Matthias refused to parley. The force he had himself assembled for the defense of the Northern Command was greatly superior to that sent to take him. He sent the Jerusalem brigade away with a flea in its ear, and history has no more to tell on the subject.

Besides, the Romans were almost upon them.

Vespasian had noted that the most strongly fortified town in the area was Jotapata, and he decided to take it. There was not much of a road to the town, which was not much of a town. Vespasian built a new road. He moved a gigantic weight of equipment up it. He threw in earthworks, battering rams, towers, a siege train and a hundred sixty pieces of heavy artillery; an operation akin, say, to taking Giggleswick by use of the entire Afrika Korps.

It took him forty-seven laborious days to do all these things and then knock the place down. It was May 29 before he walked in and set fire to what was left of it. But among neither the dead nor the few survivors did he find the commander, ben Matthias. The reason was that ben Matthias and his staff of forty were hiding in a cave outside the town. A woman gave them away two days later.

Vespasian called for their surrender, and was refused three times. On the last occasion, when ben Matthias himself was inclined to comply, he had to be forcibly restrained by his subordinates, who preferred suicide to surrender. "Not destitute of his usual sagacity," as Flavius Josephus says, the commander agreed, and suggested they draw lots to decide the order of death, the act to be carried out at each unlucky draw. "By the providence of God," as the historian urbanely records, the commander himself drew the last lot—and lost no time in surrendering. He was not put to death. Within a week he was the bosom pal of Titus and the confidant of Vespasian.

The collapse of the commander did not end the fighting in Galilee. Ben Levi, his rival, put up a rather better show, holding the Romans down till November, when he himself escaped to Jerusalem to be greeted as a hero and to become a leader of the revolutionary council, and the Romans went into winter quarters. They emerged again in the spring of 68 and Vespasian resumed his stately offensive, first mopping up other Administrative Districts, including that containing the Essene settlement at Qumran, whose inmates fled, hiding their papers in nearby caves where they remained undisturbed for a couple of thousand years.

But as he took up position before Jerusalem, express news reached the general from Rome. The emperor, thirty-one years old, had committed suicide. Everything ground to a halt. The offensive was the emperor's offensive; no emperor, no offensive. A somewhat dreary interregnum ensued. This was the Year of the Four Emperors when one son of Rome after another got into the saddle and fell out of it. Nobody bothered very much about Judea; except of course the Judeans, and Vespasian, whose enormous army was sitting around in it, eating.

The size of his army, its present geographical position, between Rome and Rome's granary, Egypt, and the presence all around of old friends, province-governing, right-thinking friends, began to give him ideas. What the old country wanted was not so much song-singing, Games-attending, suicidally inclined thirty-year-olds, as somebody, say, in his sixties, who knew a thing or two and was *stable*, not likely to go off at half cock.

Nobody ever accused Vespasian of going off at half cock. He carefully sounded out the views of his friends the provincial governors. Syria and Egypt, both O.K., and controlling incidentally just about half the imperial armies. The general acted. Establishing himself in Egypt, and directly controlling food shipments to Rome, he sent the governor of Syria with an army to Italy to oppose the current jack-in-office, Vitellius. By the early summer of 70, master of Rome and the empire, Vespasian set sail himself. He told his son Titus to finish off the Judean business as quickly as possible and join him.

Titus gladly did. The emperor's offensive was on again. With the amusing and knowledgeable ben Matthias at his side he attacked Jerusalem on the 10th May and took it just over eleven weeks later. The Temple took him longer —over a month longer, so tenacious and fanatical was the resistance of the emaciated and starving defenders. But fall it did, on the 29th August of the year 70, the 9th of Ab of the Jewish calendar, which thus began its long history as a day of fasting and desolation. Three or four weeks more, and the very last pockets of resistance, in the upper city, were silenced. It was over. The massacres took place, the wholesale transportation of the population into slavery, the parceling out of the land among the delighted neighbors. Vespasian and his jolly son, immortals both, had settled the hash of this superior and supercilious people once and for all.

All that remained was to assemble the spoil—the great Temple lamp, the Menorah, having apparently been damaged in the fighting, was away being repaired—and take it back to Rome for the Triumph. And all, in time, came about. The following June the Triumph was held, the streets of Rome running like a river with the precious spoil, as the historian Flavius Josephus observed. The proceedings closed when the last Zealot leader, especially preserved for the occasion, was ceremonially strangled.

Ben Matthias was there, too. He had gone along with Titus, still his bosom pal. Vespasian was so taken with the young man that he adopted him. Ben Matthias took the emperor's family name, Flavius; and while he was at it, dropped his Hebrew name Joseph in favor of the Latinized Josephus. As Flavius Josephus, historian, he began to write the history of his interesting life.

That was it: the story of a hopeless revolution and of a hopeful young man. But was it only this young man's winning ways that had saved him in his hour of peril?

Agrot, when he'd recapped the story at Ein Gedi, had presented another theory. The consignment that had included the Menorah had also included nearly two tons of gold. And the governor of the Northern Command, according to the priest's scroll, had got wind of it. . . . A lot of gold in one handy parcel for a man who didn't expect to win. A handsome bribe for an impecunious general who still had lingering ambitions and friends to be won. . . .

Certainly there was much in the historical record to support the theory. There was an element almost of gratitude in the way Vespasian, in his hour of triumph, had adopted his young friend. And he had not stopped short at the adoption papers. The young man had become a pensioner for life. He had died a rich and respected Roman.

How right of the young man's rival, ben Levi, to be suspicious of him; and how derelict of the Jerusalem junta to send only 2,500 men to bring him back; and how audacious of ben Matthias himself to recount the incident even though, as he wrote "the reason [for the rumors about him] was not explained." Or was this ingenious man simply coat-trailing to see if there were any of his countrymen yet alive who knew enough about the matter to postulate a reason? For, although he might have got the gold, it did not seem that he could have got the Menorah. And perhaps he still wanted the Menorah. Perhaps he had gone on wanting it, years and years after, in his prosperous Roman respectability. He'd certainly, years later, acquired titles to land in Judea. Why should he want land there, in a country he was glad to see the back of, where his name was detested?

Supposing he *had* tried to look for the Menorah, how far would he have got? He'd known the area where it was buried, because the gold had been buried in the same area. But, without any more definite indication he'd be looking for a needle in a haystack. Unless he made a regular expedition of it—which in the nature of things he couldn't—he'd have to wait until specific information turned up. And the *only* information was in the three coded scrolls written by the priest and his humble amanuensis. One of them was hidden at Ein Gedi, another a few miles away at Murabba'at, and the third high in a rock known as The Curtains. Unless he'd chanced upon that one—surely very unlikely—we were relatively in a much better position.

It seemed to be an idea to try and identify The Curtains.

In the hotel I started on my notes.

* * *

The phone went while I was still at it.

Agrot sounded cheerful.

"Be ready at six in the morning," he said. "Everything's working out wonderfully. I've managed to lay hands on an old student of mine—absolutely first class. It was a matter of getting the army to play. We're going to need a driver anyway, so I thought we'd better have one who understood the subject—a sort of assistant. I am going to have to leave you on your own for a short while. I have to be back in Barot on Thursday night. How are you shaping with your notes?"

"Fine. Who's the ex-student—a soldier?"

"Yes. An officer."

"Of course. Nothing but the best," I said, and hung up and looked at my notes again. I'd written:

1. Locate natural features described "The Curtains" with cave near the top at 600 feet.
2. Locate site of "perfumery" at "watering place" —presumably Lake Tiberias.
3. Resweep all areas already covered by Agrot (i.e., places worked by Sidqui).
4. See police files for infiltrator particulars.
5. Find out what Ike doing now.

I put a full stop after the last and, on reflection, added a new thought.

6. Up Dr. Hilde Himmelwasser!

Five

BEHOLD STRANGE WOMEN

And thine heart shall utter perverse things.
—Proverbs 23:33

1

THE POLICE STATION at Nazareth had once been a Turkish police headquarters, and still looked it. A somewhat ominous high wall surrounded a group of galleried buildings built round a courtyard that retained a flavor of First World War cavalry and of Lawrence of Arabia. We went through a malodorous outer room in which a few Arabs sat drowsing on wooden benches, to the first-floor office of the three-star pakad in charge, and in a couple of minutes were drinking Turkish coffee while I looked through the dossier of the infiltrators of last December.

It was a large one. There were depositions from Kibbutz Gesher and from the Border Police post at Ashdot Ya'acov. There was a large-scale map of the Mount Tabor area with several places pinpointed. There were photographs and fingerprints of the two men. And there was an autopsy report on Sidqui which revealed that he had been suffering from chronic bilharzia which had led to his frequent visits into the bushes and thus (as Agrot's half truth in London had indicated) to his death.

There was nothing else on Sidqui, but much more on his companion. His name was Ta'an Naif Jabel, and he'd been a member of the Hamduni tribe which had wandered in the Nebi Yusha area of Upper Galilee until the Arab-Israel war of 1948 had sent them fleeing over the Lebanon border. Naif himself had been back to Israel several times since, on cattle-rustling trips. In 1960, while serving a term at Yagur Jail near Haifa, he'd earned himself a remission of sentence by volunteering information about the Syrian Deuxième Bureau. He'd apparently been recruited into the Bureau in Lebanon. There were transcripts of all previous interrogations, but nothing on that of last December. I asked the pakad why.

"He didn't say anything."

"Nothing at all?"

"Not a word. Not even his name."

"He spoke freely enough about the earlier espionage business."

"Oh, yes. This time he had the fear of God in him. I think we'd better have the interrogation officer in," he said, and picked up the phone.

The interrogation officer, an Arab of sallow, dyspeptic countenance and brooding eyes, tended to regard Naif's mute performance of the previous December as a personal rebuke. "If I had here the latitude of my opposite numbers in Syria and Lebanon," he said, "this man would gladly have told me everything in a quarter of an hour."

"Why do you think he didn't?"

"He was frightened what his friends would do to him."

"He must have known he'd be safe enough in custody."

The Arab smiled sourly. "Adon," he said, using the honorific rather formally, "the types we deal with here aren't fools. They know the routine. We can only hold a suspect for two days, and, by getting a court order, for another fourteen. After that he has to be charged in Haifa. It's a matter of simple arithmetic. On the seventeenth day he has to be taken out of here in a van. On the way the van has to slow down maybe ten times. In Haifa he has to be taken out of the van. At any one of these points someone can get him. And someone did."

"We didn't of course realize," the pakad said quickly, "that he had such good cause to be frightened. Or precautions would have been taken."

A few minutes later we strolled back to the jeep.

"Nothing startling," Agrot said, "but a useful session all the same. At least you've made contact. You might need them when I have to leave you on your own."

"Which brings us to another matter," I said. "When you leave me on my own. There is the question of the driver."

"What's up with the driver?"

"You didn't explain she was a female."

"What's the difference?"

"Vive la différence," I said. "But I'd like to have known. What's her story?"

"No story. She's just an old student, a brilliant one. I got her deferment from the army to finish her course. Now she's doing her service and when it's over I hope she'll come back to me. I mean, of course, come back to the university."

"I know what you mean," I said. He'd sat next to her in the front seat. I'd sat by myself behind.

Agrot looked at me. He said mildly, "Don't get any wrong ideas. She's a serious young woman. Also a Yemeni. And they tend to be old-fashioned."

"So am I. Which leads to another point. I took it my mate would be a man and that I'd be sharing a tent with him."

"There's no need. She can run you to a hotel every night and go to an army camp herself."

"How old is she?"

"I don't know—twenty-one, twenty-two. Ask her."

"Is she married, engaged, what?"

"Ask her that, too," Agrot said; and just then we brought her in view. She'd been heavily shrouded in an army tunic, cap and dark glasses when I'd spotted her first at 6 A.M. Tunic, cap and glasses were off now. She was sitting in the jeep reading a book in the shade of a tree.

She was a precise, delicate, petite thing, a fine shade of coffee all over, like some figurine of the Arab Maid. Her heart-shaped face supported a small tiptilted nose and longish doelike eyes, both of these features restrained from getting above themselves by a large and rather heartening mole on her right cheek. Her black hair was straight, curved under her chin; arms and legs as they should be; khaki shirt suitably filled. The only thing I could see against her was a rather tuned-in look. As Agrot had said, this girl was a thinker.

She looked up as we approached.

"Did you have useful discussions?" she asked rather intently.

"The pakad was able to answer a few questions," Agrot said. "And now, Shoshana, Dr. Laing has some for you."

His off-center nose was twitching slightly.

I said, "Oh, mine can wait."

The girl put a marker in her book and closed it. "Why wait," she said, "if I can answer now?"

Her voice, which carried twangy cadences of Brooklyn, was less pleasing than the rest of her. I ground my teeth a little. I said, "I was simply wondering—how old you were."

"How old I am? I'm twenty-two."

"Ah."

"Is that all?"

Agrot's eyes were on me. I said doggedly, "And whether you were married or anything."

"Pardon?"

"Dr. Laing asks if you are married," Agrot said in Hebrew. "She reads English better than she speaks it," he said courteously to me.

The girl was looking at me blankly. "Married? No, I'm not married," she said.

"I see."

"Was it for some purpose of the mission?"

"No, no. Not at all."

"I am single and twenty-two years old," she said, to get it quite right.

"Well. Jolly good."

A certain silence developed. The girl remained tuned in, waiting for further inquiries to deal with. I couldn't think of a single one.

"Is this all you wish to ask?" Agrot said at length.

"For the moment."

"Then we'll go now, Shoshana, to Beit Shean," Agrot said, and turned round to face front. But his nose, I saw in the rearview mirror, still twitched slightly from time to time.

*   *   *

Beit Shean was the Area HQ of the Border Police, a trim little outpost run on military lines with a flagstaff and transmitting aerial in the center of a three-sided compound of prefab building. The C.O., a young Oriental Jew not unlike Marlon Brando in some leaner and more frenetic version, smoked tangy cigarettes and showed steel teeth in an alarming smile. But he very amiably gave us lunch, and turned over all the items that Agrot requested. These consisted of a more detailed survey of the Mount Tabor area, a duplicate of the Nazareth file, and a report on the activities of subsequent infiltrators. After lunch we signed for a couple of mine detectors, stowed them in the jeep, and set off for Mount Tabor.

"I only want to demonstrate our sweep procedure," Agrot said as the familiar rounded hump came in view. "We'll do one specimen area. I don't want to spend much time here today."

We didn't spend much time there. At four o'clock we knocked off and ran into Tiberias, where the girl dropped us at the Galei Kinneret Hotel and took off herself in the jeep for an army camp. By five Agrot and I had bathed and changed, and were sitting out on the lakeside terrace with a couple of drinks.

"The best thing I can do," he said, writing himself a note and not looking up, "is to continue making introductions and putting you in touch with the sources of information."

I didn't answer. The best thing he could do, of course, was to put me in touch with Isaac Isaacs, and Ike in touch with the unreadable skin. If only a few words could be brought up, in the right places, they would obviate the need for many more elaborate measures. In their absence we were being forced to deduce what Sidqui had found on his skin; always a tricky operation. There was something peculiarly nerve-racking in having to plan, from a reading of his apparent mental processes, a laborious series of investigations that might screw me up for weeks. There was no certainty, for a start, that he'd even hit on the right area. Scroll locations always needed "interpretation," and it was on just this kind of point, where judgment or inspired hunch was required, that Sidqui had so often come a cropper.

A consideration of these factors had inclined me to test first, from other evidence in the scrolls, whether this area should be regarded as feasible at all. Agrot, who had no doubt about it, was somewhat heavily humoring me in this.

"So," he said, looking up and crossing my line of thought at this point. "With regard to your feasibility tests. I think that for the perfumery, the best source of information will be the curator of the Tiberias museum. He's an excellent man, the outstanding authority on this area. Then for The Curtains we'll have to organize the Topographical Survey people. And at the same time we can attend to the geological thing, although you know what I think about that."

The geological thing was the layer of blue marble chips used to cover the Menorah, and I knew what he thought about it. He thought it had been brought from Jerusalem with the consignment for some priestly reason. I thought otherwise. It struck me as unlikely for any reason that heavy stone would have been carried on such a journey. In my view, if marble had been used, then geological deposits of it would be found *in situ*. And if they couldn't be, then there was something wrong with the *situ*.

We had another drink and discussed it while the light

faded from the sky. A scent of lemon and eucalyptus wafted up from the hotel gardens below. Away to the left, the old Turkish black basalt fort leaned drunkenly into the water. A few fishing boats puttered past it, making for the Tiberias jetty. All of the lake—the biblical Sea of Galilee—was in Israeli hands; but only just. Immediately over the brow of the purpling Syrian hills across the water were the big-gun installations that could blast half Galilee.

The whole lake darkened as we sat there, and we sat in the dark and watched it; till the dining room, behind us, livened up with the sound of diners. Then we went in and joined them.

2

"To me," Agrot said, "everything now looks very promising." We were sitting taking lemon tea á trois and things had been looking increasingly promising to him all afternoon as his return to Barot became more imminent. "There are plenty of irons in the fire, and I'm sure you'll have done wonders before I get back."

"About Ike Isaacs—"

"That's not forgotten. Leave it with me. If anything urgent comes up you can always get me on the radiophone at Barot."

"Supposing I need a few extra hands?"

"Apply to Beit Shean. Or if it's something the military will be better at, Shoshana will arrange it." He'd been crossing items out of his notebook, and he now crossed the last one and shut it. "I think that's everything, isn't it?"

"Except for my leave," the girl said.

"Ah, yes. Lieutenant Almogi has leave due to her which she'd like to start taking at weekends. In general you'll be able to let her go at midday on Friday and she'll be back Sunday. Of course I'll be back myself before then. The sweep equipment and the papers are on her signature, and they'll have to be turned in to the army camp. But she'll leave you the jeep. I should try not to use it too much during the Sabbath. It offends people and you don't want to draw attention to yourself."

I said all right, and a few minutes later was waving after him as the bus drew him in the general direction of Afula and the south.

This seemed to leave just the two of us. I looked at the girl. She looked back at me, very tuned-in.

I said, "What would you like to do now?"

"If there are no further missions today—"

"Not today."

"Then I'd better sign in at camp."

"How about having dinner with me tonight?"

"I'm afraid it's not possible."

Gracious as ever; Almogi had been getting up my nose all day. I said crisply, "All right. Better give me your number there."

She gave me it, and then dropped me back at the hotel.

"What time in the morning?" she said, as I hopped out.

"Not too early. Ten ought to do."

"Ten," she said, and seemed to brighten up a bit. The effect was to make her mole wobble and admit a ray of sunlight. It also encouraged me to try again.

I said, "Lieutenant Almogi."

"Yes."

"You could, if you wished, call me Caspar."

"Very good."

"I suppose I might also call you Shoshana."

"If you wish."

"Pip-pip, then, Shoshana."

"Shalom," she said, unsmiling.

A mistake; damn her.

And a mistake, too, the whole caboodle, it seemed to me as I sat on the terrace, nursing a glass of arrack for company, and watched night fall again. An air of melancholy hung over the lake, and it hung over me, too. Without the presence of Agrot, the affair seemed suddenly to have disintegrated. The curator had never heard of any perfumeries in the area, the topographical people knew nothing of The Curtains, and the geological people said there was no marble. Agrot had supported all this very cheerfully. A perfumery called for large quantities of vials, and the curator had promised to turn up sites where these had been found. The Curtains would doubtless not be today as they were two thousand years ago: it needed a piece of research. And as for the marble, he'd never expected any. For the time being there were Sidqui's workings to go on, and all that was required was patience and faith.

Well. I had the patience at least. With Almogi as mate it looked as if I'd be needing it.

In the dark, thoughts proliferated, with increasing gloom. How was Dr. Silberstein getting on with my books in places like Nottingham, Shrewsbury, Liverpool, etc.? And how was Lady Longlegs getting on with whoever she was getting on with? And what of the intake filing in to the University of Beds?

All a long way away; a long way from the lemon-scented terrace and the darkling lake. Behind me, the diners were sharpening up again. I got up presently and joined them gloomily.

3

The curator had turned up a couple of sites for investigation along the southwestern shore of the lake and we buzzed along there in the beautiful morning. Thickets of pine and eucalyptus bordered the glittering water and their sharp scent filled the air. The white cupolas of Rabbi Meir's tomb and the bathhouse of the hot springs passed on our right, straggling lines of the devout and the rheumatic waiting to enter both establishments.

Galilee is a mournful sort of place, a late-afternoon land of hill and valley in which you expect to hear the plaintive notes of pipe and woodwind wild. There aren't too many woodwinds wild. The Arabs in their picturesque squalor haven't much to pipe about, and even the birds maintain a moody reserve. A sprinkling of new hotels had opened along the lake, however, and all was looking very nice today. I sang a little as the trees and hotels flashed past. Almogi remained mute, concentrating behind dark glasses on her driving.

"Did you spend a pleasant evening?" I asked after a snatch of song.

"Pardon?"

"Did you spend a pleasant evening?" I asked in Hebrew.

"Very pleasant."

"What did you do?"

"Nothing special. The usual things people do off duty."

"What do *you* do when you're off duty?"

"Eat, read, walk, sleep."

"I suppose if you sign for a meal you've got to eat it."

"Of course. We can't waste food."

"Quite so." It struck me she might have offered this explanation last night, but I perked up all the same. "What was it?" I said.

"What was what?"

"Your dinner at camp last night."

"I don't know. I didn't eat there."

She drove poker-faced on. All *right,* I said to myself. From now on we could all be official.

Menora, the promisingly named village near the first of our sites, appeared on the right a few minutes after the tomb of Rabbi Meir. The girl checked her dashboard, drove carefully another three kilometers, and ran the car into the side of the road. I unfolded the plan the curator had given me. The site was on a hill above the road. We got out and climbed up.

It was a rounded hill overlooking the lake, and the ancient village had stood on the crest. A stump of wall here and there and a long narrow excavation, which revealed a pattern of crude foundations, were the only remains of it. I spent some time looking for the promised spring and finally found it: it had been capped by the Water Board and a short length of pipe carried its contents to an underground conduit.

I sat on a stump of wall and smoked a cigarette and looked around. Nothing here was as it should be, of course. According to the priest's scroll, he'd had to climb down to the village from a height. There was little here in the way of a height; although contours, of course, could

change. Certainly, vials had been found here in quantity
—which might only mean that there had been in the
village a retailer of such things. The whole area had been
strong in trade, and there would have been no shortage
of shops. There was a more serious objection. From the
second scroll, if we'd read its curious syntax aright, there
was a strong suggestion that the rock feature called The
Curtains would be visible from either the village or the
spring, or from some point nearby. A careful check with
the map showed no possible feature of this kind.

It seemed time to put Almogi through her official
paces.

I said, "Perhaps you'll give me your assessment of
this."

"I don't think it's right."

"Why not?"

She began to tell me. I'd noticed already that her Hebrew, unlike her English, was unusually harmonious. At
least a tone deeper and expressed in an idiom cultivated,
supple, concise and yet relaxed, it also carried under-
tones of something else; an offbeat quality I hadn't yet
fathomed. I sat on the stump and listened to it. The
reasoning was not only cultivated, supple, concise, etc.,
but also bang-on.

"Not bad. A reasonable analysis," I said grudgingly.

She blushed.

Her pigment at least turned a shade darker, while the
whites of her eyes turned a shade whiter. I regarded them
with some curiosity. She put her dark glasses on.

I said in English, "Who did you read at university?"

"Many people," she said woodenly.

"Anything of mine?"

"Oh, yes."

"Didn't you do so well with me?"

"Pardon?"

I repeated it, still in English.

She said slowly, "I did very well with you."

"That's more than I'm doing with you, isn't it?"

"Pardon?"

I didn't bother answering. I just got up and started down the hill with the feeling that there were enough problems without her. Somewhat taken aback, it seemed to me, she fell into step beside me.

She said, blurting it a bit, "I'm sorry—it's just—I expected a different person."

"Too bad for you."

"I mean someone older—"

"I'll probably age a lot while I'm here."

"And these jokes—"

"Too flip for you, am I?"

"Pardon?"

I suddenly found myself pleasurably angry.

"You work it out, love," I advised her warmly. "If you can't understand me and my simple-minded jokes we'll have to get someone who does. I can't cope with your little difficulties as well as my own."

She said in a rush and in Hebrew, "Oh, please, I have the greatest—I mean, it's just I don't know how to answer when you joke, and I don't know when you joke. You're so sophisticated and I feel you make—"

"Eh?" I said.

"Fun. Of me."

I gazed at her, much taken with this image of the sophisticated joker. "Well, I'm damned," I said.

"Pardon?"

"You're welcome." I gave her a quick hug, and it

seemed to do no harm so I gave her another. "Everything all right then, now, is it?"

"I hope," she said.

"Well, thank Christ for that," I said; and as far as she was concerned, for a few days at least, everything was.

<u>4</u>

It's necessary to get the time straight now, because soon after everything went funny. I'd landed at Lod on Sunday, and it was Thursday when Agrot took off for Barot. It was the following one when I rang him and turned the job in.

He said, "What the hell? What's the matter with you? What's wrong?"

A lot of things were wrong. The main one was a growing feeling in my bones that the area was. Every minute of every day reinforced it. But there were other things. He'd phoned me a couple of times in the interim explaining why he wasn't able to get back. The reasons were good and sufficient, but they did not make me happy. It seemed to me that if the job was urgent enough for me, then it should be urgent enough for him. Also that it was time now for him to decide whether he'd sooner ditch Himmelwasser or me. I'd wakened with the jaundiced feeling that I was being used as a witch doctor or a water diviner, and I didn't like it. I was pretty sure that chemical treatment of the scroll would bring up a word here or there. The cautious Himmelwasser wouldn't undertake such treatment. All of a sudden it struck me that, unless somebody was prepared to do *something*, I couldn't go on. Some gesture had to be made to the boutons; their moribund condition was inducing in me a state of extreme nerviness.

None of this was easy to say and I was inhibited by the need to remember we were on an open radiophone.

I could hear his heavy breathing at the other end. He said, "So what have you done so far?"

I told him a bit. I'd investigated thirteen sites. I'd examined various pillars of rock that might once have stood 600 feet. And I'd inquired zealously in Arab villages to see if the local lore provided any accounts of blue stones (the geological people not having come up with any).

"So what is it? Have you run out of possibilities—what?"

"No. I'm just not prepared to do any more."

"Come and see me."

"At Barot?"

"I can't get away. Do this for me."

"All right. I'll come tomorrow."

"Tov." He hung up before I did.

The girl had been hovering. She said, "You're going away this weekend?"

"Yes." It suddenly occurred to me that what with the blaze of industry I'd overlooked the matter of her leave.

"It doesn't matter," she said. "I knew there would be much to organize at the beginning."

"Do you want to go this weekend?"

"Yes, I'll go this weekend."

"Well, have dinner with me at the hotel tonight and tell me about it—unless you're busy."

"Thank you. I'd like to," she said, smiling. A distinct improvement had come about in the social outlook of Almogi. I had carefully fostered this by preserving a certain distance during the day, and not involving her in any activities at night. I'd had my own night activities—at the dinner table of the curator at Tiberias, and at those of the C.O. in Beit Shean and the pakad in Nazareth. High Life.

"Do you particularly want to eat in the hotel?" she asked casually a few minutes later.

"Not particularly. Why?"

"Good," she said.

We ate in a clearing of eucalyptus, on the banks of the lake, a mile or so south of the tomb of Rabbi Meir. We ate fish, steaks and fruit, and then sat back with a cigarette over Turkish coffee in the glow of the charcoal tray.

"Did you enjoy it?"

"Very nice," I said.

So it was. Very sylvan, too, the moon glinting back off the smooth gray bark of the trees and off the pebbles on the sloping beach below. The barbecue and fishing kit had come out of a lockup army hut nearby. I'd noticed a couple of sleeping bags in there, too, and had begun to wonder if this girl was as old-fashioned as Agrot supposed.

"I should have warned you about this," she said. "I often do it."

"Were you doing it the night you couldn't dine with me?"

"Yes. I'm sorry about that. I'd already arranged it. The food has to be eaten right away or it goes bad."

I wondered who she'd arranged it with, and of which gender.

"Any other girls at the camp?" I said.

"Four. They do clerical duties."

"Can they get all-night passes?"

"Rarely, unless they're officers. They aren't."

"Easier for the men, I suppose—to stay out all night?"

"Oh, yes. Much easier."

I couldn't see much of her face, which bothered me. What I could see looked merely tuned-in, which bothered me all the more. A faint suspicion developed that Almogi might be having me on.

"Why were you so happy at not having to turn up till ten next morning?"

"Oh, that. The fish round here are funny," she said, smiling. "They don't bite till about nine. I like to catch them for breakfast."

"You sleep here, do you?"

"Yes. Israelis like to sleep out when they can."

"I like to sleep out when I can," I said.

No comment.

I drew on my fag a bit and put my arm round her.

"Don't do that," she said a few moments later.

"Why not?"

"One thing leads to another."

"Why shouldn't it?"

"I'm engaged," she said.

"That's all right."

"My fiancé expects a virgin at marriage."

This statement, as incendiary as it was unexpected, set me on with greater vigor.

"I don't know if you're expert at judo," she said. "But from here I could throw you into the lake with no trouble."

"Why the hell should you want to?" I said, shaken.

"I don't want to."

"How about just relaxing, then?"

"I'm very relaxed. I don't want to relax any more."

"Okay," I said, and after a moment took my arm away.

No interloper I, except by invitation. There was also the matter of staying out of the lake. "What's this about judo?" I said.

"Any girl of the army can take judo."

"Doesn't that terrify the men of the army?"

"Some more than others. It's a brave army," she said.

I pondered this, and noticed the tuned-in look had switched on. "In your army, I think," she said, "the officer gives the order Advance. It's so in every army of the world. In the army of Israel he must order Follow Me. This tells us something, I think, of the quality."

A certain amount of this had been coming out of her of late, so no particular homily seemed intended. I looked at her curiously all the same.

"How long have you been in Israel, Shoshana?"

"Over fifteen years." She told me about her family. Her father kept a small shop in Tel Aviv, her mother had a cleaning job, an elder brother worked in a road gang, and an elder sister was on a kibbutz.

"You're the bright one of the family, then?"

"It isn't brightness. Just opportunity," she said, warmly. "I was the only one educated here. The others had no education."

"Do they look like you?"

"There's a family look."

"An Arab look?"

"It isn't Arab. There's Arab blood, of course."

"Yes." Very complicating. Was it her Arab blood that made her shake her head when she meant yes and nod it when she meant no? And which of her compound linguistic signals were meant to be read: the Arab interrogatives, which seemed to advise Come On, or the plain Hebrew words, which said Keep Off?

"What's your boy friend like?" I said distractedly.

She dug in her shoulder bag and produced a photo. An enormous bruiser, somewhat dusky, smiled dourly out of it from behind a bristling mustache.

"Is he a Yemeni, too?"

"A Moroccan. His name in Shimshon," she said, smiling.

"Samson. He's a big fellow, isn't he?" I said, faintly.

"One hundred and ninety-eight centimeters."

I bemusedly worked it out. The monster was six foot six.

"We aren't officially engaged," she said. "I think we will be officially engaged. He can pick me up with one hand."

"What else does he do? Professionally."

"He's an army officer. A regular."

"In this area?"

"No, no. In the south. The far south," she said, drawing thoughtfully on her cigarette. I looked at her. The down-turned face was grave as ever, no particular emotion, sorrowful, gladsome or sportive, crossing it.

I said, "And are you going to the far south for your weekend?"

"Only to Ein Gedi. My sister's on the kibbutz there. She's married, with a baby."

"Ein Gedi. We can travel down together, then. Have you seen the cave there?"

"No. They don't know about it on the kibbutz. It was kept quite secret almost from the start."

I gave a final glance at the man in the far south and handed him back. I said, "Would you like to see it?"

"Very much," she said, promptly.

"All right. We'll do it."

"And would *you* like—it's more comfortable on the kibbutz than at Barot, if you're staying overnight."

"Can they put me up there?"

"I could phone my sister and find out."

"Well, do that. We'll buzz off at midday."

"Good," she said, and looked pleased; but Shimshon and the judo, both, seemed to have put the mockers on this particular idyll. We left soon after.

5

It was dusk when we picked up the road to the Dead Sea, night when we finally dropped down to it. We ran along the shore, headlights blazing. It was hot, close, very still. Across the water the Mountains of Moab lay like crouched animals. It had been raining up above, but here it was just overcast.

"It's Shabat already. We won't make a disturbance," she said, pulling in under the trees at Ein Gedi. "They'll just have gone into the dining hall. We can go and wash now."

A rather switched-on version of *L'Cha Dodi*, the ancient hymn that greets the Sabbath as a bride, was coming out of the dining hall as we washed. We sat and smoked in the steamy darkness and listened to further renditions. Presently, the season of song over, we went in.

A couple of hundred young kibbutzniks of both sexes, in shorts and shirts, were at their Sabbath victuals. We made for the table under the Sabbath candles where the sister had kept a place for us, and shortly after my hand was being wrung all round the table.

All this was very genial, and after dinner became more

so, when a social do in our honor developed at the sister's place. The sister, Miriam, bearer of the family look as Shoshana had said, bore it, however, in a heavier and more lowering way. She seemed to regard me, an Englishman and a Gentile, with some suspicion as a friend of her sister's. At all events, when the party broke up she announced that Shoshana would be sleeping with her. The husband, one Avner, walked me to a guest hut.

"So tomorrow you'll relax," he said. "It's a relaxing place. Just look at us—we relax all the year round."

I'd already ringed him as the family joker, simple deadpan type, and I contributed a weary smile.

"Shoshana will show you round. She's a great kid—full of life."

"Is she?"

"Of course. It's a shame she's saddled herself with this Moroccan."

"What's up with him?"

"He's a strong silent type—a pain in the arse. Still, Miriam likes him."

"So does Shoshana."

"She doesn't know what she likes. Incidentally, get her to take you up to the Cave of Shulamit when it's cooler tomorrow."

"Where is it?"

"Up beside the waterfall. You'll like it. Shalom."

"Shalom."

In the morning I ran myself in the jeep to Barot. No account was being taken of the Sabbath there; work was in full swing. I found Agrot in the administrative tent, out of sorts. He said, "I want to give you a rundown on my problems. Then you tell me yours."

I'd been prepared for this, but I listened. His classification system had gone wild in the scramble to complete; two seasons of work were being endangered; on the results of this expedition would depend his financing for the next; etc. All good and sufficient reasons.

"Have you finished?" I said.

"Also I know what you want me to do. I want *you* to try to understand the difficulties."

I listened to them, too: the invaluability of the Faculty of Science; the need to avoid conflicts; the dangers of chemical treatment to an old skin; the fact that decisions on the latter subject were not his but the Department's.

"Is that the lot?" I said.

"Speak if you want to! We're not in a law court." He'd been hanging on to his temper, but he lost it then, and I was glad. It's easier to be angry with an angry man than a reasonable one, and I'd been feeling my own troubles drowning in the general sea of his.

I said, "Because my position is much simpler. I'm doing no good up there, and I won't until we get some more dope. I'm not prepared to stay without it."

"So we won't get excited. We'll try to stay calm. Just tell me what you think I can do. In the light of everything I have told you."

"You can take the skin from Himmelwasser and give it to Isaacs. If necessary you can allow chemical treatment on your own authority and get departmental approval afterwards."

"Even if I were prepared to do this, I can't leave here at the moment to organize it."

"I'll organize it."

"I mean organize Dr. Himmelwasser."

"That's what I meant."

He took a bottle of brandy out of a cupboard.
"Have a drink," he said.

When I left matters stood like this: I was going back to
Galilee. By Wednesday, if I was still unhappy, I'd call him
at Barot. Whatever the state of the nation at Barot, he
would then leave and join me in Jerusalem. In Jerusalem
he'd fix Himmelwasser.

I ran back to Ein Gedi not dissatisfied.

6

She didn't want to see the scroll cave in the afternoon—
"Nobody works on Shabat and it would be hard to stop
interested people coming with us"—so we went after dinner.

It was dark when we'd entered the dining hall; bright
day when we came out. I stopped, stunned. It wasn't
overcast now. An incredible moon shone from a clear
sky. With night the mountains had closed in and now the
fantastic Judean peaks seemed to be on top of us, old and
primeval and hoary in the moonlight. The folds of rock,
drenched in the pale luminescence, seemed like pock-
marks on some giant face peering down into the canyon.
Above them, the stars pulsed with extraordinary bril-
liance.

"It's wonderful, isn't it?" she said, watching me.
"Wonderful."
"We're in the lowest spot on earth—like being in a
hole and looking up. I don't think it's like this anywhere
else at full moon, is it?"
"No."

"Well, how about getting the torch, then, and we'll go."

I'd sooner have just stood and watched. A number of kibbutzniks were standing or sitting about doing the same. We went to the hut.

"Here's the electric light."

"All right. Don't switch it on," I said.

"No. You're funny, aren't you?"

"Am I?"

"There's a word in English, 'moonstruck,' isn't there?"

"Yes."

"You're *very* funny."

A lot of this seemed to be going on, but no answers were expected. We went out again.

A second look only confirmed the first. The entire rift was alive and electric in the lunar light.

To get to the canyon—the kibbutz being on a slight plateau—you have to descend. We descended. Below were the remains of an earlier pioneer kibbutz. The crude buildings of fiber board and palm thatch stood silent in the moonlight. We went past them and headed into the canyon.

We got to the ledge and climbed up. "There you are."

"How far in were the scrolls?"

"At the very end. It runs in for six meters."

"Can I go in?"

"Go ahead."

She took the torch and wriggled in; and a few minutes later, somewhat dusty, wriggled out again. I gave her a cigarette. We sat and smoked, dangling our legs over the ledge.

"It's strange, isn't it? Why should he have come from Galilee to Jerusalem via Ein Gedi?"

"Maybe troops were blocking the direct way," I said.

"And why leave the Jerusalem copy *here*?"

"It was the only one he had. He'd hidden the other two on his way south—one in The Curtains, the other at Murabba'at."

"Wasn't there a raid here round about that time?"

"Yes. From Massada. Passover of 68." The revolutionaries at Massada had swarmed down and attacked the village. The men of Ein Gedi had run away. The theory was that our character had run away with them, hiding the scroll and his money for safety.

"A very bloodthirsty one?"

"Yes. The revolutionaries were annoyed at the men running away. They took all the food and killed the women and children. Josephus mentions it."

"*Can* it have been a raid just for food, do you think?"

"How do you mean?"

"All that senseless killing. I've wondered about it. It's almost as if they were after something else, and didn't find it. . . . You don't think it could have been . . . It's silly, I know. I just felt something while I was in there, in the cave."

Silly or not, I felt my own back hairs tingling a bit.

I said, "I don't think it's silly at all, Shoshana."

"You mean it?"

"I think you might be on to something."

"Oh, Caspar, that's marvelous. Does it help?"

"I don't know. I don't know how the people at Massada can have known there was a scroll here."

"It was only a feeling," she said anxiously.

"I'm hot on feelings, love. Very strong on instinct."

"So am I."

"Are you?"

"Oh, yes. Always," she said, neat little head shaking its usual baffling negative.

We finished the cigarette and clambered down. The canyon, if anything, was brighter than when we'd walked into it. We seemed to be levitating in a river of silver.

"Where are we going?" I said, minutes later.

"I don't know. We seem to be heading for the waterfall. Where do you want to go?"

"The Cave of Shulamit?" I said, suddenly remembering.

"All right," she said, after a pause. It had struck me that the deadpan joker might well have put me on to the local romancing spot. There was nothing wrong with that, of course, and my words of commendation seemed to have put her in a party mood. We made toward it, anyway.

The soft hiss of the waterfall swelled as we drew nearer, and suddenly we saw it, flashing white down the cliff.

The biblical spring—the *ein* in Ein Gedi—spurts several hundred feet up in the hard limestone, and cascades down over a series of ledges. Some of the ledges are so big that they form large water basins; others are small grottoes. A rough stairway of stones and boulders leads from one level to the next, the path so overgrown with bamboo and tropical foliage that often it's like ascending a tunnel.

We paused at each level, and had a lengthy rest at the third, perching on a large boulder on the lip of a narrow water basin. The moonlight was filtered here by overhanging foliage from a higher level. It spread a glow so dim and astral that it was hard to tell rock from water and water from air, the whole grotto seemingly adrift in pale liquid motion.

We left it at last and climbed higher, sometimes so damply near the main flashing column, and so much a part of its muffled roar, that we seemed literally to be climbing up it.

"Hang on to me here," the girl said, some levels later. "We go in a tunnel. The surface is uneven."

She went head first into the bamboo, bent double, and I followed. The only thing to hold on to was her nubile behind, which I did, firmly. The tunnel rose for thirty feet of impenetrable blackness and then ended in a brightness so theatrical I couldn't all at once take it in.

We were in a large natural amphitheater, about a hundred yards across, a bowl of rock; a focusing bowl for the moon at the moment. We were not, evidently, at the top, for water still ran, from a higher level, but somewhere it had been blocked, and now it moved everywhere, trickling, rippling, seeping, down rock faces and across them, every facet glittering silver as it reflected back the unbelievable globe that hung over the hole in the sky.

The main stream wandered musically down the middle of the amphitheater, collecting other rivulets before falling thunderously below. Trees and vegetation grew out of the rock, and a number of boulders stood starkly shadowed like Henry Moore figures.

We went and sat on one and smoked another cigarette, staring about transfixed. There was a somnambulistic quality about her in the moonlight that seemed to preclude any advances. A good dark cave, of course, was another matter.

She pulled herself out of her trance at last and looked at her watch.

"Eleven o'clock. We ought to be going soon."

"What about the cave?"

"It's here."

We were sitting outside it, the opening entirely covered by a fan of hanging fronds. Water ran down the fronds, forming a continuous flowing curtain. I cursed a little. A beauty spot, evidently, not a romancing one.

"Why the Cave of Shulamit?"

"From the Song of Songs. The Shulamite had long hair —like that. Don't you like it?"

"Very pretty. I thought it was the kind of cave you could go into," I said lamely.

"You'd get wet, wouldn't you?"

"Maybe we ought to have brought our swimming things," I said bitterly.

She smoked her cigarette very carefully to the end, and stood up. "Let's go, then."

Half an hour later, drearily, I found myself back in the slumbering kibbutz. We hadn't talked much on the way down. I walked her to her sister's door.

"Good night, then, Shoshana."

"Good night."

She turned her face just as I kissed her, and got it on the cheek.

"What's the matter?"

"Nothing. It's late. We don't want to wake them up."

"Shoshana—"

She slipped out of my arms.

"Good night," she said, and was inside in a flash.

Somewhere, somehow, one of her compound signals had been misread. Or was her brother-in-law right, and the girl didn't know her own mind?

Next day, early, we went back to bloody Galilee.

Six

A NAUGHTY PERSON

He winketh with his eyes . . .
he teacheth with his fingers.
—Proverbs 6:12, 13

1

I WASN'T by the Wednesday, so much "unhappy" as in a state of manic depression. I'd shuttled so many times past the tomb of Rabbi Meir I was ready to blow it up; also sawn-off rocks that might once have stood 600 feet; and Arabs keen to sell me blue stones. We couldn't pass a village anywhere in Lower Galilee now without half the population running out with beads and marbles. In the morning we visited Nazareth, on what I'd already decided was the last chore—a visit to an Arab lapidary reputed to know the home of every colored stone in Galilee.

Above and beyond these problems were two others. The weather had broken and rain now fell dismally. And the girl had become suddenly hostile. This last nonsense had manifested itself on the run back from Ein Gedi, and hadn't improved. It seemed to me her sister was behind it somewhere.

I said, "Look, love, what's your particular problem?"

"I have no particular problem."

"Have you got a period or a face-ache or what?"

"Neither of these things," she said coldly, "and if I had they'd be my concern, not yours."

"I'm not an Anglo-Saxon rapist, you know, whatever your sister might think."

"And leave my sister alone."

"Well, you leave me alone," I said, and meant it. She'd already offered to throw me in the lake again, the result of an unfortunate pleasantry. "Might doesn't solve anything," I'd sneered at her; but even that didn't rouse her.

Well, damn her, I thought, and damn Agrot, too. Particularly damn Agrot. I decided to tell him so, whatever the lapidary might say.

The lapidary didn't say much. He was a little old man about ninety, a pronounced case of curvature of the spine, and his main preoccupation seemed to be with the price of reefers. He was sitting on a rug smoking one when we entered his minuscule shop, and his only interest in the visit was the possibility that I might know of a reasonable source of supply.

"They have gone mad in Akko," he said. "It's the wholesalers. Mad or crooked. Possibly both."

"It's not the wholesalers, Grandpa," Shoshana told him in her lilting Arabic. "It's hard for them, too. In Jordan they stop the hashish going out, and in Israel we stop it coming in. There are new roads at Barot and Arad where the old tracks were. The price is bound to go up."

"Yes. It's a part of the degeneracy of the age," the old man said sadly. "So what is this book you are writing?"

I told him about the book I was writing; allegedly on the biblical geology of Galilee. He didn't listen much. He stubbed out his reefer presently on his black thumbnail. "The finest marble," he said, "is in the south. You must go there to see good marble."

"What about Galilee?"

"No. There are no commercial deposits here. There never were."

"Can you suggest how I might come on even small supplies, reasonably?"

"Certainly. Hang the ringleaders," he said, taking out another reefer, and then reluctantly putting it back again. "You would find prices tumbling overnight. It would have an immediate effect on the cost of living. You don't happen to indulge yourself?" he said wistfully.

I left him a quid or two to help with the cost of living, and we went out. It was raining like hell, and we had to dash back into the suk again. We stood drearily in a café entrance, crammed between numerous sodden Arabs. In the roadway—a tiny cobbled path that ran like a ditch between the high pavements—donkeys lumbered by, hocks awash in the rain water swilling down the street, their panniers brushing past us.

"Let's go in and have some coffee," I said, and we did, coldly, the only words being mine, and to a young Arab pimp, telling him a bit abruptly to eff off. He was back again in a brace of shakes with a pal, and I told them both to eff off. The pal said he had five children, and what with that and the weather, he'd do me a nice tour of the Church of the Annunciation, the Chapel of the Angel, Joseph's Workshop and Mary's Well at half price; alternatively he'd take my photo. He managed to take it, too, before the proprietor, alarmed by the flash, threw him out. By that time the rain had slackened, so he effed off anyway, without extracting any money.

We went, too.

At the hotel the girl waited below while I went up and phoned Agrot. She was leafing moodily through a magazine in the lounge when I came down again. She looked up a bit nervously.

"Have you made the—arrangements?"

"Yes. Pick me up tomorrow morning about eight."

"Will we be coming back here?"

"I don't know."

"Will you want me next week?"

"I don't know that either."

She got up slowly, and seemed to be trying to say something. I didn't help her, and whatever it was, she didn't say it.

2

It was raining in Jerusalem, too. The girl dropped me at the King David, and teetered about a bit while the porter got my bag and I went and signed in. I didn't hurry and presently, a bit lost, she wandered over to the reception desk.

"Is there anything you would like me to do?"

"No." I was looking up a telephone book.

"Well, what do you *want* me to do?" she blurted.

"Nothing. You can push off now."

She hadn't made any arrangements in Jerusalem, and was not due on her weekend till noon tomorrow, so this stymied her slightly.

"You mean to Tel Aviv?"

"Wherever you want. You can take the jeep."

"Well. Thanks," she said, flummoxed. "Do you want me to come back *here* on Sunday?"

"I suppose you could."

She still hung about, and I looked up. "What's the problem?"

She said, gulping, "Caspar, I'm sorry if differences have occurred between us. What I'd like you to know is that I enjoy very much the work I've been doing, and I wish to continue, unless you have any fault to find with it."

"I see," I said neutrally.

"So would you like me to telephone here on Saturday night?"

"All right. I don't know if I'll be here."

"Would it be too much trouble for you to phone me, then?"

"Okay. Leave the number."

She rapidly wrote it on a scrap of paper. "It's a café, down below. I'll wait in for it."

"No need for that. Your boy-friend's coming up, isn't he?"

"Yes. He is," she said, smiling slightly.

"Well, don't waste an evening. I mightn't even phone," I said, to wipe the smile off.

It wiped off. She went unhappily. I returned to the telephone book. Isaacs, Isaac. I didn't want the number, only the address. It was there.

I walked up the Jaffa Road, raincoat up round my ears, found the old Turkish alley, and went briskly along it to the courtyard, holding my nose. The scent of sanitation and gefillte fish was, as ever, very strong. A maze of iron staircases led to a honeycomb of flats. I climbed up to the first floor and rang the bell. I heard him there presently, and he opened the door. The light was bad on the balcony and he stared hard.

"Well, you bloody old bastard," he said.

"Hello, Ike."

"What are you doing here?"

"Let me in and I'll tell you."

"Well, I'll be damned," he said.

He was large and stout, and wearing at the moment his ginger mustache, pale-blue underpants and a pair of chukka boots. The place was like a furnace inside.

"Did I catch you in the bath?"

"You must have smelled it, you frigging old ram. I've got crumpet here."

The crumpet, two separate portions of it, lay on the floor under his floodlamps, surrounded by oil heaters. The girls were even more simply dressed, in dark glasses.

"Well, I'm—" Ike said. "Here, girls—we've got the biggest fornicator in the English aristocracy. He's their Olympics champion at it. They love a lord," he said, winking at me. Even his Hebrew had a broad Yorkshire accent, and he used it fairly racily without benefit of euphemism.

The girls seemed used to his little ways and greeted me amiably enough without moving a fraction of an inch. They didn't seem to understand English, but I persevered for a minute or two to make sure.

"So what's to do?" Ike said, when he'd got me a drink.

I told him, in English.

"H'm. Himmelwasser. I know her."

He knew everybody. In the early fifties he'd been perhaps the most accomplished camera artist in Europe. He'd given up his journalistic work in Israel, but as I'd found at Megiddo, had lost none of his accomplishment, or his nose for what was going on round him.

"She's good," he said.

"Rigid."

"It's the nature of the work." He winked at me, and set about rearranging the girls while I told him the rest. Then he went behind his camera and took a couple of pictures.

"I'll tell you, Caspar," he said at length. "I wouldn't want to run foul of Himmelwasser or the university. I do a bit for them, you know."

"You wouldn't run afoul of them. They wouldn't know about it."

"What if I buggered it up?"

"You could have a look at it, see what you think."

"All right. So what to-doings have you been up to meanwhile?"

I gave him a brief rundown on Galilee and Ein Gedi.

"Ein Gedi, eh?" he said. "Find your way up to the Cave of Shulamit there?"

"Yes. Very nice," I said.

"Anybody I'd like?"

"How do you mean?"

"You went up with a girl, didn't you?"

"Yes. Is it obligatory?"

Ike looked at me. "The cave with the water running down," he said, to get it right.

"That's the one. How are you supposed to get in?"

Ike's face went a little bit bent. "You take your clothes off, you silly bastard," he said. "That's the whole idea. You mean you didn't?"

I looked at him with a faint sinking feeling.

"Oh, Jesus God," he said. "She must have been overjoyed with you. Why, you poor old eunuch, you, we'd better get you back in shape. Come back tonight and I'll keep these bints."

But I hardly heard him, remembering only the look on

her face when I'd suggested we needed swimwear, and the way she'd lingered over her cigarette, and the silent journey down again.

"I can't tonight, Ike," I heard my voice saying. "I'm tied up tonight. Agrot's running in for a chat."

"Chats, chats," Ike said severely. "You can do your chatting tomorrow. There's serious to-doings here tonight. Get rid of him early."

But I didn't get rid of him early. Agrot ran in for his chat about ten. We were still chatting at two.

What with this, and the joint frustrations of the week, Dr. Hilde Himmelwasser was due to sail into stormy weather next morning; which she did, at ten o'clock sharp. The problem was to edge her out without actually kicking her out, and though Agrot refused to do the job himself, he'd agreed to provide moral support and to approve my arguments if appealed to. He insisted that no reflections be cast on her work, but with this the only hold barred, I was off at the bell and within five minutes had her bouncing off the ropes distinctly cross-eyed.

It was all done by kindness, and though the cow was on to me in a trice, and quickly dropped her zisses and zats to engage on level terms in Hebrew, she hadn't the advantage, as I had, of having gone a few rounds with a class performer like Mrs. Birkett.

What it came down to, I said, was that she'd taken it as far as it could possibly go. There were limits to what an emulsion could do, and her techniques were the most advanced in the world. If she couldn't do the job in the time available to me, then nobody could; and time was now of the essence. If I couldn't have the words, then the physical handling of the skin was better than nothing, and this—with her approval—was what I now wanted.

By half past ten Agrot had symbolically accepted her scrollery key, and she had symbolically taken herself off with a pot of emulsion.

Agrot picked up the skin and looked at it.

"What has survived for eighty generations doesn't just belong to our own," he said somberly.

"It isn't much use to anybody at the moment, is it?"

"Other generations might find ways of making it useful. . . . The ink has oxidized right into the skin," he said, squinting at it sideways. "Apply chemical treatment and the whole lot could vanish. God knows how I'd justify myself if it did."

"Well, it's not the only copy, you know."

"It's the only one we've got."

"What do you want to do, then—leave the decision to me?"

"No. It's my decision," he said. But it took him a bit longer to make it. It was midday before I got to Ike's; with the skin.

Agrot's nervousness had made me nervous. Ike was nervous, too.

He said, "Christ, it's dodgy, isn't it?"

"There's something there."

"Oh, there's something."

It showed as a faint iridescence against the surrounding blackness. He was holding the skin in a slanting light under an arc.

"What has she done, do you know?"

"I suppose everything bar treating the skin itself. I've brought you a few of her prints," I said.

He had a look at the prints.

"Why didn't she treat the skin itself?" he said.

"She wouldn't. Also, she had no authority to."

"Does that mean I haven't got authority to?"

"No, it doesn't mean that. If it's necessary, you can."

"Who said so?"

"I did."

"Do I get it in writing, or what?"

"You just take my word for it."

He had a look at me. Then he had a look at the prints and at the skin.

He said, "I'm not actually too barmy about this, Caspar."

"I guarantee nobody will know about you."

"So what if the frigging thing just disintegrates?"

"I disintegrated it."

"I don't like it."

"Look, is it possible for any words to come up off there?"

He was always very honest, Ike. He said, "Yes, I think it's possible. I'm not saying what would happen to the skin. You'd have to photograph it fast before the lot went. . . . I'm almost frightened to touch it."

"Do it for me, Ike."

"I'll see."

"I'll call you this evening."

"I won't have done anything by this evening!"

"I'll still call you. And, Ike, have you got a safe here?"

"Yes, I've got a safe."

"Any time it's not in your hand, see it's in the safe."

Then I went back to the university, more nervous than ever.

* * *

I didn't have any lunch. I had a few cups of black coffee. Agrot had black coffee, too. We spent the afternoon in the scrollery. There was still plenty to do on the notes there, and after a while I managed to focus on something that had been bothering me all along. I got out the relevant prints, and then the relevant notes. There were several alternative readings. I sat down and worked out my own, all the same.

"No one has told me," my version went, "that our acts are [known to?] Northern Command. I cannot in my soul—— ——that this Command [authority?] in our acts. The young officer himself——not possible [to say?]"

I hadn't been wrong. There was a tone of surprise, consternation, shock here. Why? Which other Command did he expect to know about his "acts"? He was operating in Galilee, the area of Northern Command. If any Command was going to know, it would be *this* Command. Or was he simply upset that the military should be involved at all in what was a secret Temple operation? I didn't think that. He'd been too keen to set down that it was specifically Northern Command.

Agrot studied my notes. "I don't like your reading," he said. "It's too emphatic. The thing is a matter of nuance."

"Doesn't he sound surprised to you?"

"He was a priest, of a legalistic turn of mind. He's concerned to set things down exactly. All through his report he is punctilious to apportion blame—or to absolve people of it. Here he suspects a hijacking operation, and he is setting down as clearly as he can that it was officially authorized by Northern Command. At the same time, in case it should turn out to be quite kosher, he's clearing himself of any charge of obstruction—*nobody told him*. You'll notice he's very careful to absolve the young officer of any blame or dereliction of duty. The search for him, when he ran away, was properly conducted, etc. It's all of a piece."

"But he's surprised it should be *Northern* Command. He's implying they have no business to be there."

"In your reading, not in mine," he said, with a faint smile. "I came across several similar things in the Bar-Kochbah work. The style is often declamatory and repetitive. It's a tricky nuance. I shouldn't waste time with it."

This is always something that has to be allowed for with Israeli scholars, of course; the feeling that it's faintly ridiculous or even slightly improper for any Gentile to challenge their reading of the *lashon kodesh*, the holy tongue, particularly on matters of nuance or shades of meaning. All very tiresome; but I persevered.

"What time are you calling Isaacs?"

"After dinner. Do you want to get back to Barot?"

"No. Good God. I can't rest."

"He might be all weekend, you know."

"Then I'll stay all weekend."

This didn't make me feel any better either.

We ate a gloomy dinner together, and afterwards I telephoned Ike.

He said, "I told you, I won't have anything tonight."

But I could hear something in his voice. I said, "What have you done so far?"

"Christ! Won't you be told? *Nothing.*"

"Are you optimistic?"

"So-so," he said.

I smiled and felt my toes uncurling. He'd got something. He wanted to hit me with it all in one go.

"How's the skin?"

"Why don't you go and exercise yours?"

"All right. I'll call you in the morning."

"Don't call. Come round. About eleven."

"What—you really think—"

"I don't know," Ike said. "And——off!"

I went back and told Agrot. We had a couple of brandies on it.

It was still raining next morning, and I shot round there in a taxi. I'd been up at six, sleepless, and had gone for a walk in the rain with Agrot, also sleepless. I went briskly up the alley, holding my nose.

I was early, and Ike didn't answer the door himself. A little fellow in a white lab coat did.

"Mr. Isaacs in?"

"Yes, sir. It's Dr. Laing? I'm his assistant. He's through there, working. He's expecting you, Doctor. Go in."

He shut the street door behind me as I went in.

I said, "Well, you bastard—hit me with it!"

He did. Somebody did. Somebody hit me with something. My head seemed to explode and shatter in fragments. Just as I fell I had a glimpse, as if through a prism, of the little assistant, peering carefully, solicitously almost, into my face.

Seven

A Horrible Thing in the House

Israel is defiled.
—Hosea 6:10

1

I was lying under the car on the A.6 and Paula was being sick again. This wouldn't do, of course. I detached and deep-breathed, as advised, and it did the trick. No A.6. No sweaty nightmare blankets, either, though. Just mustiness, carpet mustiness. I'd passed out, then. Only where? And who was being sick? Somebody was being sick. Was it me being sick?

No, it was Ike being sick, poor old bastard. In his pajamas, too. I seemed to be up on one elbow looking at him. He was being sick the wrong color. He was lying on his side. It was all down the front of his pajamas, and underneath him. My head was a long way away and icy cold. Wherever the hell it was, it was hurting. Then it returned, and we associated, and I said, "Oh, Christ," and tried to get up.

"It's all right," somebody said, clicking his tongue. "Stay still. You'll be fine in a minute."

"What the hell is happening?" I said. My lips seemed

to be numb, and I said it in Arabic, no doubt because he'd spoken Arabic, too.

He didn't say anything, just went on clicking. It was the little alleged assistant, and he had an ice bag on my head. He was cleaning up my face, which seemed to be wet. Two others were there, heavy darkish men, mustached. They were sitting smoking, keeping a casual eye on me, and on Ike. Ike was lying under the lamps, where the crumpet had lain. He was lying in a quite relaxed way, except for a subdued twitch every now and again as he vomited. His face was sideways on the carpet, in a pool of it, eyes open like a fish and looking at me. It was not an apprehensive or an urgent look, just thoughtful, absorbed almost, as if he were metering the flow that gushed rhythmically from his mouth. I was suddenly vomiting with him, horribly.

I seemed to be in the bathroom then, and one of the men was holding me while the alleged assistant, quick as a cat, dabbed at my face with a little face flannel.

"It's all right, you'll be fine, there's nothing to worry about," he said, worried. "You just need a hat. Give him a hat," he said.

One of the men took his hat off and put it on me.

"That's fine. You look quite well. It's only to the car," the assistant said.

I was weaving about, horribly shocked, mumbling. "What are you doing? What have you done to Ike? What do you want here?"

I knew, of course—in some remote, though acceptable way—what they'd done to Ike and also what they were doing here. Knowing it didn't make it any less surrealist or improbable. It seemed important as I reeled about in my hat, to assimilate every detail of what was going on here. These characters were going to kidnap me. They were going to kidnap me in broad daylight! They had to be stopped, for God's sake. They had to be hoodwinked, outwitted, frightened off in some way. In what way, for God's sake? And by whom, for God's sake? There were two big powerful men here, and one alert little spry one, all quite plainly on top of the job.

The little spry one hadn't bothered answering me. He'd opened a medical chest and was fiddling with a pad of lint. And suddenly everything went into slow motion as my concussed and laboring brain started assimilating in a frenzy. I assimilated Ike quietly vomiting next door and the large man standing over the lavatory and wiping a knife very carefully on toilet paper; and the other one leaning in the doorway and studying a sheet of curling black card—the scroll fragment, I realized suddenly.

The little one had lifted the hat and popped the lint inside and replaced the hat again. "That's better," he said. "That will stop it. We can go now."

I said, "Look here," still mumbling at him and weaving about. "This is some horrible mistake. I don't know what you want, but you've got it wrong. You've got the wrong man. I'm—I'm a physician, a doctor," I said, suddenly recalling how he'd addressed me. "I'm simply a doctor. What do you want with me?"

"A physician?" he said, a bit taken aback, and the other two looked around, a bit taken aback also. "Well, I don't know anything about that," he said. "It's got nothing to do with me. It will all be explained."

"Explained? Explain what?" I said, but with a certain idiot relief flooding in. The man plainly didn't know me from Adam, and I'd suddenly recalled that my passport and every other bit of identifying material was safely in the hotel; also that my Arabic was quite as good as his. "You camel turd, you!" I told him. "You offal skin! You've made a mistake, can't you see? I'm an Arab, you fool—like yourself! I'm visiting this man. He's my patient. Ask anybody in the locality!"

This statement, though incoherently delivered, seemed to upset the two larger men, who frowned uncertainly at their colleague. It didn't, unfortunately, upset him. He simply began fumbling fussily with a pocketful of papers.

"No mistake, I think," he said. "No mistake my end, anyway. Seen with the man Agrot. Staying at the King David—"

"Visiting, you fool—visiting a patient!"

"—Followed here yesterday. And here—check photograph. That's him, isn't it?" he said.

His two colleagues had a look at the photo. I had a look at it, too. No mistakes his end, all right. I seemed to be scrutinizing the photo anxiously for mistakes. There I was in it, sitting at a plain wooden table, alongside a military-type sleeve, with a young Arab grinning in the background; evidently taken on some dig in Jordan. I had the same worried scowl I must be wearing now.

I said, "That's easily explained, of course."

"Of course. But we have to go now, Doctor." He was getting harassed. "All the mistakes will be settled. I'm sure you will be back here soon with many apologies. It's just a matter of control. Stand straight now. We'll walk to the car. We'll walk quite slowly. What we'll do, I and this gentleman will walk beside you. We don't want to hold you. The other gentleman will walk behind you. He's there to see you don't make a disturbance. If you make a disturbance he'll have to shoot you, and we'll run. Please don't make a disturbance."

"No, no, don't make a disturbance," the other gentleman said. It was the first time he'd said anything, and he said it in a shocked, admonitory sort of way.

I was sitting on the toilet then, my legs having folded, and looking up seriously at the two heads of the little chap, my eyes having crossed as well. He was clicking with his tongue. "Come on, now. Stand up. You can do it. It isn't far. I'm afraid you were hit a bit too hard," he said, clicking some more.

I'd been hit a bloody sight too hard. I couldn't seem to keep abreast of the situation for more than seconds at a time. Thank God Ike had stopped vomiting. He'd stopped because we weren't there now. We were on the iron stairs. We were in the alley. We were in the Jaffa Road. It was drizzling.

Mad, of course, all of it. Couldn't be happening. It wasn't me here, walking thoughtfully down the Jaffa Road with the two gentlemen. Where was the other gentleman? The other gentleman was behind. Street crowded as usual; vans, buses, housewives, old men with sticks.

"Not very far now. Just keep walking normally."

I was walking normally. I seemed to be walking normally. My feet weren't quite touching the ground. There was a reason for this, I thought, watching the windscreen wipers flick there and back. We were stopped at traffic lights. I was in a car. I suddenly remembered getting into the car. It was a big beat-up old Studebaker, parked at a traffic meter in a side street. As I got into it I remembered why Ike had stopped vomiting.

Some confusion seemed to be present here. To do with my head, of course. Except it wasn't mine, but this Arab doctor's. He'd been hit on it. Hit a bloody sight too hard.

I was full of indignation suddenly. "You *are* a camel turd," I told the man again. "A Palestinian camel turd," I elaborated. So he was; Palestinian Arab accent. The others seemed to be Jordanian. "A turd," I said again. But it wasn't him. He'd taken himself off. I was in the back with two other turds. I suddenly remembered he was driving. The whole trouble was, *lapses*. Pockets of sleep, gulfs. Like the Big Dipper, but instead of leaving your stomach, leave your senses, swoop. It wouldn't do. Had to assimilate. Street names, say. Where street names? No bloody street names.

Y.M.C.A., though; tall tower and domes, couldn't be anything else, which meant King David Hotel opposite. *Which it was.* This was pleasing. So the railway station next, if we were going out of town. Keep awake for it.

Didn't keep awake. Went off, came back, tried to think what I was supposed to be keeping awake for. We were out of town. A bus lumbering ahead. I took its route number, quick as a flash. Number seven. A very useful item. Even more useful if I knew where it was going. Turn and see the destination board as we pass. Turned, but missed it. Too much mud. Endless red mud. Where the hell were we walking to through all this mud?

"Where the hell are we walking to through all this mud?" I said tetchily.

"To the trees. It isn't far now," one of the Jordanians said. Both Jordanians were there; not the little chap, though. Taken himself off again; a spry little bastard if ever I saw one.

"Where's the car?" I said.

"We'll have another car. You'll be comfortable. You'll be able to rest first."

"Rest where?"

"Not far now," he said.

We were in a lane. I had an impression we'd passed houses. Fruit on all sides, now; stepped terraces of fruit trees, dripping in the rain. Rock walls, red earth. Where the hell were we? A truck came bouncing along the potholes in the lane. I looked to see if there was a name on it. Couldn't see. Too many trees. I was standing under one. My hat was tight, sodden from the dripping tree.

"Where's your friend?" I said. The man was holding me up.

"He'll be back. How do you feel?"

"Not good."

"Soon you'll feel better. We'll move soon."

"We'll move now," the friend said.

We started to move. The hat was tight and hot. I wanted to take it off.

"Don't take the hat off," he said.

"It's tight. It hurts."

"Soon it won't hurt."

It hurt now. It hurt like hell. I was stumbling on a black cinder track. I held my head down. My head was getting banged somehow. A tunnel of blackness, and I fell in it, fell away in it.

"I simply must have a rest," I said crisply.

"Yes, you can rest. It's done you good to rest."

"How long have we been here?"

"An hour or two. Take another rest if you wish."

"Yes," I said uncertainly, and took one.

I was still in the tunnel when I'd taken it. We were all in the tunnel. I was in a slightly fetal position, back pressed hard into the curve, hat touching the roof. They were sitting one each side of me, a pistol in each lap. I was trembling in a piercing draft. A husky resonance sounded as the wind blew through the tunnel. I said, "Where are we?"

"Just a place to rest. It was too wet in the trees. You look better now."

I didn't feel better. I felt as if a meat cleaver had been buried in my head and my limbs trussed and crammed into some compact-sized freezer. A place to rest. We must be at the jumping-off point, then; on the frontier. We were waiting for something. What? My teeth started to chatter like castanets.

"You still have some shock," the one without the hat said, watching me.

"How long are we staying here?"

"Till it's dark. In an hour or two."

"I can't stay like this for an hour or two," I said, chattering horribly at him.

"Go to sleep again."

"I have to relieve myself!"

I did, too. An hour or two! What could I do in an hour or two? What could I do anyway, with these two enormous ruffians and their pistols?

They were looking silently across me at each other. The hatless one nodded slightly and after a moment the other rolled over on to his hands and knees and lumbered up the tunnel. His face appeared in the entrance after a minute. "All right," he said softly.

The man beside me gave me a nudge, and I got over on my hands and knees, too. My head lurched shatteringly as it accompanied me. I moved into the husky resonance of the tunnel mouth and felt it vibrating my hat brim, and then wind-blown rain whipped in my face, and the man outside was helping me up. His companion was close behind me.

We were in a thicket of olive trees. Large pieces of junk lay about, a battered old boiler, a rusted cistern, sandbags. The tunnel was a section of abandoned sewerage pipe, about a yard in diameter. A zigzag ditch ran to one side of the thicket; a slit trench. We must be right on the border.

I relieved myself.. We were in a valley. Through the olive trees I could see a hill on the other side of the border, with a little blue flag fluttering at its peak. A track led up the hill to where the flag fluttered, evidently from a road in the valley, out of sight now. That would be the road where the car would pick us up when it was dark— not more than a couple of hundred yards over the border.

There was nothing to be seen on this side of the border. We seemed to be in a hollow, a no man's land. The slope cut off all signs of Israeli activity. But the Israelis worked their land close up to the border. There would be buildings and people near. How near?

The man with the knife had taken it out and was hefting it a little in his hand. He said, "Hurry up." I hurried up, and turned, and saw a rooftop, Israeli side.

A rooftop. A hundred yards away, not more. The slope of the hollow was littered with debris. Where it stopped, fruit trees began. Above the fruit trees was the rooftop.

My hands were shaking so much I could hardly zip up.

The building might be abandoned, of course. . . .

Through the wind-blown rain, the mud on the slope winked evilly in the dirty gray light. One would have to run up the muddy slope. Very unpromising.

"Ready now?"

"Not quite."

"What's the matter?"

"I feel sick," I said truthfully.

"Come back inside. You'll be better seated. There is a breeze there."

A sympathetic but firm grip. We went back inside, on hands and knees, myself in the middle. Bits of debris and builder's rubble were scattered in the entrance. My hand closed on a half brick, and let it go again. What use was half a brick? Half a brigade of guards, maybe.

I maneuvered back into the fetal position and tried to think. My head was hurting so horribly, this was not easy. *Where the hell were we?* I hadn't the faintest idea, except south. But wait. How did I even know south?

Think. I knew it because—of what? Because of the *King David,* that was it. We'd passed the King David, going south, and I'd expected to see the railway station which was farther south still. Also the bus. It was a number seven bus—the Ramat Rahel bus, I realized suddenly. You couldn't go any farther south than Ramat Rahel: the border looped round there, enclosing the Jerusalem enclave. And we hadn't got that far. I was sure of it. I had a sudden flash of the Studebaker at the entrance to a lane, and of ourselves getting out. A muddy potholed lane, going downhill. Houses in the lane, terraces of fruit trees . . .

I suddenly knew where we were; could place it precisely. You could see it from the hill at Ramat Rahel, in line with the flag I'd spotted: the flag of the United Nations post. A lane ran down into a valley, to the old truce line. There was a shell crater at the bottom, with a cluster of blasted olive trees. All along the lane, right down to the crater, were smallholders' cottages and their fruit gardens.

Plenty of cottages, plenty of people. It was simply a matter of getting there, across the crater, up the slope

. . . pursued by two men with guns, rather faster on their feet than I was, in present form; men who wouldn't hesitate to use the guns, who'd have used them in the Jaffa Road this morning, with far more people about.

But wait, I thought. There were important differences between this mud-bound crater and the Jaffa Road. They'd had a car in the Jaffa Road. They'd have run to the car and got away in it. They didn't have a car here. There wouldn't be a car till it was dark. And there was nowhere to run till then: any shooting would bring a UN jeep down the track before they'd got a couple of hundred yards. So there'd be no shooting. There'd been no shooting in the flat this morning. I suddenly remembered the man cleaning his knife in the bathroom. The guns were more in the nature of protection—possibly for laying me out again if I made a disturbance. But if I put a few yards between us—if I did it quickly, without warning?

This appraisal of the situation and the realization that I'd have to have a try within the next couple of hours threw me into such a shaking panic one of the men actually put up his hand to hold me.

"Try and relax," he said. "It won't be long now. We'll go early."

"Eh?"

"The rain is making it dark. We'll have the signal before an hour."

I was sick, in his lap. He edged away, swearing.

"Are you all right?"

"I have to go outside again," I said weakly.

They looked at each other again, and the one I'd been sick on lumbered off. Presently his head was in the entrance again. "All right."

I thought, *Oh God, this is it,* and found myself mindlessly on hands and knees padding up the tunnel. I seemed to be slavering as I padded, like some big tired dog, limbs rubbery, stomach heaving, the other man butting me from behind. Just as I got to the entrance, I was sick again. I'd put my hand down on the half brick. Then the man outside, hissing a bit in sympathy, was bending down to help me up. He had big round eyes in a big round face, and I was looking up into it, vision blurred by tears of sickness, and willing myself to do it. Then I did it.

His expression didn't seem to alter much. His mouth, circled with mud and brick dust, merely described a tight pursed O and he went backward, eyes apologetic almost, flat on his backside. Then I was stumbling round, and the other man, his view cut off, was up on his knees in the tunnel entrance, arms outstretched to steady me. "Easy now—easy," he said. "Get your balance." And I paused a moment and got it, and drew one foot back and let him have it, hard, horribly low, and his face went gently meditative. He said breathily, "Ah," and held himself, and gave a profound bow, on his knees, and then I was running, running like hell.

2

The fallacy about action is that once you're in it apprehension goes and you concentrate calmly on the job in hand. Nothing like that happened to me. I ran in blind panic, concentrating on one simple thought: *God help me if they lay hands on me.* About half a minute later I saw this was very likely. I was running the wrong way.

I'd come belting out of the trees, making for the slope,

when I saw over to the left the black line of a cinder track. It disappeared into the trees. I suddenly remembered that we'd come down this track. In the mud it was the only sensible way down—or up. I turned and ran toward it right away, and as I turned saw the man I'd hit with the brick also running toward it; and realized he'd be at it rather sooner than I would. The other man was also on the move; not running exactly. He was stumbling along and clutching himself, with a very unpleasant look on his face.

I thought *Oh Jesus Christ* and without pause swerved frenziedly back in the original direction. The slope was still nearer to me than to them. If I could only keep going I'd get there first. I had to get there first. I felt myself practically flying, leaping over obstacles, sickness gone, headache gone, breath gone too. I made the slope, thick red mud sucking at my shoes, and started up it, and almost at once began slipping back down again. I clutched frantically, at rocks, debris, was on my knees, and off them again, breath sobbing as I scrambled.

About halfway up I stopped, limbs leaden, lungs choked. I'd stopped not so much because of these physiological details as because I'd suddenly seen I wasn't going anywhere. Rocks had been gouged from the earth immediately under the top. Several were still lying around. The effect was to create an overhand that you couldn't see till you were close up to it. I was quite close enough now. Without assistance from above it wasn't possible to get up this way at all. The assistance was already there. The first man was standing watching me, not even breathing very deeply. As I looked, the second joined him. They didn't say anything. They simply looked at me, fifteen feet below. They looked at me fairly enjoyably.

I threw back my head and yelled "Help!" It came out as a falsetto bleat in the wind, and the only effect was that the man I'd kicked bent down and picked up a rock and threw it at me, hard.

He couldn't miss at that range, and he didn't. It caught me a fearful bloody thump on the shoulder. I got my head down fast as I saw the other man bending. I stayed down, spread-eagled on the slope, protecting my head, too shocked to move as both bastards began stoning me. After a witless minute or two it occurred to me they were trying to drive me down, and what was good for them was bad for me, so I started wriggling up, not able to see where I was going, just protecting my head and collecting a barrage of appalling bloody thuds on the back till I made the shelter of the overhang and crouched there, moaning slightly and trying to think what the hell to do now.

The situation was so uniquely horrible it hardly bore thinking about. All I'd done besides getting the wits stoned out of me was to ensure I'd pick up a bloody good hiding in the bargain. I'd pick that up now whatever I did. It was simply a matter of waiting for it. The only advantage of this refuge was that they couldn't get at me immediately. They'd have to get me down first or maneuver in some way round the side of the overhang.

Which side? The left side. On the right there was no slope at all, merely a drop. On the left there was plenty of slope, littered with debris and boulders. A very large boulder, immediately under the overhang, at present cut me off from this slope. I saw suddenly that it was possible for them to get round its offside without my seeing.

I edged toward it and tried to find a vantage point to look round. There wasn't one. The thing stood upright like an egg, bottom sunk in the hill, broader parts concealing the view. I couldn't get below it without exposing myself again. I tried to get above it.

I dug my shoes in the greasy red mud and edged higher, under the overhang. It smelled damp and musty like a grave. There was a gap of about a foot between the top of the boulder and the overhang. I couldn't squeeze into it. I couldn't see through it. Earth blocked the other side.

I hung there, listening for movements above my head. I couldn't hear anything. Only a gentle moaning, which seemed to be coming from me, and the deeper moaning of the wind. It moaned loud and clear all the way from Ramat Rahel, the Heights of Rachel; a constant wind. "Rachel weeping for her children," the prophet Jeremiah had said. "Refrain thy voice from weeping," he'd advised, "and thine eyes from tears; for thy work shall be rewarded."

I wondered if mine was going to be.

A faint pattering of earth fell on the slope. I twisted round and looked down. More earth fell there.

Someone coming down.

I edged out as far as I could and tried to see around the rock. I couldn't see around it. I shook the bloody thing.

It moved.

I shook it again. It moved again. Earth fell out of the gap as it moved. I could suddenly see through. I could see a foot, moving down very slowly, and then the other, and then legs, and then the rest of him. It was the man who'd copped the brick. He still carried the mark on his mouth and there was blood on his chin. He stopped suddenly and looked at me. He couldn't see me through the gap; I was in heavy shade. I could see him very clearly, not five yards away, at the other side of the rock.

He stayed like that a moment, then looked up and waved. He didn't wave immediately above my head. He waved over to the right, a long way over. They'd separated, then. Why? I racked tired brains and tried to work it out. While I did so, he sat down. He just sat on the slope and waited.

There seemed to be only one answer. He'd come down to bottle me up. If I broke and ran I wasn't going to get past him. I could only get below him. Then I'd have to run to the other side of the crater and try to get up there. The other man would be waiting there.

If I didn't do anything, he wouldn't either. He'd just wait there till it was dark and come around the boulder with his gun. No need to frig about throwing rocks then. If I ran he'd simply shoot, in the right place.

It was getting dark now. It didn't take long to do it here. One minute it looked a bit dark and the next it *was*. The choice seemed to be to run now and chance it, or run later with the near certainty of a bullet in the backside. I was a bit scrambled today, but not that scrambled. I started moving down from the rock. My foot slipped. I hung on to the rock. The rock lurched. It lurched quite strongly.

Something here; definitely something here. The thing was loose, ready to roll if I had the strength to make it.

If the bastard at the other side could only be encouraged to shift himself to a point just below it . . .

I looked down. An old toilet cistern, lidless, was half bedded in the slope. I picked up a stone and tossed it down. It clanged into the cistern and bounced out. I threw another. Then I picked up more and climbed up to the top of the boulder again and looked through the gap.

His mouth was open and he was looking earnestly down the slope. He hadn't moved. I leaned out as far as I could and pitched a couple more stones out. I sent them arcing up, and they hit the overhang first, breaking a bit off it. Then I looked through the gap again.

He still hadn't moved, but his big plain face was creased in thought as he looked down and then up, trying to follow the line of the falling earth and stones. He twisted round and tried to see the top of the overhang above me. He couldn't see it, so he stood up and tried again. He still couldn't see it. He turned and looked at the boulder hard, and I saw the succession of simple thoughts passing through his head. It was always possible that I'd found some way of getting up. I might have dislodged the earth and stones as I moved. Was I still under the overhang? I glared at him through the gap, silently urging him to shift himself down where he could see. Presently he did. He began to move down the slope, very cautiously. I watched him for a moment, then got in position behind the boulder.

It wasn't till I was there that I realized I couldn't see him now. I'd have to guess when he got in position. Also there was nothing to hold on to here. When the boulder went, if it went, I'd go with it. If I'd guessed wrongly, he wouldn't cop the boulder. He'd cop me.

I attuned to his remembered rate of progress, heart thudding powerfully. I gave him about a quarter of a minute, counted ten slowly, drew a breath, and shoved.

The thing sucked earth, tottered, went. I clutched on nothing and went with it. I saw him, not quite below, just a little to one side, but with his body angled round to peer under the overhang. He couldn't quite get out of the way in time, got a hefty nudge under the shoulder, dropped his gun, reared up and started pattering down the slope backward, still on his feet. I was pattering down frontward, still on mine. I took about twenty tiny skittering steps, unable to stop, the pair of us facing each other about twenty yards apart as though giving some fancy and high-speed demonstration of the rumba. Then I got my foot in the lavatory cistern, sat momentarily, watched him still pattering with fury backward down the slope, and was up and out of it.

3

I traversed the rest of the slope like a greyhound, made the top, peered frantically for the entrance to the lane in the sudden gloaming, saw it, and was making toward it when the other man, a hundred yards away, cottoned on and came running. He fired as he ran. I saw the flash, heard the report, and took off more keenly than ever.

The lane was empty, dark—pitch-black almost. I floundered uphill among the potholes, saw a house, the first, decided it was too convenient, and realized I'd better get out of the lane anyway. There was a pile of fruit crates in the next entry. I dodged past them, saw an open wooden door, and ran through. I was in a garden and the fruit groves ran parallel on the left. I jumped on the low wall of the first terrace and sprinted along, screened by the dripping trees, still in line with the lane. The backs of the houses were toward me, and there were lights on in them. I saw one glimmering only dimly, made for it, jumped down off the wall, into a garden, found the door, turned the knob and went in.

An old couple were seated at a table with candles—Sabbath candles, Friday night, I realized suddenly—the only light in the room. He was reading aloud from a book and she was listening to him. The pair of them swiveled round open-mouthed and sat looking at me. I said, "Blow the candles out," too choked to say any more.

"The Sabbath candles?" the woman said, and just then there was a shot, fairly close, and I blew them out. The last thing I saw was the face of the old man, disembodied almost in the candle flame, neck scrawny, lips bluish as he gaped at me.

I said, gasping in the dark, "There are Jordanians in the lane with guns. Where's the phone?"

"Where's the phone?" It was the woman.

"To call the police."

She said stupidly, "To call the police? On Shabat?"

I don't think I shook her. I don't know what I did. We seemed to be sitting on the floor in a passage, and I had my cigarette lighter lit while she dialed. In its light I could see she was wearing a wig, the *sheitel* of the old orthodox Jewess, and it was slightly askew. The old man seemed to be seated on the floor, too, and a hell of a row was going on outside, firing and glass shattering and people running. The old man was rocking back and forth moaning.

She must have made the call. I must have asked her to call a taxi, too, because one turned up, before the police; the driver on double rates for Shabat. The quality of the row had changed outside. It was all outrage and excited hubbub now, and I knew they weren't there any more. They'd be in a car, speeding into Jordan, where I would have been.

For the first time almost, I suddenly realized what had happened today, and I was faint and dizzy. I could hardly stand up. Once I was up, I could hardly move.

"Wait! Stay. You can't go now. What about the police?"

"Tell them to phone Professor Agrot. Professor Agrot, at the university, or at his flat."

"No. Please. You tell them. Don't go now. You can't go now."

I could. I did, too exhausted to argue.

"So where are we going?" the driver said.

"I want a doctor."

"On Shabat? We can see. What happened to you?"

"Just a minute. Stop there," I told him. "The telephone box."

He had to help me out of the cab and into the box. I leaned against the wall inside, sick and faint, horribly conscious of my head. The hat seemed to have gone. The lint had gone too. There was just a sticky mess there. There was mud all down the front of my clothes.

The phone answered after the first ring. Agrot said, "Yes?"

I said, "It's me. Did you find Ike?"

He said, "Caspar! Are you all right?"

"Yes. What's happened to him?"

"The police have the body. What's happened to *you*, for God's sake?"

I started to tell him, appreciating dully what he'd said. I felt myself slipping down inside the box. I levered myself up, but still kept slipping. He said at last, "You say they had a photo of you taken in Jordan?"

"Yes," I said, but in the same moment realized it wasn't. I had a sudden hallucinatory vision of him, the little grinning Arab I'd told to eff off in Nazareth, standing behind me in the photo; and of the friend I'd told to eff off, too, who'd taken it. The military sleeve next to mine; Shoshana's sleeve. I heard myself telling him it, and his precise voice repeating it. He said, "You don't sound good. Where are you?"

"In a call box."

"Do you want me to pick you up?"

"No, I've got a cab."

"All right, I'll see you at the hotel in a few minutes."

"I'm not going back there."

He started to say, "What do you mean?" and stopped and said, "I see. All right. Do you want to come here?"

"No. I told you. They were *looking* for me—"

"Look, you'll be perfectly—"

"Good-by."

"Wait a minute! Where are you going?"

"I'll let you know," I said, and hung up.

Wherever the hell it was, it was away from here. But there was my head first.

We met the doctor opening his front door, just returning from synagogue, a little elderly man. He looked me up and down in the street, and then at my head. "What's this—a traffic accident?"

"Kind of."

"People shouldn't ride on Shabat, then it wouldn't happen," he said. "Come inside."

He cleaned my head up and put six stitches in it, and then dressed and bandaged it. The room swam as I sat there. I said, "Do you mind if I smoke?"

"Why smoke on Shabat? Is it such a hardship, one day only, to keep your religion?"

"It's not my religion."

"It's not?" He had a good look at me. "So smoke."

"You have an excellent accent," he said as he worked. "Where are you from?"

"England."

"Good. That will be six pounds English. Or forty-eight pounds Israeli."

He wouldn't handle money on Shabat, so I counted it out on a small side table, and looked at myself in the mirror above it. My head was like a great bandaged balloon, very identifiable if anybody happened to be looking for a head injury. I said, "Is there anywhere I could get a hat tonight?"

"Tonight, Shabat? I don't think so."

"I don't want to go about like this."

"Go to bed. That's where you should be. I'll give you some tablets."

"I have to go out."

"It would need, anyway, to be a very big hat," he said, smiling, and then looked at me a bit speculatively, and smiled in a different way. "One moment," he said, and went out of the room. He came back in with a *shtreiml*, the big round fur hat of the ultrapious. "Try it," he said.

I tried it. The enormous thing fitted like a glove. It seemed to carry a persona of its own. I stared rather weirdly at my features in the mirror. A medieval type rabbi stared back.

"It was my father-in-law's," he said. "Of blessed memory. The Talmud enjoins that if a man lacks a garment he should be given one." He seemed to be breaking up in a quiet way.

"How much for the hat?"

"I'm not a hat shop. Bring it back."

"All right. Thanks. Shalom."

"Shabat Shalom."

The taxi driver gave a double take at the hat. He said, "Are you all right?"

"Yes. Can you take me to Tel Aviv?"

"On Shabat? It'll cost you a fortune—double fare both ways."

"How much?"

He told me how much. He couldn't take his eyes off the hat.

I said, "All right. Let's go."

"Have you got that much with you?"

"Yes." I was pretty sure I hadn't, and also sure it would have to take care of itself. I was too exhausted even to think about it.

He covered the forty-four miles to Tel Aviv very slowly, in an hour and a half. It wasn't quite eight when we got there. He gave me a shake in the back seat.

"Where is it you want?" he said.

I had a look out. We were cruising down Allenby Road, shuttered and deserted for Shabat. I said, "Is there a Yemeni quarter here?"

"The Yemeni quarter? It's behind Mograbi Square, the upper end of Carmel. Is that where you want?"

"Yes."

He turned and got into Carmel Street.

"Anywhere in particular?"

"Stop at the phone box."

He stopped and I got the bit of paper out and went in the box. He got out of the cab, too, and planted himself solidly outside to watch his investment. The phone rang a long time before anybody answered.

"Yes?" a man said angrily.

"Shoshana Almogi, please."

"The Almogis don't use the phone Shabat," he said furiously. "Neither do we."

"It's very urgent. Tell her Dr. Laing."

"Wait!"

She was there in about half a minute, breathless.

She said, "*Who* is it?"

"Me, love."

"Caspar! Where are you?"

"I'm here."

"In Jerusalem?"

"In Tel Aviv."

"Oh, that's wonderful."

She didn't know how wonderful. But this was very encouraging. We'd parted in a distinctly funny way. I'd been wondering how to go about it.

She said, "Exactly where are you?"

"In a call box." I looked out the window. "In Elyashiv Street."

"But we're just round the corner!"

"Shoshana, can you put me up?"

She hesitated just a moment. "Yes, certainly. Of course. Stay where you are. I'll come right down."

"Fine. And Shoshana?"

"Yes?"

"Bring a few quid with you."

Eight

DESOLATE AND FAINT ALL DAY

I am not able to rise up.
—Lamentations 1:14

1

THE AWFULNESS, the impossibility of having to explain creased me up as I waited for her, but in fact I had to do very little. She seemed to get it in a trice, and only goggled fractionally at my hat as we walked to the flat. She said anxiously, "The only thing is—I didn't realize—there are a few people here. They want to meet you, naturally."

I said, slowing in the street, "Shoshana, I can't. I just want to go to bed. I didn't know how the hotels would be, Friday night . . ."

"It's only relations, an uncle and aunt, my brother and his wife, their children. And Shimshon. Shimshon is here for the weekend. He won't mind sleeping on the floor, just one night. And the rest will go soon. They always come for Shabat."

"But my clothes—look at me."

"So you had an accident!"

"And my hat."

"The hat, the hat," she said rapidly. "What about the hat? A lot of serious people wear hats like that. Maybe

English professors *wear* that kind of hat. Why else would you be wearing it? Nobody will even notice the hat."

But they did notice it. It was a crammed and misshapen hovel over a humus restaurant; and the full house in it stared with fascination at my *shtreiml* as I reeled in the doorway. Only her father, a rather wizened old body, greeted it with any animation, and only then because he thought I was a *yeshiva-bocha,* a member of a religious seminary, who had somehow wandered in off the street. This old body lived only for the synagogue, I gathered, as the confused evening developed. I seemed to be sitting over a plate of soup. Everybody seemed to be talking, of accidents, police inefficiency, the Pentateuchal portion for the week.

"It's terrible the drivers here. They should put still more taxes . . ."

"For instance, in *Vayishlach* in Genesis today, something puzzles me. Ibn Ezra interprets the attitude of Esau . . ."

"*Idiot,* you've been told—he's not Jewish . . ."

"They go like lunatics. If the police prosecuted every time an accident . . ."

"She's proud to work with you, our Shana. Look at her . . ."

I looked at her. She wasn't wearing uniform now. She was in pale-blue slacks, pink jumper, tiny Shield of David on a thin gold chain round her neck, black, black hair. Shimshon was looking at her, too. A big morose character, khaki rig, captain's stars, smoldering-eyed, red beret; all the males covered in this religious household.

"So he goes to greet his brother Jacob, taking *four hundred men* with him. Why? Because . . ."

"A little chicken, a spoonful of rice—Come, what can the doctor object . . ."

"If the police won't take an action, go to your own people, the embassy. These liberty-takers in big cars . . ."

"Again, why do the rabbis put dots over each letter of *vayishakayhu*—'And he kissed him'? Because it wasn't a genuine kiss! Tell me . . ."

"How many times more—*idiot!* Excuse him—he lives only for the synagogue. . . ."

"So take my advice, make them prosecute. . . ."

"Do you want to go to bed now?" she said, brown eyes watching me.

"Yes."

"Shimshon won't mind sleeping on the floor, just one night. You won't mind sleeping on the floor, Shimshon, just one night?"

"So what does he do? Does he trust him, never mind the brotherly kiss? Does he stay with him . . . ?"

"No, not for a night," Shimshon said.

"Exactly! You see? The military mind! Which Jacob had. Not for a night even! A clever man. They were all clever men in those days. When they said something plainly, all right. Otherwise they said one thing and meant another. So explain to me, why does Ibn Ezra . . ."

"Come on," she said.

"What—already going?" her father said.

"Of course, idiot. To bed," her mother said. "He's ill, can't you see? So sleep well, we'll see you tomorrow."

"The *bocha* stays here tonight?"

"I told you already—he's the professor of Shana!"

"Fine. So we'll go together to synagogue."

"Idiot—Pay no attention. He lives only . . ."

"There's no light," she said. "I'll leave the door open till you undress."

"No, Shoshana, close it a minute. I want to talk to you."

She closed it, pitch blackness.

"Shoshana, listen, I don't want to go back yet. I've got to think. Will you fix me up with a hotel tomorrow?"

"Stay here."

"It's Shimshon's bed."

She didn't say anything. She just leaned on me, soft jumper, soft little breasts. My knees gave. I was sitting, in a jangle of springs. She was sitting beside me, lips touching mine, just touching. She said against them, "Oh, Caspar. Caspar, I'm so glad you're here," hands cool on my neck.

"Shoshana."

"Stay here."

"Yes."

I had no clear idea when she went. It wasn't so dark suddenly. I seemed to be swooping about the room getting undressed. I had my trousers off before my jacket, was in bed before I remembered the hat. I levered the hat off and lay back, in some confusion of mind.

The kiss, the crater, the gushing face on the carpet. I seemed to be obsessed with a need to return the hat, to prosecute liberty-takers. The softness of breast, of arm, next to mine in the photo, who wouldn't eff off. Would he ever eff off, sitting smoldering next door while she kissed me here? Not a sisterly kiss, or a brotherly, like the clever man, like all the clever men, who couldn't be believed unless they spoke plainly, saying one thing and meaning another.

Tablets. Needed to take tablets. I'd roused up, but sank

back again. No real need. Could manage without. Could easily manage, a filmy veil parting then, and under the veil a gulf, and down the gulf me, leaving the awful day, endlessly leaving it, endlessly floating in endless gulf on big balloon head.

2

I didn't hear Shimshon in the night and he wasn't there when I woke. Shoshana was there. She said, "Would you like tea or something? Would you like something to eat?"

"What—breakfast already?"

"Lunch already."

"What time, for Christ's sake?"

"One o'clock, for Christ's sake. You were sleeping beautifully. Do you feel beautiful now?"

"I don't know how I feel."

"You look beautiful." She was very gay, eyes sparkling. The door was shut and she gave me a quick kiss. I sat up. My head lurched and every hump on my spiny prehistoric back ached.

"Is there anything you should be taking?"

"I don't know. I have some tablets. I don't want them."

"I think a little soup and mince and then compote."

"All right."

"I'll bring you a bowl to wash in. There's no bathroom."

"Thanks."

"Do you want the lavatory? I'll show you when you want it."

I just wanted to lie there. I didn't want mince or compote or a bowl or the lavatory, and I didn't want to think about them. She went after a while and I lay and thought about Ike. It seemed like a bad, a terrible dream. I felt nauseated and oppressed thinking about it. I thought about it while I washed and in the toilet and when I ate. I scarcely answered when she spoke to me, and presently she went again.

There was a religious picture on the wall, the all-seeing eye of God looking through a cloud. Great shafts of light spread from the cloud as God looked through. I gave him a bit of a look, too.

"I think you should have a breath of air," she said. "I got most of the mud off your clothes."

"Where's Shimshon?"

"At the synagogue. He went with my father to *ma'ariv*. They'll soon be back. Shabat is out. I thought we could have a little stroll and a cup of coffee. It will do you good."

"All right." I wasn't doing myself much good in bed. I'd tried to get up, but there was nowhere to sit, no chairs, no carpet, no floor covering of any sort, just Shimshon's neatly rolled blanket and his mattress. The only furniture in the room was an old chest of drawers, piled high with brown paper parcels containing, apparently, her father's stock of prayer shawls, phylacteries and skull caps: he kept a little shop of religious articles.

I dressed and got my great hat on and met her father and Shimshon just coming in as I left the room.

"Hello, *bocher*!" The old nut was exceedingly jovial. "Did you miss some talk today! You'd have licked your fingers." He'd had a perfectly marvelous day, Shabat the best one of the week for him, scarcely out of the synagogue or the adjoining study hall for a minute of it. He gave me a lengthy rundown on the principal highlights of this day of delight, till his daughter checked him.

"We're just going out, Father. He hasn't been out today yet. We're going for a coffee."

"Fine. I'll come with you."

"You wouldn't like it. We're going to Dizengoff."

"Dizengoff, feh! It's too noisy, Dizengoff."

"I told you you wouldn't like it."

"We don't have to go to Dizengoff," she said in the street.

"What's wrong with Dizengoff?"

"Isn't it too busy for you?"

"I don't mind Dizengoff." I never did mind it. Dizengoff always had a tonic effect on me. Maybe it would have one now.

It was too far to walk so we took a taxi and got off at the Circus and walked down from there.

Tel Aviv on a Saturday night is a very lively town, of course, and Dizengoff Street is the liveliest part of it. The Circus is a hub, of treed lights, wheeling traffic, corner cinemas, stores; and radiating away from it, one of the spokes of five main streets, is Dizengoff.

It isn't very broad and it isn't very tall, but a certain dense hubbub lets you know right away that you're in one of the streets of the world. Tree-lined, café-lined—and with flats above the cafés, so that the balcony dwellers may call without inconvenience to friends in the street—it exudes a *gemütlichkeit* not to be found elsewhere. It isn't the rue de la Paix, of course, but the habitués like it better; just as they prefer soft drinks to apéritifs, and lemon tea and strudel to almost anything.

We eased our way through the swarming strollers in the neon-lit night, passed packed tables of sports and political experts, and found a place for ourselves in a noisy convocation of rabbinical students. My hat was not at all out of place here, I was glad to see, and I sat back and felt the accustomed revivifying process of a Saturday night in Tel Aviv.

There are Jerusalem people and Tel Aviv people, and it's aesthetically proper to be one of the former. I was one of the latter. It's an architectural outrage, of course, a mass of Mediterranean concrete gimcrackery, mainly shoved up too quickly, to cope with the sudden influx of people who found themselves alive when they hadn't expected to be. Teitleman and his mates had helped to perpetrate much of it; but the life of a Teitleman building, thank God, is not much above twenty years.

But it's a live town, an excitable and passionate town, swept by strange fads and fancies, dietetic, therapeutic and artistic. Any morning of the week you can see yogi and calisthenics enthusiasts intensely engaged on the beach, and any evening find packed crowds appreciating works of the most baffling obliquity in concert hall and gallery.

All over it now, its smaller class of businessman had opened up to catch the post-Sabbath trade. In every hole and corner there seemed to be an oil-lit stall selling some minute requisite, elastic, shoe laces, combs; and at every other one, bits of food, potato cakes, fried chickpea balls, fruit and vegetable juices, nuts.

It's only twenty minutes by bomber from Cairo, and there was a fair amount of khaki in the street; and with it some less definable but very Israeli quality, a certain humorous pugnacity. Toughness, self-reliance, qualities greatly prized here, had also struck an echo in the girls. There was a mischievous, tomboyish look about many of them as they passed, army hats cocked modishly over one eye, egg-brown arms round the necks of male and female comrades; a strong impression of matey solidarity.

I suddenly felt myself coming alive, with a sensation of cotton wool lifting off the top of my head. Hadn't this girl been demonstrating some rather over-matey solidarity with me of late? Was it imagination, or had she or had she not been giving me a kiss-up on Shimshon's bed?

I had a look at her. She was tidying the giant Moroccan's epaulets, which seemed to please him. He was smiling a fond darkling smile, anyway. It suddenly struck me as a bit rough on him, after sweltering for months in the south, to have won me for his last evening.

I said, "Look, I don't want to disrupt anything. I'm fine here if you want to go ahead."

"So are we," the girl said. "We wouldn't want to do anything else, would we, Shimshon?"

Shimshon opened his mouth and closed it again.

"What had you planned to do?"

"We had planned to go to a kebab house in Jaffa and after that to the Al Raschid nightclub," Shimshon said immediately.

"I see," I said, a bit taken aback by his explicitness and also by the length of the speech. "Well, go ahead. I know my way around here. When I'm tired I'll go back."

"We wouldn't dream of it," the girl said. "We'd much sooner be with you, wouldn't we, Shimshon?"

"Yes," Shimshon said, into his coffee.

I said, "Look, you'll only make me come with you if you go on like—"

"You mean you'd like to? You really feel up to it? You don't think it would be too much for you?"

"No. Yes. I don't know," I said irritably. "I just don't want—"

"Why, that would be wonderful. If you think it's right for you. We'd love him to come, wouldn't we, Shimshon?"

"Yes," Shimshon said, and looked at me briefly. "If he thinks it's right."

There was nothing ambiguous in his look at least. Two little red points glowed murderously in his eyes for a moment. But that's what we did, anyway.

3

The kebabs came up on practically red-hot skewers, and we lingered over them in the little Arab parlor, and then had Turkish coffee before wandering down the dark Jaffa lanes to the Al Raschid.

He'd booked a table, which was just as well, because it was after ten and the cellar was packed for the night. The ambiance, I noted, was strictly nonrabbinic, and waves of amazed hilarity followed us as we were led to the table.

"It's your hat," Shimshon said unnecessarily, delighted by my momentary discomfiture. "It surprises them here. You could take it off now."

"No, thanks." I didn't know what she'd told him, but my Invisible Man type bandages would surprise them even more. Also the hat had changed my face in subtle and not unpleasing ways. I'd quite taken to it.

It certainly seemed to be producing service. The first cabaret was just finishing, and the belly dancer shimmied up and to applause practically screwed herself on my knee. Also, and more usefully, it brought the wine waiter at a jovial trot as soon as signaled.

I sat and worked my way through a bottle of white wine, the others sipping abstemiously, while dancing proceeded. Nice wine, Avdat wine, from the stony uplands of the Negev. You needed to drink a certain amount to get the stony flavor. I drank a certain amount, and ordered another bottle. Sometime during the course of it I began to feel wonderful.

Much better to be alive than dead. Much better to be in Tel Aviv than, say, Amman. Much better to be here drinking stony Avdat than anything else I could think of. Life went on, of course, I thought, and sighed gustily, and watched absently as Shimshon began scooping about on his knee. He seemed to be scooping cigarette ends and ash from his knee. He seemed to be putting them back in the ashtray. Definitely something wrong with this fellow's eyes. Funny little red points in them when he looked at you.

I sighed heavily again, and saw the red points come up again as he started scooping on his knee once more. A strange sort of obsession. He was moving the ashtray away from me. I seemed to need the ashtray and took it back. Fellow didn't want to give it, playing little games on his knee again. Definitely strange.

"You are blowing the ash on Shimshon's knee."

"Is *that* what it is?" I said, and looked at him more kindly. "Good job you were there," I said obscurely.

"Are you sure the wine is good for you?"

"Something wrong with it? Tastes perfectly good to me."

"Your head."

"Ah. I see what you mean. Don't think about it," I told her. "Life goes on, you know."

Which it did; nilly-willy. Nilly-willy? Willy-nilly, back to front, say one thing and mean another, like the clever fellows in *Vayishlach*. There was something about these clever fellows that it was important for me to remember. What was it?

My head seemed to be orbiting gently like some black-ringed Saturn about a yard above my shoulders, filled with an immense life-enhancing capability. A capability for what? For posing opposings, for flashing nilly-willy-isms.

"Not dancing?" I said to the military mind opposite.

A touch of his old eye trouble came on again.

"Shimshon doesn't dance," the girl said for him.

"Nor you neither? Either? Nilly-willy," I said.

"Yes, I dance."

"How about a spin, then?"

She looked at me rather carefully, and then at my hat. "Are you sure you wouldn't be better sitting quietly?"

"Certainly not. Much better on my feet."

So I was, I thought, springing effortlessly across the floor on them. And why not? Much better to spring across a dance floor with a lissome young thing than across a crater with a bullet in the behind. As a proposition it was self-evident, and one requiring celebration; except that the band seemed to have fallen into some slow confusion.

"What on earth's gone wrong with them?" I said, not exactly put off but having to concentrate more on sudden inexplicable complications in my bossa nova.

"They're supposed to be playing a tango."

"Is that what they're supposed to be playing?" I said,

amused. But indeed, when you came to study the matter, which I did, amiably enough, nodding encouragement to the leader who seemed rendered uncertain by my patient earcupping attention, some tango-type rhythm did seem to be being attempted. The tango, of course, was my specialty, and once the facts had been established, I flowed smoothly enough into it. I fancied I knew a few steps that would interest them here.

It occurred to me while executing them that the presence of the hat was lending a certain panache to my performance, and that by swiveling up my eyeballs and gazing intently at the brim I was able not only to enhance my aesthetic enjoyment of it but also to provide what must be an appealing picture of exaltation, very pleasing to beholders. An appreciative circle began to open up round us, and encouraged by it, I smiled and allowed my tongue to hang out in a relaxed fashion, thus transforming the expression into one of mindless rapture that I was able to retain almost indefinitely; which I did, swooping sightlessly about the floor.

The girl seemed to wilt after a bit.

"Let's sit down now. You've danced enough."

"Garnch enuch? I cug garnch all ni."

"Look, the cabaret's ready. It's Yemeni singers."

"Yengengi hinger, eh? A hewy inkerechking gialek," I said, not bringing my eyes down for an instant and intrigued by the unusual problem of having to produce a succession of labials with the tongue hanging out. "Ill gey ge hinging in gialek?"

"Yes, yes. Of course. I'm sure. It will be very interesting. Come and sit down."

I sat down, exercising my tongue rapidly and blowing out my cheeks, and watching curiously as a bit of further trouble developed with her unquestionably deranged escort. He seemed to be trying to shift to another table. Shoshana seemed to be trying to restrain him. They settled in the end on shifting a couple of ashtrays instead. A strange chap, ashtray fixated; no doubt to do with his conjunctival eye condition, now chronic. But no question the night was developing in unusually interesting ways. He'd left a single ashtray on the table, but as I began to whistle the catchy little Yemeni tune, he removed that as well. I affected not to notice, scattering my ash on the table as I listened to the song.

The fellow's cavortings with his handkerchief, which he began flapping about the table, seriously interfered with my enjoyment of the number, but I was able to follow it fairly well, which was more, I prided myself, than most of the revelers in this room could do.

A tricky dialect, the Yemeni, and the words of the song didn't mean what they said. It was one of a tradition of reversal songs—the Jewish minority of Yemen, oppressed by their Arab masters, often having to conceal their sentiments, even in song—and since this was a duet involving a lovers' meefing and subsequent tiff, it was trickier than ever. By the end, when the girl, in a rage, was telling the boy to clear off, and he was electing to understand her, in the spirit of the rest of the song, as meaning him to stay, the fun was pretty uproarious. I seemed to be appreciating it uproariously, having to correct them on only minor points of grammar. Excellent actors, too, the girl particularly convincing, eyes flashing as her fury mounted, voice powerfully audible even above my own. It wasn't till she came across and struck me that I realized she wasn't acting.

Obviously some ridiculous misunderstanding, as I was

at pains to point out, in my near-perfect Yemeni. I seemed to be pointing it out to the manager, who was escorting us to the door.

I brooded over this in some bewilderment as we rode back in the taxi. Everything seemed to have become exceptionally nilly-willyish of late, *Vayishlach*-like, reversal-song-like; otherwise back to front, topsy-turvy, arse uppards. Something bothered me about this. I wondered what it was, staring out into Carmel Street. The cab turned the corner of Elyashiv, and I was suddenly aware the girl had been giggling surreptitiously for some time. I gave her a responsive snigger back and affectionately pressed her knee, almost at once receiving a paralyzing kick on the ankle as I realized too late the knee had been Shimshon's.

Reversal problems were still bothering me in the flat. I seemed to be backing discreetly out of the living room to leave them alone, backing into my own room, backing on my flaming back. What kind of conjunctival clot had left a mattress lying about in the dark? I pulled myself up off the mattress, rested momentarily on the bed and closed my eyes to reorientate. Almost immediately a dreadful queasiness came over me. I half sat up, but found this even worse. It suddenly occurred to me there was nowhere to be sick here except in the chest of drawers, so I lay down again and tried to control it. I must have succeeded.

Shimshon was at no pains to conceal his waking presence next morning. A sharp kick on the bed, which nearly had me out of it, announced he was ready to return to the south. I opened slit eyes. He was looking down at me in the gray dawn, abnormally large hands holding an Uzzi submachine gun, eyes distinctly conjunctival.

"Going off now?" I said huskily.

"Yes. I'm sorry to have wakened you. But since you are awake," he said heavily, "perhaps I will say one thing. Shoshana and I will be married."

"I know. She told me."

"I wanted to be sure you knew."

"Of course. Congratulations." My head ached cataclysmically.

"I don't suppose I'll see you again."

"I don't suppose so."

He shouldered his Uzzi. "So. Shalom."

He was holding out his hand and I took it. He seemed intent on leaving his mark there, smiling slightly as he slowly pulverized it. I couldn't feel the hand at all as I took it back. I could only feel my head. Presently I didn't even feel that.

4

I woke with the feeling that everybody had better be very gentle with me today. I felt monolithic, unarticulated, in grave danger of shattering. Last night had been a mistake, of course, and yet there had been something about it . . . What had there been about it? It seemed best not to think too hard. Dangerous stresses could be set up by thought. The mind twanged and fluttered like a cat's cradle already without any weight being put on it.

I got very carefully off the bed in a rising threnody of springs and stood for a moment with a hand on each side of my head, directing it about the room. The angle of vision seemed to have narrowed significantly. The eye of God was pitiless this morning.

"Can I come in?" She'd heard the springs.

"Yes."

She looked a bit subdued herself.

"How do you feel?"

"Strange," I said.

"Shimshon has gone."

"I know."

"He's disturbed, poor Shimshon."

Demented would have been a better word, I thought, recalling the red-eyed phantom of the dawn.

"Will you be ready to go out soon?"

"Go out?" My voice seemed to be vocalizing distantly like some middle-register foghorn. I listened to it curiously. "Go out where?"

"We'll have coffee in the street. Mr. Benyamini below has a bad mind. He knows we're here together. My mother has to work today, but tomorrow she'll stay."

"Ay see," I heard the foghorn curiously sounding.

"Have a wash, then. We'll go."

We went to Rothschild Boulevard and sat and had a few cups of black coffee. I had a couple of brioches as well and presently began to feel less detached.

"You were terrible last night."

"Yes." Vagrant snatches of it had come back to me over the brioches. I sat and mused gently. Something had got into me last night, no doubt about it. As through a mist I could recall my correction of the Yemenis' grammar, the heady feeling of being in possession of all available knowledge. The recollection strangely brought no familiar heartburning. Odd. Very odd. Odder still, vestigial feelings of knowing my onions still persisted, together with a calm conviction that when the present disorders should pass all would be found to be well. Why? No use to inquire now. The mind would have its own no doubt deluded reasons, I thought, nodding slowly at my coffee.

"Do your stitches hurt?" she said, misinterpreting the nod.

"No. Not really."

"You'll have to have them looked at. We'll go to a doctor here."

"I've got to take this fellow's hat back." Snatches of my tango recurred then, together with thoughts of the doctor's father-in-law of blessed memory. The old chap's gear was certainly having a turn or two in its latter days.

"What do you want to do now?"

She was in her tuned-in mood of inquiry. I wasn't sure what I wanted to do. We decided in the end that what I wanted was a little walk, and we had one, down the swarming lanes off Carmel. The day was assuming its own dreamlike character, outside time. About two o'clock I had a sudden mad craving for a plate of cold borsht and a tomato. We found a place and I had them, the girl watching with some amusement and attending to a much heartier plate herself.

"Shimshon likes such little meals," she said. "I didn't think you would."

"A plate of borsht wouldn't go far with Shimshon."

"Well. He's a very unusual person. Of course he doesn't talk much—"

"Thinks a lot, though, eh?"

"And acts," she said with some acerbity. "Don't be humorous about Shimshon."

"What is it he does?"

"I don't know. He won't talk about it. I know it's secret and sometimes dangerous. Once he had to cross the border. Maybe he's done it many times."

"In the south?"

"I don't know. He used to say the south."

"What do you mean?"

"If it's something they don't want you to know, they say it's in the south. It's all desert there, so who knows?"

"Doesn't he ring you up?"

"Of course. It's a military line and they never say from where. All I know, sometimes he says he's coming and five or six hours later he arrives—whether from the north, the south, I don't know. Probably north, since he wants me to think south. I don't ask now. I know he can't speak plainly."

"Oh, Jesus Christ," I said, spoon poised and staring at her.

"What?"

"Oh, bloody hell."

"Something's wrong with the soup?"

"It's back to front!"

The proprietor was eating a plate of klops at the next table and he got up and had a look at my soup, a bit sharply.

"It's what?" he said.

"Back to front. It shouldn't be north. It should be south. I need a map," I told him urgently.

"You need a sleep," he said, after examining both the soup and me again, and went back to his klops.

"Yes, come, we'll go now," the girl said with some anxiety. "We'll go back, never mind Mr. Benyamini."

"I need a frigging map! I need it now, this very minute,

right away, instantly!" I declaimed, dropping the spoon in a frenzy.

"Yes, yes, we'll get a map. We'll get it in the street," she said, wiping borsht off her blouse. "Come now."

She still hadn't latched on when we were outside, so I filled her in, boutons flashing in a nuclear burst of revelation. They'd flashed last night, of course, under cover of the stony Avdat. They'd quite possibly flashed the night before under cover of the concussion.

Vayishlach, reversal songs, and now today Shimshon . . . an old and continuing tradition of people forced by events to speak unplainly, to say the opposite. As the priest had said it. He hadn't gone north from Jerusalem; he'd gone south. No marble in the north; plenty of it in the south. No identifiable rock peaks in the north; numerous in the south. And no reason why Northern Command troops should raise an eyebrow in the north—but every reason in the south.

Of course! It wasn't enough simply to decipher the coded document. You had to decipher the man himself. You had to strip the layers off the onion skin. He'd set out to deceive. And he'd still deceived, two thousand years later. He'd got the measure of bloody old Sidqui, anyway, and bloody old Sidqui had led us all astray.

The girl had paled a bit under this incoherent flow, and she began looking distractedly about her. "A map, a map," she said. "I don't know where we can get a map here."

"Where are we?"

"The Carmel market. There are no bookshops. . . . Wait a minute," she said. "Would any map do? Like a Bible map?"

"Of course it would do. Certainly it would do. I *want* a Bible map!"

"This way. My father's shop. He has some."

We nipped down the back doubles to it. It was a disintegrating bicycle-shed type structure, wedged in the entry to an alley. It was locked. I nearly kicked the door down in my fury, screaming at him to come out.

"It's no good. He does this. He just locks up and goes to synagogue. What time is it?"

"Three o'clock."

"He'll be at *mincha,* the afternoon service."

"How long for?"

"I don't know. *Mincha* doesn't last long. But it's always possible," she said, looking nervously at me, "that he'll decide to stay on for *ma'ariv,* the evening service. He often—"

"Where's the synagogue?"

"Right opposite."

"Go and get him out!"

"But he's with his cronies. I don't like to—"

"All right," I said, and gritted my teeth, and went across myself.

He wasn't in the synagogue; he was in the adjoining *bet ha-midrash,* the study hall, with a dozen other little old men, taking in snuff and the words of Obadiah, whose prophetical portion was the Sephardic one for that week. The old buffer was delighted as ever to see me. "Hello, *bocher*! You picked just the right moment. Settle an argument. The phrase, 'How are his hidden places sought out—' "

"I want a map," I said.

"A map?" he said uncertainly. "It doesn't need a map. The prophet is speaking—"

"Give me a map!" I snarled.

"One of the roll-up maps, for the children's classes," the girl said, having hastily come in behind me. "You have them in the shop. It's to settle another point."

"Ah! A map. To settle another point. Of course. But we've reached here such an interesting—"

"The map!" I said through clenched teeth, and would have picked him up and run across the road with him if he hadn't come then. But he did come, and half the study circle with him, to help discuss this further interesting point.

The interior of the shop was a choking camphorated darkness, revealed, when he lit a dangerous-looking oil lamp, to be in a state of post-holocaust confusion. The stock, of prayer shawls, shawl bags, phylacteries, books, vest fringes, mezuzahs and skullcaps, was in a single heap as if flung there by some passing congregation in flight. The eye of God, however, the twin of the one in my room, was keeping an eye on things, and perhaps enabled him to find where the maps were buried; which he did after some minutes, while I waited sneezing evilly and treading on various old men in my agitation.

"Here we are. Maps," the old man said, rather surprised. They came in individual cardboard boxes and he blew the dust off and took one out. "Four pounds. Or half a pound English."

"Father, he doesn't want to buy it!"

"Of course. Would I sell him? It's just a matter of interest. It's very reasonable. For a map," he said.

"Very reasonable," a couple of the old men said. All of them were trampling about pricing the stock, and finding all of it very reasonable.

I took the map with trembling hands and unrolled it. It was marked in tribal divisions.

"Have you got a ruler?"

"A ruler? I don't think I've got a ruler. Do I sell rulers?" he asked the girl.

He didn't sell rulers, but one of the old men had a tape measure with him, and I managed with that.

It went thirty centimeters from Jerusalem to Mount Tabor in the north, so I swung it round and found thirty centimeters from Jerusalem to the south. It landed in the Wilderness of Zin. Could there be a habitable place in this wilderness?

There was a habitable place. There was the oasis of Hatseva; the ancient watering place of Hatseva.

Nine

THE WILDERNESS OF ZIN

Southward.
—Joshua 15:1

1

WE MET AGROT there about four o'clock on Monday afternoon. He'd been driving since six from Nazareth, across country almost cut off by floods, and he was wet, tired and bad-tempered. The oasis of Hatseva was, as oases go, far from being romantic. A rather dreary though dense tangle of eucalyptus and other flora, it sat weirdly in a featureless expanse of geological rubble, at the moment lashed by rain and howling winds.

When last used to any purpose it had been a Roman military post, and today it was an Israeli one. From midday onward, Shoshana and I had sat in a little prefab hut, listening to the rain drumming on the roof and making conversation with the commander, a keen Bible collector. He was hunting around for "a really nice specimen of an early Latin Vulgate," misplaced somewhere in his kit, when Agrot arrived. Agrot had a private word with him, and then a few minutes later we were sitting alone in another room.

I'd swapped my *shtreiml* for a large black sou'wester,

and he seemed to find nothing odd in my sitting around in it. He simply said brusquely, "You don't look so bad. I've got news."

It concerned the Arab who'd photographed me in Nazareth. The Nazareth police had picked him up late Friday night. They'd picked up a few other street photographers as well, only this one had been clot enough to have the negative still in his possession. By breakfast time Saturday seven of his associates were in the clink with him. Quite a lot had been found out by now.

I said, "What is it—a Jordanian government network?"

"It's a syndicate. A private syndicate."

It was a Jordanian-Syrian syndicate, started apparently in 1961, when a sharp upturn in scroll prices had attracted business brains in Amman and Damascus. One of the members, an Amman bookseller, had contacts with the Ta'amireh Arabs, and had been able to organize a first look at anything new that was found. They'd bought and sold three or four things at very much better than normal academic prices before the priest's scroll had appeared—to present them with a poser. They hadn't dared take a normal option on it—as they'd hitherto been doing before raising a buyer—in case it somehow got away from them. In the end they'd had to buy it, outright, for £9,000.

"Who advised them?"

"Sidqui. He was the best they could get. Apparently the earlier stuff had gone abroad, illegally, so they couldn't trust anyone attached to the university. Sidqui was a good bet. He'd got grievances against the university. They'd retired him early because of ill-health. He was fine for them."

"For us, too," I said jovially. "Well, now they're barking up the wrong tree—"

"Let me finish," he said wearily. "There's the military angle."

The military angle came from the Syrian end. One of the Damascus backers was connected with the so-called Palestine Liberation Army, some of whose more militant members were springing the raids from Jordan. The syndicate couldn't buy themselves a raid, but they could buy advance information and also the right to participate if necessary.

"It's proved necessary," Agrot said. "A bunch of their men is coming in with a raiding party this week—either Tuesday, Wednesday or Thursday, according to weather. No—please," he said, as I tried to speak. "Just listen a minute. I'm very tired. I was up all night interrogating these men, and I've been driving all day. We'll take a helicopter back—I've asked the commander to whistle one up. The roads are impossible. We have to be back there tonight."

"Who has?" I said.

"We have. You and I. It's not as simple as it sounds. It's going to be a problem of deduction. They have three parties coming in, and the question is—"

I said urgently, "Look, the bloody thing isn't up there!"

"You'll tell me on the way."

"But it's down here. I told you it was down here."

I hadn't in fact told him that. I couldn't tell him it on the phone. I lost no time telling him now.

He barely listened. He sat staring at me with lackluster eyes. At the end, he said, "You could be right. I don't know. They've got more of the scroll. . . . All I know, we've got to attend to this first. That's obvious enough, surely?"

"No. It isn't," I said. "For reasons that I'm trying to—"

"I'm too tired to differentiate between your reasons and their reasons—"

"Well, I'm not," I said briskly. "Which gives me a slight edge in evaluating them, and also brings us to a point. Much too much nonsense has been going on here." And so it had, I thought, enraged suddenly by the recollection of all the berserk things he'd involved me in. Clambering up and down the Ein Gedi canyon, frigging about in Galilee, getting myself assaulted and abducted in the Holy City. It was time now for all this to stop. The scholars had to put their thinking caps on.

I told him this, at length.

He sat looking at me, blinking slowly. He said, "Well, I can't make you," and paused. He looked out the window. He said, "How much work do you expect to do here in this weather?"

"What do you expect to do in Galilee? The weather won't be any better, and didn't you say the raid was contingent on the weather?"

"Yes. I can't argue with you," he said simply. "I just thought since you were so involved . . . They'll certainly come one of these three nights."

"Won't you get warning?"

"There'll be a warning. There's to be a system of flashlight signals the night before."

Very typical. I could see myself cowering evilly on some wind-swept hill, waiting for an almost certainly hepped-up Arab across the border to remember to flash his little flashlight, probably with a failing battery and from dense cover. The least I could see in it was a nasty cold.

"They won't be coming tonight, then."

He said, "No, not tonight. . . ." and trailed off, and I suddenly saw he was at rock bottom, slumped in his chair, mustache and twisted nose both drooping.

This led me to rashness. I said, "Look, I don't want to waste time! If and when these bloody Arabs are ready to buzz, let me know and I'll come."

"It would be too late. It's got to be planned. . . ."

"I couldn't help with the planning. I'm no military genius. When you tell me what to do, I'll do it."

"All right. If that's as much as you can offer . . ."

It already seemed a bloody sight too much, but before I could qualify it, he was asleep; and half an hour later was gone, whisked away to northward, by whirlybird.

2

A gray and lowering sky sat over the desert next day, but the rain was off. We were out in it early, with a laden jeep. I'd sat up late the night before brooding over the commander's large-scale map. If a spoke was to be put in this Galilean lunacy, the Menorah obviously had to be located smartly. This called for energy and a pioneering spirit. There were two days' rations and a couple of tents in the jeep in addition to a handy prospector's kit comprising pickaxes, a mine detector and explosives.

The Wilderness of Zin was the southern limit of the territory variously ascribed to the tribes of Simeon and Judah; the northern one of their much-abused neighbors the Edomites. They were all of them quite welcome to it. It looked perfectly hideous this morning, the great rubble-strewn plain colored a diarrheic green by the torrential rains. Away to the left three thousand years ago had passed the enormous horde of the Children of Israel, whose appalled reaction seems well reflected in Moses' plaintive cry in the 17th chapter of Exodus: "What shall I do unto this people? they be almost ready to stone me." The Children had a point, of course.

In the moisture-laden air the whole eastern section of the wilderness stood revealed with startling clarity. It looked distinctly implacable. Under the thunderous sky, the mountains seemed to have moved angrily forward as though to inspect this intrusive and noisy insect that was buzzing over the silent plain. We were buzzing westward, as rapidly as the suspension would bear, to the nearest high ground.

There was plenty of it, I was glad to see, to both west and north; no shortage of peaks, either, that on closer acquaintance might be recognizable as The Curtains.

I had a pretty good idea of what the procedure should be. The Galilean experience had shown, at least, what kinds of spots Sidqui had looked out for. They'd all been a kilometer or two from some central high point; in rock foothills; in a fault in the rock.

This made sense. With the primitive tools available to the priest's party, nobody was going to start digging holes in solid rock. They would naturally look for a fault, and with their crowbars and hammers widen it, and crack the rock and lever out the pieces, and then replace them when finished. So I wanted a vein of blue rock, with a fault in it, and in the fault a number of broken slabs; possibly overlaid, by the workers or by time, with rubble.

As we drummed closer it was possible to see that there was plenty of colored rock here. The rain had brought out the stratification quite clearly, and dull veins of maroon, pink and dark green were visible. There didn't seem to be any blue; but this wasn't discouraging. Blue marble was a rarity anywhere, and I'd already decided the priest had specifically mentioned it as a further point of identification. It would need a bit of looking for.

The rain had decided me on my course of action today. While the rock was wet and the colors so clearly discernible, it was obviously an idea to cover as much ground as possible. Even a cursory inspection would show much more today than a closer one when the rock had dried to its normal brownish-gray. So with binoculars and a tankful of petrol I hoped to cover—at least to cast eyes on—all the high ground from Har Marzeva in the southwest to Ma'ale Akrabim, the Scorpion's Pass, in the north. This would still leave the rocky elevations around the Makhtesh Hakatan, the highly interesting crater to the east of the Scorpion's Pass, to be covered the following day. I had high hopes of this makhtesh. I'd been to the bottom of it a couple of years before. I was still using as a paperweight a stone I'd picked up there; a blue stone. This didn't mean that the surrounding high ground would have a vein of blue stone. But it was a nice sort of pointer.

"So why don't we go there right away?" the girl said on hearing this reminiscence.

"I know where it is. It's a better idea to see the rest while there's a chance. We might not have such good conditions again."

"You just want to leave it to the end, to look forward to."

"What's wrong with that?"

"You're a baby."

"Don't you like having things to look forward to?"

"Of course. You're still a baby."

It wasn't the only thing I was looking forward to. I allowed my mind to wander ruminatively over the tents and sleeping bags in the back, while scanning the hills of Zin through binoculars.

We'd covered the immediate southwest by ten-thirty, and turned north, gingerly crossing a couple of flooded wadis. About half past eleven we stopped to eat. We stopped by a curious table-like eminence of rock.

"Which mountain is that?"

"Mount Hor," I said, checking with the map.

"Oh!" She swallowed her mouthful guiltily. "We shouldn't picnic here."

"Why not?"

"Aaron the high priest died here," she said, looking at it a bit superstitiously.

I looked at it a bit that way myself. A gloomy place, an exceedingly Genesis-type place, half as old as time. It wouldn't have looked any different the day they'd taken him to the top and stripped him of his vestments and left him there. The House of Israel had stood and watched. They'd stood and watched here, and mourned him for thirty days.

The sky overhead had turned a subtle shade of black, and a couple of rays of light shot through to spotlight a tiny patch of wilderness on either side of the table of rock. It wouldn't have surprised me to see the single eye popping through as well to see who was sitting here eating *wurst* sandwiches in this place of awe.

We stayed all the same. Once you stopped there was a curious lack of will to move. The silence was so gigantic you found yourself straining to hear something through it. There was nothing at all to hear through it: no breeze, no trees, no birds, no life; nothing. A vast waste of gloomy desolation, dead flat under the gray sky; watched only by washed mountains. I had an awareness, never so totally realized, of being on a planet, of being a speck of consciousness dropped on the planet and blinking this way and that to orientate. Here indeed was context and reality, the planet as it was; as it still was beneath the green growths that had sprouted elsewhere. Unsettling.

We finished the sandwiches in silence and had an orange each and somewhat broodingly proceeded.

By two o'clock we'd covered the ranges of Rekhev, Halak and Golehan, and were looking for a place to ford a wadi flooding out of a ravine. Beyond it was the Ma'ale Akrabim.

"Venosav lachem ha-gevul mi-negev le ma'ale akrabim," God had said. "And your border shall turn southward of the ascent of Akrabim." And here it was, unchanged in name, only slightly changed in feature, the Scorpion's Pass. The British had built the first road through it. It rose twelve hundred feet in just over half a mile, by way of twenty-two hairpin bends. On the western side was the precipice known as the Frog's Head.

It was after three before we ground to the top, and almost too dark to see anything. The overcast was lower still here; it was sitting almost on the Frog's Head. The only illumination came from a single shaft of sunlight that cut apocalyptically through the gloom. Following it down, you could see it shining like a silver sixpence on a spot of valley below. It was raining in that valley below; not yet here. We turned and went back.

Large single spots of rain began to fall as we descended. It seemed wisest to make for the ravine. We'd noted as we passed that there were overhanging shelves of rock there that could provide shelter. We dropped cautiously down the hairpin bends to the plain, came out on it and made for the ravine.

The wadi was running in spate down the center of the ravine, red-brown water gurgling. There was still room on the right bank for the jeep to proceed. We nosed slowly along, found an inlet that sloped gently upward, ran the jeep up it and got out. It wasn't raining here yet. The air was warm, close, palpable as cotton wool. We got the tents out of the jeep and pitched higher up, under the overhang, and then laid out the rest of the kit. There were groundsheets, waterproofed sleeping bags, a paraffin lamp, a small pressure stove and a barbecue set.

It was still not four o'clock, too early to eat, yet weirdly, almost luminously, dark. I lit the paraffin lamp and in its yellow conspiratorial glow wrote up my notes while the girl made coffee. The day had been useful. There were three or four places where green veins in the rock might have blended into blue, where the funny light had made it hard to tell anyway. None of these places was more than fifteen miles from Hatseva; Mount Hor only eleven. Could Hor possibly be the point of reference, the eminence from which the distance had to be taken?

It would certainly have been an important eminence to the priest, and to his priestly superiors who had authorized the disposal of the consignment. No fighting would have been expected here. The Menorah could lie in peace. And certainly it was the kind of "difficult terrain" the priest had mentioned. He might have plodded with his ten men and his twenty pack animals through this very ravine; have camped in this very inlet. Could this have been the "first halt" on the way back where the work had been done "with cords, and to the letter"? It was just about one halt distant from Mount Hor; six miles . . .

The hairs on the back of my neck began to bristle. I suddenly knew in my bones the area was right. We mightn't be in the exact vicinity, might be ten, twenty, thirty miles from it. But it was here somewhere, in the south, the harsh prophetic south. I knew it, had sensed it in the priest's coded words, had been feeling it more strongly all day. I'd felt nothing in the north, the merely melancholy north with its many springs and green fertility. It was in the south that Israel had found its ethical purpose, to the south that it always looked for renewal; renewal seen in terms of hard rock and desert austerity, not Jordan water and baptism.

I'd sensed myself this morning the foursquare rocklike quality of the old religion, its permanent air of having survived a catastrophe and of having to lay down survival laws for the sojourners on the planet. The planetary sense was very strong in the desert. This was the desert inheritance. When affairs became complex and uncertain one made for the desert to find reality again—one made for the south.

In the south, too, that first Menorah had been made. It had been made from the earrings and the bracelets that the women had brought from Egypt. They had given up their ornaments in this austere place; had had them melted down and purified and fashioned into "one beaten work," an ornament for the people, a light for Israel.

It was here. If it was anywhere, it was here, in the south.

I couldn't sit still. We drank the coffee and clambered down the bank and wandered into the ravine. We took

the lamp with us. It was pitch dark now, not merely overcast; no moon, no stars. It was much cooler, too, and I
put an arm around her. The ravine went into a couple of
S-bends, widened, narrowed, widened again. The water
gurgled steadily, rain still sluicing off the mountains,
draining through the runoff wadis into this main one.
From the state of the wadis we'd seen earlier I'd expected
this one to be much higher. Water was evidently trapped
somewhere in the mountains, in a catchment of rocks.
Another good rain in the night, and that would probably
come down, too—a flash flood.

The prospect wasn't disturbing. We were high enough
up the bank with the jeep, and the ravine was wider
there. We turned presently and went back. I washed out
the coffee things in the wadi and then set clean water to
boil on the pressure stove while the girl got the barbecue
going and rubbed mustard into the steaks.

We ate on our sleeping bags, and by seven were happily
digesting. "What do you want to do now?" I said.

"I don't know. What about a game of cards?"

"Have you got any cards?"

"A soldier always carries cards."

We had a game, on a groundsheet; not at all unpleasant in the yellow light. She played with immense concen-
tration and rummied out in about five minutes.

"Hollywood system?"

"All right."

"What stakes?" she said keenly.

"Strip stakes."

"Which stakes?"

"Haven't you heard of strip poker?"

"Oh, that. I'm cold enough already."

"Why don't we go in a tent?"

She looked at me a bit carefully. "All right."

It wasn't any warmer in the tent, but it was a lot more snug. She took half a quid off me and was shuffling for another rubber when I leaned over and kissed her. She didn't exactly repel me, but she didn't do anything else much, either. When I drew back, she started shuffling the cards again, erratically.

I said, "Leave the cards."

She said, a bit wobbly, "Don't you want another game?"

"Not that kind."

"Caspar, let's just be—friends."

"I'm friendly as hell."

"I mean—what is it?" she said, licking her lips distractedly, "—chums! I want you as a chum."

"Were you only feeling chummy at the Cave of Shulamit?"

"We didn't go in the Cave of Shulamit."

"And you were very angry."

"Not at all."

"Are you sure?"

She dropped half the cards and started picking them up again. "Yes," she said doggedly.

I said, "All right. Chum," and leaned over again.

It was longer this time, and she didn't mess about with the cards. She said presently, a bit wildly, "Can't we be like brother and sister?"

"We're not brother and sister, Shoshana."

"Caspar—"

I moved the lamp out of the way and lowered her on the sleeping bag.

She said, "No, no."

"Why not?"

"Caspar, stop!"

"Shana."

"Please—"

I kissed her while she was saying it, and felt her tongue. She didn't withdraw it, and presently her arms went round my neck. This was nothing but food and drink to the old Adam, who in course of time began steamy maneuvers. Her face swiveled sharply round under mine. She said, "No!"

"Yes."

"You mustn't. Stop it."

"You want to."

"I *won't*!"

"I adore you," I heard the old Adam frowstily muttering, short of wind but on cue.

"No. Stop. It's wrong. Shimshon!" she said wildly. "You know Shimshon. You met Shimshon!"

Frig Shimshon! I cried silently, from the very depths of being.

"Shimshon loves me. He needs me. He expects a virgin at marriage. How can you make me break a trust?"

All this was becoming very nerve-racking and I drew back presently, breathing heavily.

She said plaintively, "Oh, Caspar, I'm sorry. I'm very sorry."

"So am I," I said.

"I did tell you. I tried to tell you. I truly love Shimshon. I can be quiet with him."

She was right there, but I didn't pursue the point, staring like a maddened bull at the buttons I'd undone and which she was now rapidly doing up again.

"I'm not like this. You only make me like. this," she said. "You don't truly know me, and you don't know Shimshon. He's like a great rock to me."

"He's like a great rock to everybody," I snarled, enraged at the way the absent behemoth was dominating the conversation. "And, anyway, one thing has nothing to do with another."

"Oh, yes, it has," she said, and then I fell on her again, aware that all was lost when the action stopped; and that the action, moreover, had been neither totally unexpected nor totally unknown to her.

In five minutes we were back at the pre-Shimshon position. She said shakily, "You only make it more difficult for yourself."

"So long as it is for you, too."

"Yes, it is. I tell you that. But I still won't."

"Wanting to is the same as doing it, intellectually."

"So be satisfied, intellectually."

"It's bad to deny yourself. It can have the most appalling effects."

"No, it isn't. It's very good. It's good for the character. It can only have a good effect to resist temptation."

"So why don't we get in your bag and really give the devil a run?"

She moved urgently underneath me. "No. Go to your own bag. You need to sleep now."

"It's cold in my bag. You'll be cold in your bag. Where's the sense in that? We could both be warm in one bag—and improve our characters."

She could see it wasn't really on now, and she smiled, efficiently buttoning up again. She sat up and gave me an affectionate kiss on the nose. "The sleeping bags are of kapok and will soon warm up. Go on now, Caspar. You'll soon sleep."

I did go presently. But sleep took longer.

3

We were' up betimes next morning and off on a tour of Akrabim. It hadn't rained in the night and the skies were still heavy. It was warmer than the previous day, and every now and then there was a spot of moisture and a sudden slight shift of air from the north, not quite a gust, more like a little shock wave, as if a giant door had been slammed in the mountains. This was not promising. Torrential rains and howling winds could spring up in a jiffy, as they already evidently had somewhere in the north.

We labored slowly up the hairpin bends, stopping for binocular work, and continued on to the Frog's Head. There was an incredible view from the precipice: Mount Hor, the 'Arava, the Mountains of Edom, all black under a black sky. We stayed about an hour, and then, the slight shock waves coming more frequently, decided to press on. We'd have to go on foot into the crater. It wouldn't be pleasant to be caught there in a deluge.

There was a track down to it at the other side of the pass, and we went slowly through. A check with the map and a few physical hints showed where the track had been. It wasn't there any more, buried under boulders and scree washed down by the floods. We picked a way through them and came to the crater.

The Makhtesh Hakatan is seven kilometers long and four wide; three hundred meters deep. At the bottom is a narrow ravine that drains much of the area, passing the water through the plain of the 'Arava into the Dead Sea in the northeast.

Numerous small waterfalls were trickling down the sides as we began climbing down. The flow seemed to increase about halfway and I stopped.

"What's the matter?" the girl said, behind me.

"It doesn't look very healthy."

The footing below was increasingly slippery. If more water started washing down, there'd be a problem getting back up again. I had a look down through my binoculars. A general mess of reddish-brown below. There *was* blue stone there, of course; I'd seen it. It looked as if we'd have to make do with tracing the vein, if any, outside the crater. We turned and went back up. At the top we stopped and had a cigarette. It was still only ten o'clock. I felt as if I'd been up half the day.

"Aren't you tired?" I said to the girl.

"No. I slept well. Didn't you?"

"No."

"I was driving all the day."

"And driving me mad half the night."

"I left you with a clear conscience. That ought to have helped."

"It didn't."

"So tire yourself out and you'll sleep tonight."

"All right. Let's get on with it."

I tired myself out prowling about the head of Katan for a couple of hours, then we went back to the jeep and ate. Afterwards we did another hour, then pressed on for a closer look at yesterday's points of interest. We were doing that at four when the sky fell in.

It came down as if a giant tank had overturned above, a sheet of water that seemed to fall solidly out of the air, slapping down on the crags of Golehan, where we happened to be standing, bouncing up underfoot, drenching every exposed part. We splashed in our oilskins back to the jeep, clutching on to each other in the cyclonic turbulence of wind; made it, and plowed slowly through the lashing deluge, buffeted by the wind, to the ravine.

We drove with the headlights on, peering out the open sides, the wipers unable to cope with the river of water pouring down the windscreen. The plain was so fantastically awash with water, we were in the middle of a wadi before we realized. The four-wheel drive dragged us out of it, and then another, before we found the ravine entrance, and with a homing sigh sailed into it.

Incredibly, all was a haven of peace within the rock walls, the wind rushing past outside, and even most of the rain, apparently, being blown across the gap. The wadi, however, was ominously higher and we drove with the nearside wheels in the water, feeling the tug and often slewing round into it as the tires lost their grip.

Thunder had been roaring and booming outside, but here it had a different sound, crackling and grating.

The girl was muttering to herself as she looked out her side of the inlet.

"Have we passed it? It surely wasn't this far."

"All right. Take it easy." She'd nearly had us in the wadi. "Watch your driving. I'll look."

"If I jump out, you follow me—all right? Don't try to save anything—just jump."

"What are you talking about? It's only thunder. No panic."

"It's water."

"It's what?"

She didn't answer, wrestling the jeep out of the wadi,

and just then I heard it myself, heard it properly. It wasn't thunder. It was a flash flood, battering its way along the S-bends of the ravine. I'd seen these things before. It happened like lightning—literally in a flash; a sudden explosion from some high catchment area; a dirty speckled head of water and boulders that elongated as you watched, to race like lava erasing everything in its path, roads, buildings, farms. It could transform a countryside in a matter of minutes. It could transform us, of course, in much less time than that.

We were too far into the ravine to back out. The only thing to do if it appeared was to get the hell out of the jeep and try to scramble up higher—as she'd already worked out.

The shock wave was already thrumming in the water. We could feel it in the jeep.

She said, "Thank God—there!"

The inlet. It was a tossup who'd make it first, we or the unseen water. The spray was already standing in the air above it.

She was mumbling. I caught the words. *"Ve-im hamavet . . ."* Yet if my death be fully determined by thee, I will in love . . . The prayer at the approach of death.

I said, "Jesus Christ!" somewhat altering the addressee. "Get your foot down! Move!"

She got her foot down. The jeep seemed to jump in the air sideways like a cat. It slewed round, back end in the wadi, shimmied, lurched—*moved*. It moved like a rocket, wheels suddenly gripping. We made it a fraction before the water. It caught the rear of the car a solid thump, slewed us round broadside, but didn't tip us. The girl overcorrected on the wheel, and went almost vertically up the steep rock wall, till the jeep stalled. She yanked on the hand brake, left it in gear, yelled "Out! Out!" and scrambled out herself. I seemed to flow out of my side, not quite sure whether I was on my knee or my elbow.

The jeep was already skidding backwards. It slid about a couple of yards and stopped, bits of equipment tumbling out of the back. I saw the mine detector go and a pickax and the barbecue. The girl practically threw herself on the barbecue, spread-eagling herself over it on the slope. All below was an inferno, a boiling froth with giant boulders lazily tossing like corks. Above the Wagnerian uproar I could hear her piping, "The tents! Watch the tents!"

I watched them, with some fascination. The two bulky bundles, erratically weighted by the sleeping bags, were lolloping slowly down the slope in fits and starts like a couple of Mexican jumping beans.

I went slowly after them, managed to grab one without effort, and with just as little effort let the other go.

The paraffin had gone, too, but there was plenty of petrol in the jeep's tank. It made a nice blaze for the barbecue. We kept it going for quite a long time after we ate.

Later, I had news for Shimshon.

The water went down in the night. We sat and watched it, smoking a cigarette. We sang, "Where have all the flowers gone?"

Later, she said, "How did she die?"

"It was a road accident."

"Are there any children?"

"No."

"I suppose that's a blessing."

"I suppose it is."

"Yes. How old was she?"

"Twenty-seven."

"Were you in love?"

"Yes. We were."

She gave me a little hug.

Then we sang a bit more and went back to the bag.

We heard the distant booming soon after dawn and sleepily listened to it. A new storm rumbling in the hills. Then she sat up suddenly and got out of the bag at a hell of a lick.

"What is it?"

"Come on. They're calling us."

"Who are?"

"It's a Tannoy. Coming up the ravine. Get up quickly. They mustn't find us like this."

She kicked the tent down and got it in the jeep. We were both barely dressed before the staff car rumbled along, all six wheels awash in the water. The commander was there himself, with a couple of soldiers. He called up, "Hello! Are you all right?"

"Yes, thanks. We managed to get out of it."

"That's good. I was worried about you."

"Was the storm so bad?"

"Oh, yes. The worst."

"Nice of you to come to the rescue.."

But he hadn't come to the rescue. Agrot had been on the blower at four. The signal had come. His bloody Arabs were set to buzz tonight.

Ten

A SORE BOTCH

An astonishment, a proverb.
—Deuteronomy 28:37

1

OF THIS NIGHT'S DOINGS so little remains in the memory, and that of a hallucinatory sort, that it might easily have happened to somebody else who'd merely told about it. I was drunk, of course; had been from about midday onward, having hit the bottle (of fruity Stock brandy, thoughtfully placed in the helicopter by the commander at Hatseva) shortly after Agrot arranged for me to have lessons in the use of the Uzzi, the walkie-talkie, and night-stalking procedure. About four in the afternoon, when I was supposedly having a snooze, I managed to nip out into the village and buy another bottle of Stock. Half of this one was still left, in my water bottle, at half past two in the morning. I was sitting on a bare hillside then, in pouring rain, overlooking the village of Menahemya, singing a little and exchanging reminiscences of Golder's Green with a jokester called Shapiro. Even now that I know what happened there's no coherent picture; only foolish flashes. . . .

"The position is," Agrot said, pink-eyed from lack of

sleep but otherwise very cheerful, "that three parties are coming in and we're not sure which one is going for the Menorah; hence the need for elaboration."

There was a fair degree of elaboration. The usual procedure with military infiltrators is to let them in, shut the gate and clobber them. In this case, because it was necessary to let whichever turned out to be the Menorah party get as near to their goal as possible, the clobbering operation couldn't commence at once. Instead, a careful assessment had had to be made of all possible saboteur targets, and adequate protection arranged for them. This called for a lot of soldiers: for the targets, for covering Agrot's experts, and for shadowing the infiltrators. A special communications system had had to be devised, and also a special drill to ensure against the soldiers shooting each other in the dark.

I lost track of it at an early stage and concentrated earnestly instead on what Agrot had in mind for me.

The infiltrators were coming in across a fifteen-mile stretch of border, from a spot near Sha'ar HaGolen in the north to Yardena in the south. A certain paucity of targets before the group in the center inclined Agrot to believe that this was the likeliest to go for the Menorah. They would be coming in along the track from Naharyim on the Jordanian side, to cross the lock gates of the disused hydroelectric canal, and would most likely be making in the direction of Menahemya.

"Just here," he said, pinpointing it on the map. "Now, then, bearing in mind that they'll have chosen this route because it's the shortest to their objective, where you do think they'll be making for?"

I studied the map. The nearest high ground to the lock gates was the southerly slope of Mount Yavne'el, barely three miles away. It couldn't be that, of course. It was quite ten miles from Tabor, much too far from Sidqui's workings.

I said so.

"Well, now," Agrot said. "You covered this area pretty thoroughly. Just refresh me on the kind of ground there is on this slope of Yavne'el."

"I can't," I said. "We never covered it."

"Exactly," Agrot said, his nose almost doubling back on itself in pleasure. *"We never covered it.* No blame, to you, of course, or anyone else. It was that noodle Sidqui. He was wrong about Tabor. It's quite obviously Mount Yavne'el—just as well known to the sages. The trouble is, we didn't devote nearly enough time to finding other points of reference. You were too busy looking for extraneous things like The Curtains and the perfumery. *Not that I'm blaming you,"* he said with the greatest good humor. "Almost certainly you'd have hit on this in the end. I know I would."

"Just a minute," I said anxiously, feeling everything slipping away again. *"You* think that the *Arabs* think that the Menorah is somewhere on Yavne'el?"

"Well, it certainly won't be any farther. They're coming in at two, and they'll want to be back by first light. Allow an hour on the site and what have you got left?—just a couple of hours for them to get there and back. Anyway, I'm putting you *here,* overlooking Menahemya. When they pass, you follow them. I'll be *here.*"

He'd put himself on Yavne'el, and other of his experts strung out at four other spots.

"Cheer up," he said. "Remember, scholarship depends on the ability to make these little adjustments. I know what hopes you had of Hatseva. To the scholar there can be real benefit in a dead end."

"All right, one more run-through. Here's your palm grip and here's your trigger, and remember to press them both or it won't fire. That's your safety element. A beautifully safe little gun. Now your clip, twenty-five shells. Slide and lock. And observe something—no obstruction below. You can fire from the ground, you can fire while you're crawling. Finish the clip—throw it away, slide in another, and no need to raise your head for a moment. The finest light submachine gun in the world. All right, we'll do it by numbers now. At the order one, on your belly. Are you ready?"

"You know, I'm not sure I absolutely need—"

"One!" the sergeant said.

"Caspar, are you awake?"

"Yes, love. Come and have a drink."

"Caspar, you're supposed to be sleeping. I only looked in to see that you were."

I hadn't seen her since we'd got in. Her eyes were somewhat shadowed, as well they might be. I said, "Why don't you have a nap?"

"I'm going to."

"Have it here. Nobody will disturb us."

"How much have you been drinking?"

"Not as much as I'm going to."

She was looking at me a bit anxiously.

"Do you think the Menorah really is here?"

"I don't know, love."

"Does Agrot think so?"

"Oh, yes, he thinks so."

"Caspar, don't drink any more. Nobody could have done more than you. If it does turn out to be here . . ."

It suddenly occurred to me she thought I was drowning professional sorrows in drink. I reached up to her but she retreated to the door.

"Just you go to sleep now. You've got to be wide-awake tonight."

I let her go and looked out the window. I was in a camp bed, in an office, in Beit Shean. A lot of other people were at Beit Shean today. They were hurling themselves about the compound with their Uzzis. Too many many men and too many Uzzis which were much too easy to fire. An incautious move out there tonight and a man could easily get himself shot. I watched the scene with foreboding and took another swig at the Stock.

Dusk brought on the walkie-talkies and the night-stalking, and at nine there was a briefing conference over supper in the C.O.'s office. There was much talk of reception committees and silent combat and everybody was very keen and very jolly.

"What's the matter—you're not eating?" Agrot said.

"I'm not hungry. I'm tired."

"Don't decide to take a nap when the infiltrators come through. It might be a long one."

This was an enormous joke, and everybody laughed enormously. I laughed as enormously as anybody. I heard myself whickering away, the note of quiet hysteria mercifully undetected by the others. It was doing good work, the Stock, but a long pull still lay ahead. I promised myself a really long one as soon as supper was over.

2

"What I used to like," Shapiro said, "was going down Swiss Cottage on a Saturday night, or up west, to these clubs—you know, the ones that used to advertise in the J.C. 'For the Older Crowd. Teen-agers Definitely Not Admitted. A Really Sophisticated Evening to the Music of Fabulous Bands.' Jesus, did we take the Michael! We used to chat 'em up, these old bats out looking for prospects. Boy, they were man-eaters! Ah, well, happy days," Shapiro said, and had a drink out of his water bottle. I had a drink out of mine.

"What you got in there?" Shapiro said. "Fruit juice?"

"Very fruity juice. Have some."

Shapiro had some and liked it, and later had some more. He was my cover, Shapiro. We'd been sitting there since midnight. The jeep had dropped us at the other side of the hill and we'd climbed up, in our dull plastic capes and hoods, our faces blackened to prevent reflection. There didn't seem much possibility of reflection. In the fine teeming rain the night was pitch black, no light showing even from the village below. With the Uzzi slung on one shoulder, the walkie-talkie on the other, night glasses round my neck, and a few further Stocks under my belt, I was feeling not unlike Barlasch of the Guard. It didn't seem at all now an unreasonable way to spend an evening.

Shapiro, who had been whiling away the time with this easy flow of reminiscence, was twenty-four, a kibbutznik now doing his national service and seconded to me for his supposed familiarity with both English and Hebrew. The only thing I could see against him was a certain keenness for action, but under the influence of the fruit juice he slowed down. I plied him with more, and as the night wore on added to his linguistic abilities with a few pleasantries in Arabic. We were engaged on that at half past two when the walkie-talkie suddenly came alive and Shapiro, hiccuping slightly, crawled erratically back fifty yards up the hill to cover me. The infiltrators had arrived.

With a certain weird disbelief I suddenly saw them on the road below, a number of little bobbing figures, evidently trotting, bunched together. Just before the village, and exactly as Agrot had calculated, they left the road, mounted the hillside and disappeared for some minutes into the scrub, before appearing again on the little track directly below me. They disappeared briskly off in the direction of Agrot. I lowered the night glasses and looked round for Shapiro, now due to rejoin me for the shadowing operation. Nothing happened. I wondered hopefully if he'd gone to sleep, and after some moments half rose to see. There was a rustling in the dark and he said throatily, "Keep down."

"What's up?"

He was beside me, looking furtively about. "How many came through here?"

"I don't know. I didn't count."

"I counted five," Shapiro said.

"Oh."

"There was supposed to be six."

"Maybe only five came."

"No, they didn't. They passed six through to us on the blower. Didn't you hear?"

"No."

"Well, they did. Where's the other bastard?"

We were silent for a while, peering about in the rain for the other bastard.

"Are you sure you counted five?" I said.

"No question."

I looked at Shapiro. The only question was whether he was in condition to count up to three. The men had been much too tightly bunched for any adequate count. It seemed a God-given delaying factor, however. I said, "That puts a different complexion on things, doesn't it?"

"Right."

"They could have left him as a cover."

"Ready to jump anybody who made a move."

"Check. Be best for us to stay here, then."

"I don't know," Shapiro said.

"If we don't want to cock the whole thing up," I said.

Shapiro mused, the Stock fragrant on his breath.

"I tell you what," he said. "I'll go for a shooftie and sort him out."

"Do that," I said keenly. "I'll wait here and keep watch."

"No, you go on. And don't bother about night-stalking and that. Get right down on the path and show yourself. When he moves, I'll sort him."

"Oh, now," I said. "I think we'd better work this out a little."

"Come on, mate. For Christ's sake," Shapiro said passionately. "Give me five minutes and get moving. I'm off now."

And off he was, surprisingly fast, leaving only a cloud of Stock to mark the space he'd occupied. I took another myself, and pondered. Shapiro would come to no harm, of course. I, on the other hand, could come to plenty. I was being asked to take to the track recently traversed by the infiltrators, and due to be retraced by them—perhaps sooner than expected if anything should alarm them ahead. This was plainly ridiculous. It was ridiculous anyway, but with Shapiro as my protector it was nothing short of madness. It wasn't the only danger, either. There was no infiltrator on the hill, and if there were, Shapiro was in no condition to sort him out. He was much more likely to lose his way, come round in a circle and sort me out. *That* was the real danger. I sagely put the stopper in the bottle, turned over and began crawling, away from Shapiro.

It occurred to me after some moments' crawling that Shapiro, although undoubtedly far gone, might all the same be keeping an eye on me. In this case it would be better to make *in the direction* of the track; and then get a sprained ankle. To simulate it convincingly, of course, I'd have to get on my feet. Was it a risk worth taking? I paused and had another drink and considered. I'd sunk a lot of Stock, a bottle and a half at least. I was showing a tendency to keel even while crawling. Could I even get on my feet?

I carefully took off the Uzzi, the walkie-talkie and the night glasses and laboriously stood up. The hillside lurched. The sky flickered before my eyes. I closed them. When I opened them again, the sky was still flickering. It kept on flickering, in the direction of Yardena, and shortly afterward a thin rattle of automatic weapons became audible. Almost at once the same thing started in the direction of Sha'ar HaGolen. A brilliant pinpoint of light suddenly broke in the sky, and then another. Flares. Very pretty. I found myself stumbling enthralled toward them through the lancing rain, until I fell over and continued at the crawl.

I began to wonder after a while where I was crawling. I seemed to be crawling down. Surely I should be crawling up? I shambled round and began crawling up. This was tiring, of course. Very tiring indeed. What was needed here was a good St. Bernard. The thought no sooner occurred than it came to me that I was that good St. Bernard, succoring cask around neck. Except the succoring cask had gone. What sucker had succored off with my succoring cask? I looked bemusedly around, and found it in my hand. This was rich! so rich my limbs gave way completely. I was laughing richly as I began tumbling slowly down the hill; still at it as my head thumped solidly on a rock and I passed out.

A thunderclap and bright lights disturbed the peace. The thunderclap was roaring my name. It metamorphosed into a loudhailer. A loudhailer with spotlights. A loudhailer with spotlights mounted on a half-track, ambling across the hill. I got blearily to my feet, and immediately fell down again. But I'd been seen. Through waves of nausea and vertigo I saw the half-track change direction and amble toward me. It was still night, and still raining.

"Wonderful, marvelous, what a night!" Agrot said. "Have a drink. Oh, they've given you one already," he said, upwind of me. I was back at Beit Shean. "So how did you get yourself in this pickle?"

"I'm not too sure," I said cautiously.

"You've got a bump on your forehead like an egg. You must have been knocked out by the infiltrators. They must have disarmed you, too. We found your equipment on the hill."

"How's Shapiro?"

"A flesh wound, it's nothing."

"From an infiltrator?"

"Not at all. A stupid accident. He mistook one of our boys in the dark and swore at him in Arabic. No one realized he knew any Arabic. Anyway, the man shot him in the leg. Never mind. It's our only casualty—a small price to pay for the Menorah. Hey, sit down. You're really groggy."

I sat down because I really was.

I said, "You mean, you've found it?"

"There's a guard over it now. We'll take it out when it's light. Which leaves you just time for an hour's sleep."

But time too for gloomy retrospect. I'd been wrong, then, and they'd been right. *North,* the scroll had said, and they'd gone north, and struck rich in the north. Why had I thought south? A hunch, nothing more. A *Vayishlach*-type hunch. But Agrot knew his *Vayishlach,* knew it better than I; as evidently he knew his syntax better than I. So did they all, these Semites. Why not? It was part of their consciousness, of their way of thinking. If Agrot had said the priest had been expressing not astonishment at the presence of northern troops in his area but only a legal precision, why hadn't I accepted it? If *he* hadn't felt in his bones that the Menorah would have been taken to the south and not to the north, why should I have done?

Why indeed? There'd been nothing to support the hunch. Nothing at all had come up during the three weeks I'd been in Israel. No contradictions in the priest's scroll, apart from the one disputed phrase. . . . I'd been away from it too long, this kind of field work, had sought subtlety where none existed; I'd been flogging a dead horse. The thing had been here all the time, under my nose, and no boutons had flashed.

I felt sick suddenly; of romantic notions of the south, of hunches that deceived, of subtlety in every form, of myself.

I slept a bit, all the same.

3

Agrot was still in a state of garrulous euphoria as we bounced past Menahemya at twenty past six. "The stuff is quartzite, of course, bluish quartzite, but exactly the kind that might have deceived the ancients, very hard and with a fine grain, not at all unlike marble. Quite obviously they had a tip-off from local Arabs that a vein of it was here— hence the mine detectors. We got a simply fantastic reading last night—I told you we took a reading last night?"

I indicated a nod without actually nodding. I couldn't remember feeling worse in my life. A scalding mug of black coffee had done something to revive feelings of life and humanity, but not enough. My head hurt hopelessly. This was due not only to the rock but to the bottle and a half of brandy. In a vague and unlocalized way I felt incurably ill.

Beyond Menahemya the road degenerated into a track, and a mile farther we turned off it onto the open hillside. A square canvas tent had been rigged in an outcrop of rocks, and a number of soldiers and vehicles were gathered round it. We drove up to them and alighted. Rain slanted sharply in the chill gray morning and woodsmoke drifted dismally from a nearby Arab village.

"Okay, we're here, let's go," Agrot said, and walked

into the tent. I walked in with him. "We're going to need more light. Let's have the roof off for a start." Willing hands took it off. On the ground an area some nine feet in diameter had been ringed with white paint, and around it stood buckets, tarpaulins and picks. The tumbled rock, still wet from days of constant rain, showed a dull bluish-green.

I sat on an upturned bucket and watched while Agrot and a couple of assistants began clearing the top rocks. Underneath was rubble and a number of large cracked slabs. All these were carefully manhandled to one side, and then they began excavating more rubble below. There were four or five feet of it, at first coarse stuff, and then fine. They'd been loosening it with the picks, but Agrot halted the work then.

"All right," he said quietly. "From now on, by hand."

There were six hands in the hole, but it was Agrot's, appropriately, that found the first item: a crumpled blackened twist of material. He produced a little eyeglass and examined it carefully, and then smelt it.

"Leather?" somebody whispered.

"Fabric," Agrot said softly. "Oiled, but very brittle. We'll go very carefully now, please."

They resumed work. Everybody had stopped talking, in the tent and outside it. The only sound was the soft scrape of chippings being brushed away by hand. I got off the bucket and knelt over the hole.

The twist of fabric was sticking an inch or two out of the chippings. Agrot didn't tug at it. He worked below, and presently stopped again, running his hand up and down something. He said, "Wood. Rotted."

A handful at a time, they cleared the chippings and came down to the wood level. The wood had been smoothly planed, in thin planks, to form a case. The whole lid of it was presently visible, dark and long-rotted, and slightly out of position on top of the case so that the corner of oiled fabric was sticking out of a gap between it and the sides.

Agrot examined the lid minutely. The problem was to lift it off without its disintegrating. He got a couple of fingers under and tried. A corner crumbled and broke off. He rested for a moment, and wiped the sweat out of his eyes, and tried again. He didn't lift this time. He got his fingers in, and then his hand, and then his whole forearm. The other two people swiftly had their arms in the gap. With infinite pains, they raised the end of the lid, and then spread out to distribute the weight, and lifted the whole lot off. The waiting soldiers above accepted the burden, and, hardly breathing, laid it with veneration on tarpaulins.

I was hardly breathing myself. I could feel the blood thumping sluggishly in my temples.

Agrot slowly ran his hands down the oiled material. It was the loose end of a wrapping that totally bound the contents of the case. He began to unwind it, working with a beautiful and economic precision of movement.

He only had to unwind a few turns, and then his back went stiff, and he turned, with this same economic precision of movement, and actually smiled. He couldn't quite manage to speak, though. There were nine rifles in the case, Austrian Mannlicher rifles, as used by, and doubtless stolen from, the Turkish army round about 1915. The rifles were in nice condition.

Half an hour latter, back at Beit Shean, and also back in bed, I drifted off to sleep with a tiny smile on my face. Hard cheese on Agrot, of course, but scholarship, as he'd said, depended on the ability to make these little adjustments. And the benefits, if any, had certainly come to him in one generous helping. I was already feeling a little better myself.

4

I woke at three, much refreshed, and ate a small meal assembled by Shoshana, and then went in search of Agrot. He was lying under a blanket with his boots on, hands locked behind his head and eyes screwed up watching a column of smoke rising from the cigarette in his mouth. I sat in a chair and lit one of his cigarettes and waited for him to speak.

He didn't say anything till he finished his cigarette, then he leaned over and stubbed it out and said conversationally, "So what do you propose doing now?"

"Going back to Hatseva."

"Not by air. The pilot couldn't get back before Shabat, and there's no urgency."

"That's all right. I'll take a jeep."

"Yes. There's nothing at Hatseva, you know."

It seemed unnecessary to remind him that there wasn't anything here, either. I said, "It's a hunch, to be pursued."

"You still want to do it, despite my views?"

He'd told me his views yesterday. They were: (a) that in all recorded history Hatseva had never been anything other than a military fort and a staging post and that nobody in his right mind would consider growing flowers there or starting a perfumery; (b) that it was in the center of a plain and there could be no question of the priest having to make a descent to get at it; and (c) that at the period in question it had been in Edomite (i.e., thieving neighbor) hands and therefore unthinkable as a hiding place for the Menorah. He'd told me all this in a quite jovial way as though correcting some well-intentioned child. He'd had his own (as yet unexploded) hopes then, of course.

He didn't have them now, and he was nowhere near so jovial, so I told him my views. These were: (a) that, although Hatseva might not itself be the "watering place" referred to, it seemed to me to be in the right area; (b) that blue marble was present in the area in quantities that made a thorough examination feasible; and (c) the "watering place" might prove to be one of the ancient springs of the Negev that had become lost and were only now being rediscovered, together with their related industries.

He closed his eyes while I talked, and didn't open them when I'd finished. I said, "Have you any other line we might pursue?"

"No," he said, sighing. "I haven't. I couldn't argue with you if you said you wanted to go home now."

"I haven't said that."

"At least we know the Arabs are no wiser than we are."

"I never supposed they were."

"I did. That's why I brought you in. It seemed urgent at the time. Now, of course, it isn't."

"Are you saying you want me to go?"

"It's a matter of priorities. For me, Barot is now the main priority. You will have others yourself in England."

"You hired me for a specific period. The period doesn't come to an end for two weeks."

"There would be no quarrel about the fee," he said.

I was suddenly bloody angry.

I said, "Stick the fee. And try and open your eyes while you do it. If you want me to stop work here, say so."

He opened his eyes and gazed at me mildly. "Don't get so excited," he said. "I thought maybe that bothered you. What do you suppose is going to happen in two weeks? What should happen? You told me you're not a wizard or a water diviner. It needs work—months, perhaps years, of study and exploration. A single setback doesn't mean we have to fly like madmen looking here, there. It's in the north—I'm sorry, that's my conviction at the moment. I believe the scroll means what it says. Perhaps I'm wrong. We'll see. But the single reason you've adduced—the one phrase of text that I believe you've imperfectly understood—this doesn't convince me otherwise. Maybe there are some contradictions we've overlooked. Maybe we'll find other things in the text. Maybe the Jordanians with their better text will find them first. But this is a matter of time. For the moment, there's no urgency. This is all I'm saying. I myself, when I've interrogated the prisoners, will go to Barot. But if you want to go to Hatseva—go."

And half an hour later I did.

We were past Peta Tiqvah and circuiting Tel Aviv, headlights on and wipers clicking, before I ventured a remark. I said hoarsely, "Can we get a cup of coffee anywhere?"

"It's Shabat already. The cafés are shut."

"What about a hotel?"

"I don't know. But if we're going into town we might as well go home."

"All right, forget it."

"What's the matter?"

"Nothing."

"We'll *go* to a hotel, then."

"I said forget it."

"It was only a suggestion."

"I'm sorry. I don't want to talk to anybody. I'm out of sorts."

"You shouldn't drink so much."

"It isn't that."

"What is it?"

"Isn't this bloody rain ever going to stop?" I said.

Round about Lod I suddenly remembered I hadn't asked her if she wanted weekend leave.

"Never mind."

"Was there anything you'd planned?"

"Nothing really."

"What?"

"Nothing."

I put the interior light on and looked at her.

"You're very uncommunicative."

"I thought you didn't want to talk."

I put the light off again.

By Beersheba my mouth was so like an old Arab latrine we had to stop. She found a hotel she knew and the proprietor mingled us among his Sabbath guests. It was nearly nine before we were out, and still raining. A fair number of Sabbath-breakers had been keeping us company on the road, hurrying to weekend haunts, but in the desert we were alone. The rain blasted monotonously on the windscreen and drummed on the canvas roof as we bored through the miles of darkness. The lights of Dimona came and went.

She said, "Have you thought what you'll do in Hatseva in the rain?"

"No."

"It will give you time to think."

"I don't want to think."

"What do you want to do?"

"I don't know."

"Well. There won't be a lot else."

True. Damnably true. There would also be the Bible fanatic and opportunity for hours and hours of chat. I said, "How long do you think the rain will go on?"

"Who knows? It's very unusual. The papers are saying how unusual it is. Everybody's remarking on it."

I remarked on it.

"You shouldn't swear so much," she said. "You need a rest."

"Yes."

"It isn't raining at Eilat," she said.

She said it after a small pause, and another one followed it. I put the light on and looked at her.

"What about Eilat?" I said.

"It's on the Gulf, on the Red Sea."

"So?"

"It's just a place where it's not raining."

"How far is it?"

"From Hatseva a hundred and fifty kilometers."

"Would there be enough petrol to get there?"

"Oh, yes. There are four cans in the back."

H'm. I said, "What's it like there?"

"I found an old leaflet in the car, which reminded me. It's under the seat," she said.

I put a hand under and found it. It was the Eilat Tourist Office's leaflet, and not all that old. It had been issued by a travel office in Tiberias. It had been issued, according to the date stamp, that very day. I assimilated this slowly, and also the information contained in the leaflet.

"It sounds a bit lively for my state of health."

"Oh, it isn't so lively. People go to bed early in Eilat."

"Do they?"

"Oh, yes," she said.

I looked at her again. The small neat head was facing front, serenely watching the headlamps dip and roll through the rain-laced desert. I put the light off again.

"Quite early," she said thoughtfully, in the darkness.

We got there well after midnight.

She was quite right about Eilat.

Eleven

THE SECRETS OF WISDOM

> *They are double to what which is!*
> —Job 11:6

1

WE STAYED TILL MONDAY and then the wireless said the weather had changed in the north, so after lunch we went. We slept on the beach in the morning. We'd been sleeping on the beach every morning. With bedtime at half past nine, there'd been a lot of sleep to make up for.

We got there about five. A journey through the Negev inspires a mood of contemplation at any time, but this time, as we passed through one stark and tawny wilderness after another, contemplation had curdled into inspissated gloom. As the familiar outlines of Zin hove into view, my weighed-down spirits sank quite suddenly like a stone.

There was a lot of it! A lot of emptiness, of vast tragical nothingness, utterly dead, no vitality in it whatever; an oppressive sense of all passion having been spent a long time ago; of momentous things in the history of the planet having happened here; things that had drained it, de-energized it, left it for dead, to wheel round through all eternity, out of bounds to the human race.

Agrot was right. Who would have grown a flower here, who have started a perfumery? As well run a dancing school in a graveyard or a circus in a plague town. It was inappropriate. It was not right. It was all bloody wrong.

I thought *Oh Jesus Christ,* scalp crawling, toes curling, teeth nibbling frenziedly as sinking suspicion became solid conviction. How had I ever come to conceive it, this monstrosity of an idea? No wonder Agrot had hardly troubled to listen. No wonder he'd sooner I went home and stopped bothering him. It had been a mistake. The flaming boutons had flamed in error. I'd pressed them too hard and they'd come across with the symptoms instead of the goods, like some phantom pregnancy.

And yet . . . And yet . . . The south. It was in the south. I knew it, instinctively, beyond knowledge. . . . I had to get at the text again. I had a feverish urge to get at it now, instantly. Where had I gone wrong? The reasoning was right. The marble. The reversal of north to south. The necessity of finding a "watering place" at the stated distance. At what point had I launched off into the high blue lunacy that had brought me here? There would be a clue in the text. There must be a clue there. Instinct couldn't have let me down so badly. But Agrot had studied the text, had studied it endlessly, taking the words apart and dusting them over and putting them together again, without finding anything. . . .

All right, this immediate area was wrong. Maps, then. The largest scale of map, to trace the smallest ditch of wadi to its tiniest possible source. A watering place, however long lost, there *had* to be; somewhere in a line sixty-five miles from Jerusalem. Away from this immediate doomlike area; to the west perhaps, or the east. Isolate that first. Isolate all possible places where it might have been. Maps.

Away on the horizon the scruffy little fuzz of eucalyptus grew larger.

"Hatseva," the girl said.

2

At eleven o'clock, eyes sore and back aching, I was still bent over ruler and protractors when a knock on the door announced the C.O. He'd been dodging about since dinner, lying in wait for a promised chat about his Bibles. I'd had to pass his room door (companionably left open for me) on the way to the toilet, the first time with a jolly nod, and the second with pensive face downturned in cloudy abstraction.

"Come, Professor! You've worked enough. It's time for a drink now."

"A drink? Good. I could do with one. What time is it? Good heavens!" I cried with well-simulated astonishment. "Eleven o'clock! But I've got to be in bed."

"In bed?" he said, jaw dropping. "But my collection. I've got it all set out for you."

"The collection!" I cried, clapping a hand to my forehead. "And I wouldn't have missed it for worlds! I'll tell you what I'm going to do. I'm going to steal twenty minutes!"

"Twenty minutes?" he said, crestfallen. "What can be discussed in twenty minutes? Still, come on," he said hurriedly, seeing even these twenty minutes rapidly vanishing. "They're here. See."

They were on his bed, together with a set of dealers' certificates and pedigrees of ownership. He began handing them over with gloomy haste, anxious that none should be overlooked, while I downed a couple of Stocks and made appropriate exclamations. It was a valuable collection, a very valuable one indeed to find at an army camp.

"Where else should I keep them?" he said. "I'm a bachelor. I love to have them near me. See this Yacov ben Manasseh, Troyes."

"Magnificent. A beautiful black letter."

"Undated but fully attested. Here is Magnus's appraisal."

"No doubt about it, then. Well," I said, looking at my watch, "very regretfully I have to—"

"Take something with you. Examine it in bed. Here—" he said hastily. "A Johannes Schleef."

"Oh, I'd be afraid to—"

"Please. I'd value your comments. And the Thomas Skelton. You'll find a minute."

"Well, thanks," I said, and got out of the room, and into my own, and locked it.

A minute later he was there again, tapping.

"Excuse me, the ben Manasseh. I can't see it."

"Oh, yes. Sorry. I took it in error."

"Keep it, keep it. You'll find a minute."

"Oh, really, I—"

"Good night, good night."

"Good night."

I waited till the sounds from his own room had died down, and then put out the room light and continued with the desk lamp. I kept at it for another hour, till I could hardly see, then I sat back and smoked a cigarette and brooded over what I'd done. They were photo copies of hand-drawn military maps, very large scale, 1 in 30,000, a couple of inches to the mile. I'd sat under the desk lamp and wandered over every foot of the way, climbing the lines of altitude, peering over Slopes/Cliffs into Gullies, Dry Wadis, Boulder-Strewn Gulches, by way of Second-Class, All-Weather, or merely Dry-Weather Roads. I'd filled a couple of pages with coordinates and notes. I felt flat as a bloody pancake.

I stubbed the cigarette out and sat for a few minutes longer, at a low ebb. All this to be covered in two weeks, in less than two weeks, in ten days now. It wasn't on, of course, unless some fluke drew me to the lucky spot right off. Well. Flukes had happened before.

I got up and put the bed lamp on and the desk lamp off and undressed and crawled in. I wasn't going to sleep for a bit, eyes hot and jumping, mind still traveling over the dotted lines of the wadis. I lit another cigarette, but almost immediately put it out again, mouth foul. What was needed was a drink to relax me; but no drink here. I picked up the Johannes Schleef from the bedside chair instead.

Almost at once the lovely thing began to work its wonders, the very paper calming to the touch. BIBLIA SACRA. Johannes Schleef, Mainz, 1594. A Vulgate, of course, the Latin periods as emollient to the mind as wine to the palate. I browsed through it. *Canticum Canticorum. Liber Threnorum. Prophetae Posteriores. Prophetae Priores.* Already the dotted lines were dissolving, the all-weather roads and dry wadis floating away to hell and beyond. I began to leaf through. *Jehosuah, Judicum, Regum . . .* The pages rolled like the sea, snug, slightly crimped in their binding, the black beetles of German type clear as the day Johannes Schleef impressed them. Imperceptibly the timeless Latin structures built their sheepcotes around the brain, the weary mind relaxed within and sleep began to drone through the words.

"... *donec venundaretur caput asini octoginta argenteis, et quarta pars cabi stercoris columbarum quinque argenteis* ..."

I was nodding. Everybody was nodding. Johannes Schleef had nodded. I came awake slightly and read the words again. How many argenteis? *Quinque.* Five. H'm. An interesting slip. The Johannes Schleef was worth more than its proud owner realized. The figure should be ten, of course, not five. The original was quite clear on the point. Beside me on the chair sat the original, in ben Manasseh's solid Hebrew. I picked it up and riffled through. Where were we? *Regum.* Kings. *M'lachim.* I found the passage.

"... *Verovah ha-kav hir'yonim ba-hamishah khasef* ..."

How many *khasef? Hamishah?* Five? This was ridiculous! Both of them wrong. I'd read the passage only recently. The price should be ten pieces of silver, surely, not five. Where had I read it? In the English version—the Authorized King James Version. This version, fortunately, was also to hand. I picked up Thomas Skelton. Second Book of Kings, chapter 6, verse 25.

"And there was a great famine in Samaria: and, behold, they besieged it, until an ass's head was sold for fourscore pieces of silver, *and the fourth part of a cab of dove's dung for five pieces of silver.*"

Eh?

I read it again. *Five* pieces of silver? Five, not ten, for a quarter of dove's dung.

I'd been smoking too much. My heart was going too fast and my lungs not fast enough. I felt mildly suffocated. Lights flashed. Everything flashed, including that area around the boutons.

I thought *Oh, for God's sake, no. Not that again.* But it was. A blinding electrical storm of bouton activity.

I'd suddenly recalled that I was remembering the passage not from the Authorized Version but from the priest's. I had the clearest possible image of it, and of the umpteen transcriptions: all agreeing on this point at least. "That former occasion when even birds' dung had to be sold for food—at ten pieces a quarter, as history records," the priest had written.

What former occasion? And where did history record it? History, as the priest understood it, had recorded it in *Sefer M'lachim,* the Book of Kings; and it had recorded the price as five pieces of silver, not ten. Could he have made an accidental slip? Could a man so pedantic in every other detail have erred on this one—on a point of holy scripture? Or were there other occasions when birds' dung had been sold as food?

I was out of bed, in the passage, barefoot, hammering on his door.

"What? What is it?"

He had his teeth out. He was wearing pajama bottoms and an old beat-up slipover, upper arms surprisingly hairy and muscular.

"Have you got a Concordance?"

"A what?"

"A Concordance—to check a biblical reference."

"Ah. Yes. Of course."

He'd got an old Cruden, second edition, 1761; sound as a bell. I tore frenziedly into it.

"What is it? What are you looking for?"

"Dung."

"What?"

I'd found it. *Any thing that is nauseous, or loathsome.*
Cow's. Men's . . . My eye raced sickly down the column. Dove's: *the fourth part of a cab of dove's d. 2 Kings
6:25.* Any others? No others. Plenty of other dung. No
other birds' dung. In the thirty-nine books and nearly a
million words of the Hebrew Bible, only one reference to
it. And he'd used it, precisely, critically, ingeniously. I
knew him, damn it; I *knew* him; hadn't been wrong.

"Please. What's wrong? A misquotation?"

I was grinning up at him, grinning like a slice of melon
on a plate, unable to stop, limp, utterly spent, gloriously
spent. His eyes were searching mine like a couple of
brandy balls.

"What is it? What's the matter? What's happened?"

"He's doubled up. He's doubled his figures!"

"He has? Who has? What are you talking about?"

"A crafty old bastard. A lovely old cunning old bastard."

"Look. You'd better have a drink. Here. Hold the bottle. I'll get a glass."

"Never mind about the glass," I said.

It was already going down; down throat, down chin,
down either side of the great slice of melon that wouldn't,
that couldn't, unsmile itself.

3

Ten o'clock sharp found us bowling on to the campus and, a few minutes later, beating on the door of Dr. Hilde Himmelwasser.

"Ah. Dr. Lenk. It's a surprise," she said, as ever unsurprised and gravely peering from storklike legs. "I thought you were to England returned."

"No, no. I'm here. Wanting to get into the scrollery. I understand you can get in."

"That is so. Professor Agrot requested that I start up the photo laboratory again. I will do so perhaps in two days."

"Fine. Can I borrow the key?"

"From me, not."

"You don't have the key?" I said politely.

"I don't have it."

"Who has the key?"

"The Key Security."

"Will Key Security give you the key?"

"Of course," she said, gravely amused. "How else could I get into the scrollery?"

"Then perhaps you'll be kind enough to get it and let me in."

"Ah. That I cannot. Not without instructions."

"From whom?"

"Professor Agrot."

"Where is Professor Agrot?"

"In Barot."

"Then may I use your phone?"

"With pleasure. . . . You are thinking of ringing Professor Agrot?" she said, the thought suddenly striking her as I lifted the instrument.

"What a good idea!"

"Ah, but he is very busy. I don't think he'll come to the phone. He is accepting only important calls."

"Perhaps he'll find mine important enough."

"So?" she said seriously, and waited attentively to see, subjecting me to an unwinking stare while the connection was made.

"Barot."

"Professor Agrot, please. This is Dr. Laing."

"He's not taking calls today."

"Just tell him," I said, very slowly and very calmly, "that Dr. Laing is calling from the university and wishes to get into the scrollery right away. He'll understand."

"Wait."

I waited. Himmelwasser waited. Shoshana waited. After five minutes Shoshana sat down. After ten I fought an obsessional urge to mount Himmelwasser and gallop her round the room.

"Hello."

"Yes!" I snarled.

"He'll call you at two. Leave word at the exchange where you'll be."

"But listen—"

Click.

I nearly smashed the phone in fury.

"He wasn't available?" She'd been standing two yards away.

"No . . . No," I said, thinking better of it.

"No. He is busy this week. He's taking only important calls. There is something else I can do for you?"

There was, but before I could tell her I was led trembling from the room.

"Never mind," the girl said, outside. "She has her instructions, and they have their work. In ten days Teitleman will—"

"For God's sake I've *got* to get in the scrollery."

"An hour or two. Come, we'll have coffee."

"But I can't wait till two! I'll go off my head!"

"Your head. A good idea," she said. "We'll go to the doctor."

She'd been showing an obsessional interest in doctors. She'd taken me to one in Eilat. He'd removed the bandage and applied a big adhesive dressing. He'd advised that the doctor who'd stitched it should have another look at an early moment. The moment seemed to have come. Half an hour later I was in his surgery.

It wasn't till I was actually in position that I remembered the *shtreiml*—left in Tel Aviv. I apologized.

"Never mind the *shtreiml*," the doctor said. "Who has done this? It won't do." He ripped the offending plaster off and fixed something of his own, a pad of lint held loosely in position by strips of tape. "Here. I give you more of it. You can change it every day or two."

"Thanks. I'll return the *shtreiml* as soon as I can."

"No hurry. So long as it was of use. My father-in-law of blessed memory has no need of it now."

Then I was outside again, and there were three hours to kill. We walked in them. We had more coffee. We had lunch. It was still only half past one when I was back at the campus, prowling like a tiger. But at two sharp, as promised, Agrot rang; and at five past I was in the scrollery.

4

When I'd finished with it a couple of hours later I let out a long and fairly lingering sigh. I'd translated in my own version everything that was known in as near to a modern idiom as I could get. I'd underlined certain of the phrases. I was quite sure now, and because of it, curiously flat. I lit a cigarette and looked at my handiwork. It read:

I came out by the north, it has to be understood, *and turned north, myself, ten men and twenty pack animals with thirty days' rations.*

We ate frugally, each man in his heart———— ————that former occasion when even birds' dung had to be sold for food, at ten pieces a quarter, as history records and as we understand it.

We traveled by night, the consignment as follows: in plain *terms, each beast one hundred kilograms, all ingot, private ingot.*

For———— ————the sergeants carried the OEED and the corporals its equipment. The lowest soldiers carried the implements, shovels, picks and crowbars.

In 65 miles, as understood, *we reached the area and buried the OEED. For the highest security the lowest soldiers and myself only were parties to this operation. It was not witnessed. It is here: at a depth* in plain terms *of two meters, with good———— ————a layer 20 centimeters thick, of crushed marble, of blue marble, and protected by slabs; the disposition according to separate————.*

The ingot in another place————will find [?]————in separate.

After all the work we returned, more plainly *myself, two officers, two sergeants, two corporals, four men. At the first halt the sergeants and corporals call to the lowest two [?] and strangle them.*

At the second halt the animals eat and a corporal works by one and falls under the sergeants in twos [?]; it is with cords and to the letter; all buried in the manner [the true?].

At night also in our camp as the sergeants sleep, upon them also, in twos, the knives of the officers; it is to the letter up to [and they were buried]——of [the true?].

The two officers [have eaten?]. The guilt is——not [?].

Immediately at the finish we make and go but about midnight there calls——and we stand——a mounted party, a great party. Their leader, their captain—our officers have known—is plainly of Northern Command, I repeat it, of Northern Command, has signed orders making us to him at his command place.

When it is read [?]——no one had told me that our acts are [known to?] Northern Command. I cannot in my soul—— ——that this Command [authority?] in our acts. The young officer himself——not possible [to say?] But he has said that we must——the consignment and the men to his command. But it is not possible although everything is within the law and to the letter.

Therefore I refuse to see him and he takes me and we go till two o'clock and reach a night camp in the rocks and stay.

The young officer is of [clean?] heart at all times and the guilt is [not?] his. He will not make me sleep with the lowest, although he has made them to stand over me who also fear me and allow me behind the rock with the animals when I must make—— ——which times I mount and run.

The alarm is immediately made and I was in the chase but in this difficult terrain I know [the secret?]——dark——dismount and send the animal one way while I——.

They chase in the [true?] and——without guilt. I saw from a height till midday when the alarm is made and they make and go.

*I have no food or water. I stay till night. I am weak——
——and fall and break my arm——to the bone——.*

*I am in heat and made worse. I cannot see how——the
return, therefore I go to the watering place where the people
know me.*

*I descend in a feeble state, afraid of violence. They keep
watchmen watching. They are in fear of——.*

*I lie till it is safe and enter the village secretly and go
toward a light and to my joy it is the old perfumery. The
watchman is making the——.*

*He knows me from old times, a good man, not unlet-
tered, and he is [good for it?]. I [in his mouth?] and he
takes me in. If I have done against the law——without
guilt.*

He said to write down the day he died so they
will——. It is four days after he come, the 22nd March,
he died. He said he tell me what when I bury him but he
never, he has evil spirits, so I took him at night in the
flower basket and bury him behind the spring.

I said peace on his soul and God be merciful he is a
good man, a priest.

He not—— ——help when his arm [of evil?] not tell
any man, but I tell the priest who come for flower oil and
he said I said right when I——which I hope, but that
come for the flower oil not a real [priest?] they keep a
different date.

I write twice what he write, I make my best. He said to
say where I put. I put one in The Curtains, high, two
hundred meters, the Curtain you cannot see from here,
it is turned away. It is in the first hole, you get down
from the top. I put another farther on, down low, the
bottom of the cliff, beyond as you go.

That was it; a code within a code; clear enough when you spotted it. It had been studied hundreds of times without anyone having spotted it. *"It has to be understood,"* *"as we understand it,"* etc., obviously meant the words had to be understood differently; and *"in plain terms,"* *"more plainly"* and so on that these words were "in clear." What had to be understood differently? Directions, obviously—south for north—and also figures. And the biblical reference, clear as daylight to his priestly colleagues, indicated what had to be done about the figures. They had to be halved. So it wasn't sixty-five miles south of Jerusalem that the stuff had been buried, but half that. Which watering place came within this new area?

I hadn't slept in the night, and I'd not thought of much else since, but I went to the wall map and checked, anyway. It was there on the map, of course, there where it ought to be, where it always had been, sitting under our noses. I got out a pencil and put a little kiss on the spot, but it looked like any other cross on a map. Then I went and phoned my busy friend Agrot.

5

"It's the right distance from Jerusalem—slap bang in the area where all the other finds have been made—"

"Right."

"It's in 'difficult terrain,' you have to 'descend' to get at it—"

"Right. Right."

"And it wouldn't need any other designation than 'the watering place.' It's the *obvious* watering place."

"Right. Yes. So?" he said tetchily. It was hot as hell. The sweat was pouring off me. It was pouring off him, too. He'd just climbed down from the top, still too busy to take the road around; he'd "stolen" a couple of hours and nipped over the plateau in a jeep.

"Also," I said, "the curious detail in the addendum about the other priest—who came for flower oil, who wasn't a 'real' priest because they kept a 'different date'—"

"All right—what?"

"Doesn't he sound to you like a priest from Qumran—an Essene maybe? They kept a different religious calendar. They were persecuted for it by the authorities in Jerusalem—don't you remember? It's part of the basis of their apocalyptic literature, *The War of the Sons of Light Against the Sons of Darkness*. Doesn't this sound to you like—"

"I know what it sounds to me like!" he said furiously, dabbing his forehead. "So? So?"

"So if you happen to be in Qumran and need a spot of flower oil, where are you likely to go? We know that Professor Mazar excavated a perfumery in 1960—"

"I know what Mazar did in 1960!"

"—here in Ein Gedi," I said.

He dabbed at his forehead. "All right. What else?"

"What else do you want? Marble? There's the biggest deposits of marble in the country. Why the scroll was found here in the first place? Because it was written here. Look—look," I said. I felt dizzy. "There's a lot more. Plenty more. If you don't like it, then I don't—"

"But I do," Agrot said. "My God!" He was sweating like a bullock, rubbing it out of his eyes as he stared wildly about him in the flickering heat haze of the canyon. "I like it so much. I'm frightened how much I like it."

"Well, thank Christ for that," I said faintly. I sat down, more than usually bushed. It was over for me, of course. I'd told him a bit on the phone in the afternoon, and a bit more later, about eleven at night. I'd been at Ein Gedi then, sick and faint with excitement, not really able to stay away. It was over, and I'd known it last night, but I still hadn't been able to sleep.

"But where?" he said, looking up to the plateau. "Where?"

This was the nub, of course. There were miles and miles of suitable depository ground up there; marble in abundance, eminences in all sizes. Of all the places in Israel it was the most likely to hide the Menorah, and of all the places the least likely where you might expect to find it. Without further directions, without the portion of the scroll the Jordanians apparently had, it could be a lifetime's task; as Josephus perhaps had found.

"There's the possibility," Agrot said slowly, assimilating this for himself, "of working out the route he must have traveled, and from this, perhaps, the distances. Almost certainly he would have observed the Torah regulations for animals—work periods, distances, speed and so forth."

"He's vague on times before he was rounded up. It's impossible to say how many days he was on the job."

"Maybe we can work back after he was rounded up. My impression is the period was very short between the depositing of the consignment and the ambush."

"It's just an impression. There's nothing specific in the scroll." I could see he didn't really expect much in this line himself. He was talking merely to give himself time to think. And there wasn't, as far as I was concerned, much to think about. He looked at me for a bit.

"It's a lot of work," he said.

"Yes."

"A program."

"Yes."

We remained looking at each other.

"I'm sorry," he said.

"Maybe I'll be there when it happens," I said. "If you ask me back sometime."

"So come and have something to drink at the kibbutz," he said. "Barot can wait. We have a lot to talk about."

But, again, we didn't really. He was simply being decent. Knowing how much he wanted to get back to Barot, I thought he was being very decent.

I slept like a log in the afternoon, and after a cold drink and a shower at six, slept again. They'd given me my old guest hut. It was dark when I woke the second time, but I had an idea the light had been on seconds before. I said, "Shoshana."

"Yes. I'm sorry. Go back to sleep."

"What is it?"

"I brought you a drop of brandy. I thought you might like some."

"Quite right."

I sat up. She put the light on. She'd brought herself a drop, too; which was unusual. She poured out the brandy and sipped her own solemnly as at the early stage of some wake; which was not amiss the way I was feeling.

"What's to do?" I said at length.

"I wondered if he said anything about me."

"No."

"I suppose I'll have to return to duty, then."

"I suppose you will."

"Oh, Caspar."

"Now now."

"Do you want me to lock the door?" she said in my ear some minutes later.

"Not really. Not tonight."

"All right. . . . What do you intend doing now?"

This was a question. Agrot didn't see his way to starting the action for five or six weeks. He'd seen, very roughly, a preliminary season of ten weeks which would take him into May; after this it would be too hot on the plateau and he'd have to wait till November. He'd seen it as a fairly full-scale operation for a team of fifty or so, with army support. Against this background of planned activity I felt a bit spare. Tomorrow was Thursday, and I was due anyway to go back a week Sunday. Why wait?

"I don't know," I said. "I thought I'd work things out after a sleep."

"Would you sooner I went now?"

"I'd sooner you got some more brandy."

"And I'll tell you one thing," I said, when she'd got it, quite a nice lot of it, and we'd had another one each, "I think you were dead right about that raid on Ein Gedi from Massada. I'm sure it wasn't for food. It was for this. I've been thinking about it."

"Have you, love?"

"Yes, love. Do you want to hear about it?"

"I'd love to hear about it, love." The brandy had been one too many for her, and she was kissing my nose as she said it. But I told her all the same.

The problem had been to account for the Zealots at Massada knowing about the priest at Ein Gedi, and I thought I'd accounted for it now. To explain, it was necessary to recap briefly the recorded events of the period.

Joseph ben Matthias had been appointed to his command in February, and a couple of months later, at the instigation of his rival, ben Levi, the Jerusalem junta had unsuccessfully tried to arrest him. Shortly afterwards ben Matthias had gone over to the Romans, and a little later ben Levi had escaped to Jerusalem to take high office in the government. Just a few months after, the revolutionaries of Massada had carried out their savage raid on Ein Gedi.

This was fact, and to it I added my own hypothesis. The junta had wanted ben Matthias because they'd learned he'd ambushed the treasure party. Since ben Levi had tipped them off, *he* knew about the treasure party, too. When he later joined the government he found that the priest in charge still hadn't returned and that no report had been received from him. A study of the area where he'd gone would have shown rapidly enough where he must have sought a haven. So the raid on Ein Gedi had been authorized from the nearest revolutionary fortress —Massada.

Josephus in his history has described the raid as one by terrorists for food and booty. But Josephus was politically opposed to the Zealots of Massada. Why should even a gang of terrorists slaughter the people who could continue to supply them with food? And yet slaughter them they did. They slaughtered seven hundred, all who could not run away. Why?

Might it not have been during a mass interrogation— for information more important even than a continuing supply of food? Experience of more sophisticated wars since has shown this type of interrogation to be by no means out of the way when the information sought is of sufficient value.

And the villagers, doubly luckless, wouldn't even have been able to give the information. Only one man could have given it, and he'd run away. He'd run into the canyon; after fulfilling as much of his task as he could.

He'd "written twice" what the priest had given him. He'd placed one copy "in The Curtains" and another "farther on, down low, the bottom of the cliff, beyond as you go" (evidently the one found at Murabba'at). The priest's original, still undelivered, he had stuffed hastily into the cave in the canyon, together with his money, probably on this very night of the raid, and had never gone back for them. So the villagers of Ein Gedi had died before their time, and nobody had discovered the priest's secret; and perhaps now nobody would.

She'd stopped kissing my nose while I unloaded this lore, and at the end she shivered. "The land is soaked with blood," she said, quoting somebody, Isaiah possibly. I'd taken a few nips during my recital and no longer had a fine grasp of quotable sources or I'd have capped it. I felt like capping it, my mood no longer flat and dismal, but now finely elegiac. Nothing came to mind, however, so I said, "How about locking the door, then?"

And in a finely elegiac mood herself, she did.

Twelve

BEFORE I GO

I may take comfort a little.
—Job 10:20

1

THE FINELY ELEGIAC MOOD had gone by morning and only the flatness remained. I hardly felt like getting up at all; but I did, at ten, well soused with sleep but still gravely unresolved. It was hot. I showered, shaved, managed to get myself some coffee and yoghurt in the dining room, and went and sat outside to wait glumly for the girl. There was a lively hum of agriculturalists at work. It's a pretty little kibbutz, Ein Gedi, with its trim lawns, shade trees and chalet-type buildings. Under the blue sky and wedged between mountain and sea, the plantations of palm and catch crops looked like an illustration in a child's book. Just such a picture of primary-colored bliss the People of the Land must have carried with them in their cold northern exile; Paradise Lost indeed as viewed from the stinking ghettos of Europe. This picture, and another; the older emblem, that had preserved their consciousness more surely; the emblem of a people, of a light in darkness, a seven-branched light. And incredibly the light had not failed. It had gone on shining through the ages of darkness, perpetuated in the homes, synagogues and tombstones of the faithful, the countless million descendants of those who had been here before, who had actually seen the thing itself.

More incredibly still, the thing itself still existed; it was up there somewhere on the plateau, the fantastic old artifact, older than the Caesars, older than almost anything. What hadn't happened since it had lain there! The planet had spun and the cup had filled and run over for The Children. The frenetic neighbors had taken sides in their family quarrels, shouldering one of them to divinity and kicking the others into the incinerator to affirm his message of brotherly love. What a darkness this lamp had revealed, what a conflagration it had started! And it was still there. And legend had it that it would remain there till the Jew returned to reclaim his own. Well, he was back now; but reclamation might take a little longer.

A trailer truck rumbled past interrupting these musings and Shoshana jumped off the back, like a coffee-colored sprite, in her working shorts. "Why are you sitting here like a monk?" she said, blowing on my tonsure. The head dressing had got wet in the shower and I'd taken it off.

"I feel like a monk."

"Learn to act like one," she said softly in my ear, and stuck the dressing back on. There was still a bit of stick left in it.

We went up twice that day, in the morning the hard way via the canyon and the cliff, and in the afternoon by jeep and the new road. There was a certain satisfaction in regarding the size of the job that lay before Agrot; albeit of a sour kind.

I'd hoped, of course, to get a paper out of this, but it was obvious now I'd simply be there in the foreword, the man without whose remarkable insights, etc. . . . Years ahead one could see the eventual publications; the folio academic works done up to the knocker with diagrams, figs., and plates (the work of Dr. Hilde Himmelwasser). And the later lusher coffee-table books. And the television talks, and the newspaper interviews. . . . A whole new field of lore lay waiting germinally here for the harvesters. A further required subject for the syllabus; to be taught to the budding social pests by such as me.

A sour look at the field before it was plundered, a last lingering glance over what might have been; these were the only fruits for me. Dead Sea fruits, of course, that vanished in the mouth to leave only a nasty taste; but no less resistible for that.

I phoned El Al in the evening and told them to book me on a plane on Monday.

"Which class?"

"Tourist" sprang aptly enough to the lip, but I stopped it in time. To feel like one didn't mean I had to travel like one. "First," I said firmly. Out like a lord, anyway. In three days time.

2

We took the jeep again next day and hit the plateau from a new angle, climbing almost to Arad before turning off. The trouble was to know which way the priest had come. He'd certainly climbed down the canyon, but after traveling from where—north, south, west? We were having a go from due south.

Almost at once the track vanished and we were on a fantastic switchback, the jeep rising and swooping through an incredible maze of towering rock walls. We went through Biq'at Quannai'm, the stark Valley of the Zealots, passed the squat sugar loaf of Massada, away on the right, and came out on the plateau.

On all sides the solid mesas of rock stood like ruined castles, reddish-brown in the baking sun. The geological structure here was very complex. As Agrot had said, there was everything, billions of tons of workable rock of all kinds. A handy hosepipe could help to bring up fleetingly the color of the marble. Without it, you could only guess at the true shades: the clay browns that might be beige or red, the dull charcoals that could be green or blue. The great flanks of rock sat baking in the sun.

We neared the area of the canyon and stopped while I checked with the map. A point that had to be watched here was to keep on the right side of the border. There was very little indication of it, just a line of oil drums, spaced at wide intervals. From the canyon it ran in a straight line southwest. We seemed to have room to spare.

We got out of the jeep and continued the somewhat meandering procedure of the previous day. This was to leave the jeep in a central position and cover a square all round it, jotting down on the map promising areas for Agrot's brigade to investigate. It didn't take long to see that from this southward approach very few of the areas were unpromising. The plateau was mainly hard limestone, much of it almost certainly colored. It stretched for miles, to Barot and beyond, broken here and there by great strands of rock in every known formation.

After an hour of it the girl stopped singing out, "To your right," "The hill over there," and such, and I stopped making marks on the map. There wasn't really any point. You could look left, right and center and not run out of promising places for weeks. You could probably approach it from several other directions and find just as promising places. Almost every yard in an area of several hundred square miles had to be regarded as promising.

We'd walked quite a long way from the jeep and weren't bothering about the "square" any more. I was simply swiveling the binoculars this way and that to see how much more there could possibly be. I was doing that when I saw it. I wasn't looking for it. I wasn't even thinking of it. It hit me like a hammer blow between the eyes.

I'd swung past it and had to swing back and hunt for it again. I found myself trembling all over. My hands were trembling. They were trembling so much I couldn't keep the binoculars still. But I found it again. A tall spire-type formation; a column of rock vertically striated, like a stalactite.

Through the shaking field of vision I looked to right and left. It was part of a group. The others, almost end on to me, were in a zigzagging crescent. I was looking at the far end of the crescent. The rocks stood in fluted columns; like folding doors; like curtains.

I went there and back and up and down, and stopped. I'd been holding my breath, and it came out then, slowly. I thought I'd glimpsed it the first time. It was centered in the field of vision now: an oil drum. The group of rocks was beyond the oil drum.

I let the binoculars hang and wiped the sweat out of my eyes and found the spot on the map.

"What is it?"

"Interesting range of rock."

She had a look where my pencil made a shaky ring on the map.

"That's no good. Nobody's going there. It's over the border, silly."

"So it is," I said, and crossed the ring off. The cross was pretty shaky, too.

In the afternoon I sent her off to sketch a range of hills to the south, and nipped off myself in the jeep back to the north. I found the spot and studied it.

Four distinct peaks, three in the zigzag, one squarely toward me. They lined the western side of a narrow gorge, three or four kilometers across the border. It was utterly deserted, not a bird in sight, all bathed in calm sunlight. An hour's walk. *Could* this be The Curtains? And if so, which one?

"The Curtain you cannot see from here, it is turned away," he'd written.

Turned away from where?

I got back in the jeep and drove to the top of the Ein Gedi canyon, stopping from time to time to keep the thing in view. From the top of the canyon I could see the peaks of two; just the peaks. Which one was "turned away"? It was impossible to say.

Down below the kibbutz swam in the rising air currents. The biblical village had lain farther to the north, beyond the canyon. It had been near the spring. I looked down to the site. Bare now, simply a waste of salt mud, but once covered with palm trees. The groves of Ein Gedi had been famous; the groves and the sweetly scented camphire (the Semitic *kufra,* the perfumer's chypre).

I suddenly recalled the phrase that had awakened a song in the flinty heart of Teitleman, the "pleasant fruits and camphire, in a fountain of gardens, a well of living waters." No question what the poet had in mind. "My beloved is unto me as a cluster of camphire in the vineyards of Ein Gedi," he'd written. Of course! The well of living waters of Ein Gedi—the waterfall. Wasn't it up the course of the waterfall that the priest had been carried in the flower basket, to be "buried behind the spring"? Wasn't *that* where The Curtains had to be viewed from— the top of the waterfall, above the Cave of Shulamit? All at once everything seemed to fall in place, the rest of the man's account of his stewardship. *"I put another farther on, down low,"* he'd written, *"the bottom of the cliff, beyond as you go."*

Exactly. Exactly beyond as you go. He'd written an entirely factual account of what he'd done. Start off in the direction of The Curtains—if this was The Curtains— and "beyond as you go" you'd hit Murabba'at. I could almost see it from here, the place itself just blocked by a small headland. Beyond it, clearly visible, was the bulge below Qumran. No doubt he'd been going there, to call on his oil-using, wrong-date-keeping customers; and had found time to dispose of a couple of scrolls on the way. Well. The Arabs had one now, containing the full coded directions that Sidqui had misunderstood. The other, presumably, was still where he'd left it, high in the dry preservative air of The Curtains.

H'm.

3

I still hadn't said anything to her by the evening. I sat pensively through the rendition of *L'Cha Dodi*. I fell abstractedly on my Sabbath victuals. I was still brooding as I left the dining hall.

"Miriam has a party," she said.

"I thought you weren't talking to Miriam just now."

"Miriam is too interfering. But a party is a party."

"I'm not in the party mood tonight."

"Broody bear, why are you so broody?"

"I'm tired."

"Too tired for a walk even?"

"Much too tired."

"But it's a quarter-moon. We could go to the Cave of Shulamit."

"No, thanks."

"That's not very flattering."

"I'd never manage it."

"Never manage what?" she said.

We didn't, anyway. We went to the shore instead and watched the quarter-moon from there. It was farther down the lake, the crescent moon over the lands of the crescent; over the crescent of rocks. If one could only get to those rocks, there might be no need for the work brigades, the army support, the weeks, months, years of laborious exploration. . . . Why not tell her, then? What instinct of self-survival, duplicity, secretiveness prevented me?

I'd been pondering this. The thing at the moment was mine, all mine; to brood over, worry about, marvel at, adore. To tell her, to tell anyone, was to take it out of the

realms of fable and speculation. And there was still much
to speculate about. *Were* they The Curtains? Was there
any certainty the thing was still there? And either way
was it proper or even reasonable for the professor of
Semitics at Beds so much as to think of . . . ? These
were good questions. The wrong answers could easily
land the professor in the manure.

Supposing the madness came on me, and I decided to
go. To tell her was to risk having her try to stop me or to
come with me. The latter certainly wasn't on. A British
tourist caught straying over the border was one thing; a
female Israeli lieutenant quite another. Yet to go alone
and not tell anyone might be more unpleasant still. It was
dangerous country. Dangerous things could happen in it
to the solitary cliff scaler.

"Broody bear, what's the matter?"

"Too much exercise. I can hardly keep my eyes open."

"Come back, then. You're no answer to a maiden's
prayer," she said dolefully.

But I was, in a gentle way, in the guest hut.

But I still hadn't told her when she left.

4

I was up early on the Saturday, trembling finely all over,
much oppressed.

"What do you want to do?" she said after breakfast. I
hadn't had much breakfast. I'd had a cup of coffee.

"Nothing. You'd better have a sabbath."

"What do you mean?"

"Take it off, love. Relax. Have a layoff."

"What are you going to do?"

"I am going to be a broody bear," I said.

"You don't want me?"

I did. As some men fly to food or sleep at time of trouble, I flew to females. She was all legs, eyes and hair this morning, excessively female in her shorts, shirt and sandals. I'd seen her whip out of this ensemble in less time than the telling. Reason called on me to get her at it and keep her at it till plane time Monday.

"Not today," I said.

"What will you do?"

"Mooch about and think."

Twenty minutes later I was doing it, in the direction of the waterfall. I mooched like a broody bear, but once out of the kibbutz, smartened up.

By ten o'clock I was on top, observing the Curtain that was turned away.

There wasn't really any question about it. From this angle they were more like curtains than ever, four flowing folds of rock, and only one turned away—the first of the zig-zag, nearest the border.

Through the glasses it was possible to see a series of ridges running laterally across the faces of the others; they were quite climbable. What about the one that was turned away? *"It is in the first hole, you get down from the top,"* he had written. How? From the back? The side? Certainly not this side. What I could see of it dropped steeply in an unbroken line.

The gorge was not in view from this position. Yesterday's position offered a better view. It also offered a view of the back of the Curtain. I made a quick sketch of what was to be seen from here and then moved along there.

A warm wind blew on the plateau, and I was thirsty. I

hadn't brought a flask with me. It was half an hour before I remembered the spring, and then I couldn't be bothered going back. The morning was getting on. I'd have to wait till lunchtime. One conclusion at least had been arrived at. Nothing was going to be done about The Curtains today. Tomorrow, perhaps, but not today. Today was Saturday, and the kibbutzniks were at large.

I hadn't brought a hat and sweat was soon trickling down from my head. I could feel the dressing there, unpleasantly hot and itching. But the walk brought its reward: a splendid view, altogether more explicable now, of the gorge and the zigzag of Curtains. The first, its back now squarely toward me, showed a faint diagonal ridge and then a series of sharp knobs that continued to the top. The ridge wound round from the far side, the beginning out of sight.

I moved farther to the left and up to the border for a better look. It was only fractionally better. I couldn't see any more of the ridge, but got a rather clearer view of the section already visible. It seemed very narrow, and also very smooth, no doubt from erosion. It was always possible that the lower section had been eroded away completely; that the thing was no longer climbable.

I lowered the glasses. I was on a slight elevation and could see the whole length of the gorge. The wall opposite The Curtains was lower and broken by clefts in the rock, through which water would rush in time of spate, across the plateau and down to the Dead Sea. No water rushed now. Nothing at all moved, except the slight hissing wind. All quite still in this dead deserted land.

I looked at my watch. Half past eleven. Time I was getting busy with a sketch. It would take me an hour and a half to get back; for the late lunch. I didn't actually feel like any lunch. I didn't actually feel thirsty, either. Inexplicably I was shaking all over. This was ridiculous, of course. Excitement had to be kept firmly in check. A steady hand was needed for the sketch.

I actually had the pencil in my hand when I walked over the border. I walked over it in a state of cold fright. What was this? Not today. I'd *decided* not today. Back, then. Down, Rover!

Rover didn't go back or down. After some moments I even felt a certain mild elation. It wasn't such a bad idea after all. To plan, prospect a route, and do it all in one go was asking for trouble. It was obviously a better idea to do it in bits. Find the best way to the gorge and the ascent up the rock one day, and do it the next. Here was sense. And one side of the border was no different from the other. The difference was purely technical. Any infringement was purely technical—supposing there was anybody to notice; which there wasn't. All the same, it was obviously prudent to keep one's head down.

I kept my head down, in the lee of the jumble of rocks, and scurried briskly to the gorge. A certain amount of weaving was necessary. Even so, without undue exertion or even hard breathing, I made it in three-quarters of an hour. A quarter past twelve. Very nice.

From close up, the gorge was not as straight as had appeared. There were two quite pronounced bends in it, and also a sharp inlet, immediately this side of the first Curtain. I observed this from behind a rock. I waited for some minutes, listening. Then I came out of cover and entered the gorge.

Not even a fly disturbed the massive calm. But it was as well to be careful. I nipped lightly over to the opposite wall where, dodging in and out of the small inlets and occasional large clefts, I was able to look up at the line of Curtains. They stretched for a quarter of a mile, enormous monumental walls, their fluted faces turned geometrically in toward each other, very somber. Here and there, high up, were "windows," evidently the eyries of birds. None of them looked particularly difficult to climb; except the first. This one rose sheer for quite six hundred feet before turning outward in a sort of small lip like the curling crest of a wave. There were no windows here. Holes, if any, must be above the lip.

I waited a moment, listening again for any slight click of stone, and then padded briskly over to the other side and entered the inlet at the side of the first Curtain.

The monumental flank was less smooth here, more pitted and craggy, but still, on the face of it, impossible to climb. There was, however, the ridge. I couldn't see it from this angle but I knew it was there, a hundred feet above me. I followed the Curtain round, a couple of hundred yards around its base, climbed a mound of crags like a heap of giant broken dinner plates, and found the beginning of the ridge.

It started thirty feet or so up the rock, easily approachable by tumbled boulders, and by no means as smooth or as narrow as it had appeared. Perhaps it became narrower. It seemed a good idea to find out. Perhaps I'd be able to see if some simple aids such as rubber shoes or a bit of rope might be necessary for tomorrow. There wasn't any danger of exposing myself on the Jordanian side. This face of the rock was turned to the frontier.

The ridge ran like a normal mountain track, the usual litter of rubble and fallen stones underfoot. I concentrated on not kicking them over, preternaturally anxious to avoid sound. I hadn't much of a head for heights. The thing to do was to keep one's eyes firmly on the track.

The track did seem to narrow after a bit. I couldn't notice any actual change in the dimensions—it had begun to swim slightly owing to a certain fixity of vision—but was conscious presently of my shoulder against the rock, and the need to go a bit more slowly.

I went a bit more slowly. I tried to reason whether I was going more slowly through choice or because a sharp change in the angle of ascent had made it necessary. There was no doubt it *was* a bit steeper. I could feel it in my legs and in my wind. The best thing might be to take it a step at a time. This was difficult. It was suddenly hideously difficult. I seemed to be engaged in some precarious balancing act, the whole act of walking suddenly highly complex. Absurd, of course. It was only because of the illusion of height. The thing to do was to put this illusion out of mind. I was simply having this slow sort of walk along a ledge a few feet off the ground, and the only difficulty was the proximity of the wall. It wasn't a *real* difficulty; plenty of room, if somewhat smooth now and less secure underfoot. Perhaps it would be best, all things considered, if I turned in to the wall and went sideways. No difficulty at all then; how could there be?

I turned in to the wall and went sideways, arms outstretched on the rock. There was no difficulty except the mental one of preserving the idea that I was just a few feet off the ground. The sudden effort required from the right leg indicated quite clearly now that I was climbing, and climbing very steeply. I shuffled sideways for a few minutes more, and stopped for a breather, and incautiously looked down through my legs, and saw the gorge about two miles below and nearly fell off.

I leaned sickeningly in, head on the rock, and felt it lurching and wheeling as I fought the sick horrors of vertigo. I was stuck on the rock face like a fly on the wall. My knees were trembling, delicate fly's knees, and they'd give in a minute and I'd drop, drop, drop . . .

They were giving. I could feel them giving. There was nothing to hold on to, nothing to lean in to. The rock itself was leaning out, and I was leaning out with it, stuck there for seconds only by tactile adhesion, by the pads on my fingers, by the film of sweat . . .

The rock swung, and I fought it, and it leaned in again and I could lean in with it, shaking all over, wet with sweat and suddenly very cold. I could hear my teeth rattling above the calm hiss of the wind.

Still now. Stay quite still. Everything was all right. One had simply to collect oneself and start edging back. One got led into these things without preparation. It needed preparation; mental preparation. Enough had been done for today. One had got the flavor. Another day.

I stayed there collecting myself, aware even as I did it that nobody was being fooled. If one thing was more certain than another it was that once I was down nothing on earth would get me back up again. I couldn't do it; couldn't make myself do it; would work out all manner of reasons why the thing couldn't be done. And it could be done; I'd done it; had got myself in this position at least, more than halfway up; more than three-quarters perhaps. Why not continue, as far as possible? I'd never be in this position again.

I'd got my eyes closed, and they were still closed as I started moving again, upward. The thing to do was to put everything else out of mind, to concentrate simply on the physical act of moving one foot and then the other, with the certain knowledge that I'd be doing it once only, and that if it proved impossible, then I'd *know*.

Showers of small stones fell as I moved. I couldn't be bothered about them now, all my earlier fears, of noise, of exposure, left behind, as I concentrated simply on the primary task of staying on the narrow ledge, shuffling sideways, eyes closed and arms embracing the rock.

I stopped presently and opened my eyes and looked up. The series of knobs was still some way above, fifty feet perhaps—above and to the right. I could see them standing black against the sky, reassuringly wide slabs of rock. The ledge had narrowed still farther and was no longer flat, the exterior edge rounded. I wasn't going to look down. I could feel well enough with my feet. No occasion for another fit of the horrors here. I wasn't going to fall. I was going to go as far as I could. There was a certain technical interest in seeing how far I could go. The rock face must certainly have changed since the man came up it with the scroll. Technically speaking, the thing wasn't climbable at all now. No experienced climber would tackle it, anyway, without crampons, ropes, iron pegs.

I went on, shuffling very delicately, eyes open now, not taking the weight off one foot till I was quite sure of the other. With three or four yards to the first projection I stopped and had another breather and considered.

The ledge was narrowing quite sharply now. Right at the very end it narrowed to a mere bulge in the rock and merged into the projection and didn't continue again at the other side. By that point one could practically fall across the projection. It stuck out for six feet or so, quite flat on top. The question was, how to get back? One could fall *on* the projection. One didn't want to fall off it. How to get down from it again onto the narrow ledge?

I got my breath back and stood in the crucifixion position, and tried to work it out. I'd have to get down off the projection backwards, and feel with the left leg and for a moment carry all my weight on it while the other rested on a mere bulge. I would still, however, be within arm's reach of the projection. If I teetered, the projection would be there. I could teeter by the hour, of course, before nerving myself to take the one farther step that would put me out of reach of it. How safe was it to take that step?

I knew I was going to leave it till the moment came. I was too tired now to frig about rehearsing the move. Some faint signal beep-beeped in my brain that I was burning my boats this way, that I ought to try it, that it was lunatic to go up before ensuring that I could get down again. But I moved anyway. I moved without breathing, just clinging, till my right foot brushed the bulge, and I got my arms down from the rock and just laid them on the flat slab of the projection, and bent over it at waist level, face on the warm rock, enormously relieved. I suddenly realized the impossible strain I'd been under, perched on tiptoe almost, arms outstretched, every muscle protesting. Then I hoisted myself onto it, stood up, found the whole series of projections, going up like a giant staircase; and I went up them, and found myself on top, and for the first time looked around.

5

There was no vertigo now; only a sense of weary wonder that I'd actually made it. The incredible landscape slanted below as though seen from a wheeling plane. To the east, three-quarters of a mile below, lay the still blue pool of the Dead Sea, while to the west the maze of tumbled rock rolled away higher and higher, somewhere among it a tiny glimmer of white buildings and flashing glass pinpointing Hebron, fifteen miles away. The road ran north from there to Bethlehem and Jerusalem; both out of sight now in the faint apricot haze that hid the division between rock and sky.

On the plateau floor stretched the usual lunar confusion. A stark place; but not a lowering or a hopeless one like Zin. Here was the Judean wilderness; a lion-colored wilderness; a place of prophets. If a landscape could be said to have nobility, then this one had it. No life here, so no death; no growth, so no decline. And yet, curiously, no sense of sterility, either; only of calm wonder and of the seamed face of reality. As ever the place hit me like the breath of a baker's oven, agelessly fresh, like its enduring Children.

But this was no time to be admiring noble wildernesses. The top of the Curtain was flat and grained like a lump of sugar, and descended in two steep steps to the sheer face that was "turned away." I lowered myself down. There was a cave at the first step. There was a cave at the second. Which was the "first": the first up the rock or the first from the top? There was certainly nothing below, anyway. The second step formed the overhanging lip that I'd seen from below. I decided on this one first.

I got my lighter out, bent and crawled in. There was a

musty, sickly smell of droppings inside; all pitch black. I lit the lighter.

Farther in, the cave widened and heightened. Something fluttered and brushed my head, and all of a sudden the dimness was full of fluttering; scrofulous, membranous things, queerly angled, flapping about. Bats. Scores, hundreds of them, fluttering in the air, startled by the light, others stuck on the walls, wings heraldically stretched. The commotion stirred up clouds of the sickly stench, so nauseous I found myself gagging, on my knees.

While I was doing it, one flew directly at the lighter, knocking it out of my hand. At once, some dozens of them seemed to beam in at me, dusty bodies knocking into and skittering about my head and face. I struck out and kept striking out, still gagging, till the cloud cleared.

I breathed through my mouth and mastered the nausea. It was possible to see now that the cave wasn't entirely black. A faint glimmer was coming in from outside. I looked toward it and saw the bats in a dense mass at the entrance, scuffing and squeaking as they jostled to get out. They were streaming out, twenty, thirty, forty of them, wheeling in the gorge. I turned back and found the lighter, but didn't light it this time. Now my eyes were accustomed to it, there was enough light to move by. I raised myself slowly, found I could stand upright. I moved to the end of the cave.

It was a long one, easily thirty feet. If the scroll was anywhere, it would be at the far end; as the Ein Gedi one had been. The floor was springy underfoot; the droppings of thousands of years. It would have been just as soft when he'd left his package 'here. The true bottom would be several feet under.

Not all of the bats had gone. A somnolent rearguard

remained, hung on the walls and in the crevices, twitching slightly as I passed. The roof began to lower, and I had to crouch again, till at the end I was on my knees. I lit the lighter.

The ground was level, and I felt it carefully all along the line of the back. Uniformly spongy, no spot showing any particular firmness. I put the lighter in my pocket, and, feeling with my hand, began to scoop up the muck for a distance of a foot from the back. The surface was dry but slightly glutinous on its underside, warm to the touch, and drier as one went deeper. At about four inches it was powdery, at between five and six too compacted to shift. I excavated to here and continued right along the line, the back of my hand flat in the channel and scooping the soft muck upward. The width of the cave here was some seven or eight feet, and after about four I found it.

I just touched the edge with my fingers, and whipped the hands back as if burnt; and sat on my backside in the dark, mouth wide open. I couldn't believe it. I simply couldn't believe it. I was afraid to light the lighter in case it wasn't. But I did, and it was. The edge of a scroll, inside a piece of rotted linen; tightly curled, still springy, still elastic.

I let the lighter go out, and sat for a few moments, and then very carefully lit myself a cigarette and sat and smoked it. I could see my hand trembling in the glow from the burning end. It had never happened to me like this before. A piece of pure deduction, and it had worked. I felt I should be bounding about the cave screaming with joy. I sat and smoked the cigarette and felt sick.

I smoked it to the end, and stubbed it out on the wall,

and then lit the lighter again and carefully dug the scroll out. The linen crumbled away, but the skin itself seemed to be in good condition. The dung had been the finest preservative, moist when fresh, drying slowly, never wholly parched on top, never wholly damp below; practically museum conditions. The only danger was that the phosphates and ammonia in it might have worked through the skin.

I delicately opened it. There were three sections, as at Ein Gedi. The middle one slipped out, and I examined it first. The priest's introductory note, poorly copied. The second—the same order in which we'd got it—the footnote from the semiliterate. I opened the third with my heart thumping dully. The list of places. Crystal clear; clear as the day it was written.

I rolled the skins up at once, unbuttoned my shirt and shoved the roll inside. Home, James.

Half a dozen of the bats were still clinging to the entrance as I emerged. They fluttered off, joining the others that still wheeled in the gorge. I got a toehold on the first step, fiddled the roll more snugly under my armpit and started levering myself up. I was doing that when the shot rang out.

I didn't, all at once, identify it as a shot. I didn't identify it as anything in particular. I turned to see what the hell it was, and was in time to see the flash of the next. A uniformed man was standing on a rock platform of the opposite Curtain firing a rifle. He was firing it toward but not at me. His voice came thinly over the intervening hundred yards or so, in Arabic. "Narcotics Patrol. Stay where you are."

I didn't stay where I was. After one glazed moment, I turned and scrambled like a madman up the step. I hadn't got half up it before another bullet whined and whanged; this time from a different direction, and this time at me. Rock splinters from it actually hit me in the face. I looked toward where it had come from. Not twenty yards away another man was standing, on a broad ridge on the next Curtain. As I looked he studiously sighted and fired again.

I came down off the step faster than I'd ever moved in my life, and nipped back into the cave.

Bloody hell.

Thirteen

FEAR AND TREMBLING

Which made all my bones to shake.
—Job 4:14

1

THE BATS, OF COURSE. The flaming bats! I'd forgotten the great police narks of the area. All along the cliffs of the Qumran section the authorities kept an eye open for bats, to check the Ta'amireh in their illegal scroll hunts. No doubt the Narcotics Patrol did the same. Looking for caches of hashish, of course. No hashish here. More important things than hashish. Mustn't find it. What in God's name to do with it?

I'd scrambled frenziedly to the back of the cave while these thoughts flashed through my head, with the deranged notion of simply burying the thing again. No point in that, of course. They'd go through every inch of the muck. What then?

I couldn't think. The only clear picture in my mind was of the studious look on the face of the man who'd tried to shoot me. He'd really tried! And if I poked my nose out he'd try again. The proprieties had been observed; they'd warned the smuggler and he'd disregarded the warning.

Now there was simply the enjoyable job of shooting him and impounding his hoard.

This was terrible. I had to make it known I wasn't a smuggler. I had to make it known I was ready to surrender—immediately. But not the scroll! I was damned if I'd surrender that. Not here. Not in The Curtains—so that whoever finally got it would be able to work out the implications. I'd sooner burn it first.

I was on hands and knees, turning distractedly this way and that like a mixed-up dog when this unacademic solution occurred. I stopped, chittering to myself with horrified obscenity. Burn it? Unthinkable. What a pass we'd come to! We couldn't go about burning priceless old scrolls. The thing to do was to memorize the contents, then try to hide them. If all else failed there was always the possibility they'd get it wrong.

In a trice I'd whipped the roll out and moved nearer to the patch of gray light in the entrance. The list was whippy, coiled tight as a spring and difficult to keep open. The abominable handwriting danced before my eyes like black spiders. Hebrew letter, back-to-front Greek; copied from the priest's original. Hard enough to decipher in the calm of the scrollery. Here, with the gunman a few yards away keeping my hands rhythmically aflutter, it was impossible. I couldn't do it, couldn't get a single word. No time to copy it. No time to do anything now but try to hide it.

I was turning to do this when sounds outside indicated the gunman was no longer a few yards away. I heard him yelling, heard both of them yelling, quite distinctly. I peered cautiously out of the opening and went out, flat on my stomach. He was going down the ridges of the next Curtain, going down fast like a man on a ladder, evidently familiar with it. He was having a shouted conversation as he did it with his colleague high on the opposite Curtain. I listened.

He'd seen how I must have got into the cave. I'd got into it from the rock he was on. It needed ropes and hooks. I must have them in the cave with me. He was going down to radio to Hebron for more men, and ropes and hooks.

I edged forward and had a look down. Miles below, a little toy jeep stood on the floor of the gorge. He was scrambling rapidly down to it.

"Tell them to bring lights!" the other man yelled down to him.

"Of course lights!"

Lights? I looked at my watch. Incredibly, it was three o'clock. It would be dark in less than a couple of hours. It would take them nearly that getting anybody over from Hebron. But why hadn't they found the way I'd got up? Perhaps from the Jordanian side the ridge looked very much worse than it was. Perhaps it had always been thought to be unclimbable. Whatever the hell they thought, it looked as if I had a couple of hours' security, at least. I went back into the cave with a certain heady relief. Two hours. Time, anyway, to have a more reasonable go at the list. Time to find some reasonable place to hide it. It suddenly seemed important to secure this first. I lit the lighter and had a look round.

There was no shortage of crevices in the place. The cave was seamed with crevices. The bats fluttered in them as I went carefully around. The difficulty was to find one that wouldn't show disturbance to the experienced eye. I went slowly up and down the walls with the lighter. The crevices ran down to floor level. Doubtless they continued underneath. I became suddenly excited. How about tunneling underneath the muck to find one? No disturbance would show on the surface then.

I found a promising-looking crack in the wall, followed it down to floor level, and starting a couple of feet away, began excavating. Four or five inches down I turned inward and made toward the crack, careful not to disturb the spongy surface. In no time my fingers were touching the wall. I searched carefully with them for the crevice, found it, began to scoop out the muck. A wide crevice; beautifully wide. It went in a long way, too, which was all to the good. It seemed to go in a hell of a long way. I was having to stretch full length on the floor now, my arm in almost as far as it would go. Still filled with muck; all muck. Suddenly there wasn't any muck. There wasn't anything. There was moving air on my fingers.

I lay stretched out on the floor and considered this. How could there be moving air in the crevice? Did the crevice continue in some way to the next cave above? Or to some unknown one below? But even if it did, why was the air moving? It wasn't moving in this cave. It was still and dead, though outside it was blowing quite strongly. It suddenly struck me it was blowing quite strongly against my fingers, too. I thought, *Oh, Jesus Christ,* and pulled my arm out, and with mild hysteria began using both hands to dig like a dog. It didn't take five minutes to see it was no crevice but a sizable hole in the wall. At the other side of it was the gorge.

I had a quick cigarette to steady my nerves, and while I was smoking it, worked on, enlarging the hole. I had to use my penknife to chip out the hard compacted stuff underneath. Here was very ancient muck indeed, Davidian, possibly Abrahamic. Certainly it had been here when the man had popped in with his scroll—no sign of the hole would have been visible then. Millennial ages of bats had fouled it, sealing it up entirely.

There was no need to dig far into the lowest reaches. I made an opening about eighteen inches and stuck my head out. Dizzyingly far below was the front end of the jeep. I could suddenly pick out the minute figure of the man who'd gone down standing there. He seemed to be smoking a cigarette. Just as I looked he gazed casually up and away, and began strolling up and down.

My heart was bumping erratically. Just below me, below and to the right, I'd spotted something else. It was a knob of rock, one of the steps of the "staircase." The rest passed at an angle. This one projected laterally across the rock face. It projected to a point only a yard to the right of the hole. It was, however, five yards below. If I could only get at it, I could get to the staircase, to the ridge, and down to the gorge below. . . .

I knew I couldn't. My heart failed me as I looked at it. There was no way of doing it, anyway. I couldn't lower myself to it. There'd still be a gap nearly ten feet. I couldn't drop to it. It was a yard to one side. I couldn't jump to it: it was suicidal. It needed a rope. I could perhaps make a rope, of trousers, shirt, belt, and secure it to something in the cave, and lower myself on that. Perhaps I could. I'd been up to any number of Boy Scout feats of late. I knew I wasn't going to. The thing was a piece of breath-taking lunacy. There was a much better than even chance of killing myself here, and for what? To spare myself trouble with the Jordanian authorities? To win a bit of glory with the scroll? To ensure that Israel got it instead of Jordan? Who cared who got it, so long as somebody did? Anyway, with the jeep sitting below, the thing wasn't feasible. It wasn't feasible during daylight at all. And even to think of it in darkness was such a mind-reeling absurdity that I pulled my head in again, palpitating.

I crouched there for a moment and then shambled to the front and had a look out. The other fellow was still on the rock platform of the opposite Curtain. He'd made himself comfortable there and was having a leisurely cigarette as he lay, legs crossed and back to the rock, taking in the late-afternoon sun. He saw me, but didn't bother picking up his gun. He was simply keeping an eye on the front door. He knew there was no other way out.

I went back in and sat on the floor and had another cigarette myself. I didn't look at the scroll. I didn't even think about it. What I was thinking about precluded thinking about anything else. I just sat and dragged hungrily on the cigarette, palpitating.

2

The reinforcements from Hebron turned up in a couple of jeeps around half past four. I remained inside the entrance and heard them. In the sunset the jumbled peaks of Judea had turned to coppery cinders. I couldn't see the man who still remained on the opposite Curtain, but could hear him well enough. He was carrying on an interested conversation with the men below, to ensure they not only had lights to illuminate the scalable rock, but one for him on a long lead so that he could keep me under observation. They apparently had it, and started up with it.

I withdrew into the cave and hopped about, shivering.

With evening the air had turned brisk, and I was hopping about in shoes, socks and underpants. The rest of my clothes were tied together in a bulky and dangerous-looking rope, at present fixed to a spur of rock at the bottom of the back exit. The only other article I carried was the scroll, now strapped to·my chest with the adhesive tape the doctor had given me in Jerusalem.

My teeth chattered in short rhythmic spasms as I sprang about. It would almost be better to be getting on with it than to hang about here. But I hung on a bit longer. The sun was setting fast; but it was setting against my back exit, at the moment beaming in through it like a blood-tinted searchlight. Anyone chancing to look up from below might see the fluttering rope and the figure dangling from it, like some maniac taking the short route from the eighty-eighth floor.

In the front the peaks were already turning a plummy maroon. Energetic cries came from the men climbing up with equipment. I scurried from one exit to the other, teeth horribly achatter, trying to gauge whether it was dark enough. Below in the gorge it was gray-purple dusk. As I looked down, through the back exit, the headlights sprang suddenly to life on the jeep and the thing moved. It turned in a couple of sharp movements like some ray-eyed insect and went back the way it had come, no doubt to add more candlepower to the scene at the front. At the same moment the entrance of the cave lit up with a pale milky luminescence. The lamp in position on the opposite Curtain: not long before they'd be climbing around. Now, then. With the strangest sensation of watching the thing happen to someone else, I went numbly into the routine. I gave a series of strong tugs on the rope to see it was thoroughly fixed. I tugged sideways, downward, jerked the thing from side to side. Then I hung on to it and went backward out the window, kneeling, feet first. I got one foot out and then the other, and lay over on my stomach and wriggled the rest out, till I was on my elbows; and then slowly eased off them, too.

I went down the rope hand over hand, feet walking down the rock, till I'd come almost to the end of it; then I let my feet down and dangled.

My teeth had stopped chattering now, and I wasn't shivering any more. With the weirdest sensation of normality, I hung from my familiar trousers over the gorge, and felt sideways with my foot for the step. The step wasn't there. Not far enough over.

I came up a bit on the rope, got my feet on the rock and walked myself farther over to the left. It was a long way over, farther than the yard I'd estimated. I could just feel it, feel the beginning of it with my toe. I let myself down on the rope again, got my foot flat on the step, tried to get the other one on, couldn't, was suddenly swinging on the rope, both feet away, swinging nightmarishly on a pendulum, knees barking on the rock, hearing the hideous creaking of the belt above, and a peculiar stretching sound from the shirt next in line to it.

Still now. No floundering. No further strain on the rope. Just hang. The pendulum came to rest. I hung. Shoulders, arms, wrists, ached as I hung. Sweat trickled into my eyes. What, in God's name, now? Hanging, I tried to work it out.

I could very carefully get one foot up on the rock. I could very carefully walk myself over and make another try for the step. If no good, back up the rope as soon as possible, while arms still capable.

Very carefully I got the foot up. Very carefully I walked

myself to the left, felt with the left foot for the step, and found it. Then the right foot, agonizingly careful. My arms seemed practically out of their sockets, fully extended and straining on the rope. Just as I got both feet on, perched at an angle and ready to swing if I lost the foothold again, I heard the shirt slowly rip.

Wordless prayers at once went up. There wouldn't be any swinging now. There wouldn't be any climbing back up, either. One way or another, I'd be going down.

With mindless horror, teetering at an angle of forty-five degrees with my hands grasping my trouser turnups and my feet just on the step, I saw the sequence of operations. I was going to have to throw myself to the left. One enormous heave on the rope, and with its last bit of goodness working for me I'd be over there, to land on my stomach. It wouldn't do the scrolls a lot of good if it worked. It would do me so much less if it didn't that there was really no thinking about it. I simply did it.

With a single grunt and a disk-slipping heave, I pushed off from the rope, lurched over, and turned in to the step. I didn't roll, trip, slide, bounce, judder, ricochet or do anything else Charleyish. I simply landed, flat on my stomach, with a dismal crackling from the scroll on my chest, and lay there, horribly winded. I lay for several minutes till the night air on my underclothed torso awoke a realization of the position. We weren't home yet. We were simply alive. Any minute now someone would enter the cave and find my trousers, belt and shirt (an Israeli shirt, acquired in Tiberias), and realize not only how I'd got out, but where I'd be heading. This was an evil turnup. I'd planned to unhitch the clothes. They were fluttering now out of reach. The thing to do now was to try to get down before they got up.

I picked myself up on the step and got moving. The passage from the bottom step back to the ledge, after all my qualms, was no more difficult than it had been getting up, and in no time I was shuffling briskly down, the thing such a piece of cake after my ordeal on the rope that I wondered why the hell it had given me any bad moments during the ascent.

Shouting had been going on from above as the men flung hooks, but nobody seemed to have entered the cave yet. I climbed down from the crags, moved cautiously up the inlet and peered out. The three jeeps were in a semicircle, nosing in to the front of the Curtain, headlights on and motors running to provide the power for the lights that were beamed up on the rock. Two men were standing gaping up at the operations. I bent low and nipped across to the other side of the gorge, made the opposite inlet and paused there a moment, looking up.

They'd got one hook attached. A man was swinging on the rope now, pulling himself up onto the lip of the Curtain. In minutes he'd be calling down. No time for me to run for the border. The jeeps would get there before me; at an obvious advantage on the plateau. What I'd better do was get off the plateau; down the cliffs to sea level where my slight start would be of some use.

The inlet was a cleft in the gorge, open on both sides. I went haring down it, came out onto the plateau and made off to the east toward the cliffs. I ran till I was out of breath, and just as I slowed down, heard a tumult start up behind me, and took off again. It was dark, very dark, and in the maze of rock very easy to run in a circle to where I'd started. I found a wadi bed and ran beside it: the wadi was bound to lead to the cliffs. And presently it did. It was half past six by the dim figures on my watch face as I came out to the Dead Sea. Across the gap, slightly darker than the dark sky, the Mountains of Moab crouched.

I went down the cliffs via the wadi bed, on my backside. My legs were already badly scratched and bruised, and my behind was soon worse. But the journey was enlivened by noisy goings-on on the plateau. Distant cries had been audible, and before I hit the bottom a burst of firing broke out. God knew what flights of fancy were being indulged or what poor bastards were getting it in the neck. They were liable to be Bedouin bastards, of course. It suddenly struck me there might be some here, along the shore, offshoots of the Ta'amireh. And that a stranger dressed mainly in a valuable scroll would appear a veritable gift from Allah.

I came out onto the dark shore and looked very carefully around. Away over to the right, in the direction of the border, something was gleaming. It might be phosphorescent rock. Or it might not. My own underpants were glimmering in the dark. I took them off and shoved them under a rock. It was warm down here, a sulphurous closeness in the air. The border, slanting sharply up to the sea, couldn't be more than a kilometer away. A dangerous kilometer. All manner of authorities might have been alerted on the jeep radios by this time. It was nearly a couple of hours since the Israeli spy had made his escape. Crossing the border was not going to be such a piece of cake, apart from the Bedouin-type hazards of getting to it.

I was looking at the sea when this thought occurred, and I started walking down to it. I'd certainly never be better dressed for it than now. The salt flats on the way down, crisp and sun-cracked on the surface, gave underfoot and I was soon clumping leadenly with my shoes covered in the underlying black bitumen. I kicked them off. I picked the adhesive tape off my chest as I walked, and reapplied it with the scrolls to the more familiar position on top of my head. While I was doing it, my socks got sucked off too, so that by the time I entered the water I was clothed only in the holy tongue. Let it be unto me as a shield, I thought, and kicked off.

3

The water was warm and greasy, with the consistency of blood, and the sea bed was a sediment of thick slime; both so peculiarly repellent I nearly got out again. This wouldn't do, of course. It had to be borne. I'd seen the patients lolling in it at the health station of Ein Bokek farther down the coast. But nobody forced them to swim a couple of miles in it at Ein Bokek. It looked to me now that I'd have to swim at least that. The border wasn't discernible, and Ein Gedi was three kilometers past it. There was no way of gauging distance here. Until I saw the lights of the kibbutz it wouldn't be safe to come out.

Some of the water had splashed in my face at the first kick and I could taste it on my lips, bitter rather than salt, a flat acrid bitterness; manganese and potash. Trying to swim in it was like striking out in a vat of treacle; dark chemical treacle. The stuff was so uncannily buoyant that at waist level it was a major job even to touch bottom: you simply bobbed up like a cork. Swimming on your front simply gave you a crick in the neck and a sensation of doing push-ups. I turned on my back.

This was definitely better. It wasn't swimming. It was

more in the nature of punting, but it certainly got you along. Restful, too, after the exertion, if the stuff didn't also have the effect of seeking out every scratch and abrasion on the body. My behind came practically on fire suddenly; arms and legs meticulously flayed. I punted on, hissing with the maddening irritation, eyes on the beach. The little gleam had come closer. I could suddenly identify it as a fire, a tiny fire smoldering, occasionally flickering with flame.

I stopped, sitting in the water, and peered at it. Nobody seemed to be at it, nothing at all near it; but the Bedouin tents were black, black as the night: somebody had lit the fire.

I swore softly to myself, wriggling with the exquisite agony. Nothing to be done about it. There was certainly no getting out here. I'd have to put up with it. Maybe it would ease off when it had done its worst. I lay back and punted a bit farther out, watching the fire. Nothing moved; not a soul to be seen. But were eyes now curiously regarding me? I punted far enough out to be lost in the darkness and then turned parallel with the beach again. Could somebody be keeping pace with me there in the darkness?

I concentrated on making no disturbance, pushing very slowly, legs kept effortfully under. The fire passed. The exquisite agony passed slowly with it, leaving just an overall rawness. I punted slowly on. When you came to think of it, it was more like riding a bicycle, slowly, backward. The stars came out. I lay back, and watched them, and rode the bicycle backward, through the warm sulphurous night.

* * *

I fell into a short doze about ten o'clock, and came out of it with a jaw-snapping jerk. My head was lying gently on the water. The scroll! The scroll was all right; farther up on my head. I looked at my watch. Ten minutes past ten. It had been ten when I looked at it last. It couldn't be doing the watch a lot of good, of course. It wasn't doing me a lot of good, legs now like lumps of lightly pickled meat. I got back on the bike again and shoved off.

I'd been humming the "Eton Boating Song" when I dozed off, and I picked it up again. I hummed it to the moon. A last-quarter moon. Was it only last night I'd watched this moon with the girl farther down the shore? How much farther down the shore? No lights yet. I'd been in the water over three hours now. It didn't seem that I'd ever been anywhere else; warm, womblike. You could sit in it, lie in it, sleep in it, ride your bicycle in it . . .

Humming the "Eton Boating Song" I passed slowly along the moonlit pit of the world riding my bicycle, backward.

It was eleven o'clock when I saw the lights. There weren't many lights. They'd turned the outside ones off. There was an occasional gleam from an uncurtained window. There were other lights I couldn't understand; two or three little lights moving like fireflies on the clifftop, and others coming down the canyon. Could the Narcotics Patrol possibly have crossed the border? Could they still be after me here?

I couldn't cope with this; wasn't able to concentrate any more. I simply had to get out of here. This was understood. I turned the bicycle cumbersomely round and pedaled in. I kept on pedaling after I landed. Slow on the uptake. No more pedaling needed. Switch off motors. I switched off, turned around, faced front to the beach and stood up. The idea was to stand up. For some inscrutable reason I wasn't standing up. I was flat on my face. I tried again, observed with scholarly interest that I was still on my face, and made one of those little adjustments that scholars must learn to make. I went up the beach on my face.

The crunchy surface gave under me, covering me in the black mud. I picked up so much I had to stop altogether after a while and content myself with watching the little moving lights that had moved now down the cliff and were proceeding at a briskish pace toward me across the moonlit beach. It had struck me what these lights might be, and I began calling to them.

I kept calling till Shoshana and Avner and two or three of the other searchers had almost reached me, and only gave up then because of enfeebling waves of laughter. The professor, no doubt about it, had landed himself in the manure after all. It seemed a uniquely memorable moment. And there'd been a few to choose from, taking it on the whole, today.

4

We didn't do it at Barot. We did it at the university, in the scrollery, the two of us, with the door locked, the following day. It took us about an hour and a half to make certain, and then we just looked at each other. Agrot turned away after a moment and took another sheet of paper and studiously made out a fair copy of one paragraph. Then he read it, very carefully, and pushed it over.

"You agree?" he said.

I read it carefully, too.

"Yes, I agree," I said.

It read:

> Between the round venerable mound [Arad] and the
> long venerable mound [Barot]. From the long mound,
> one thousand cubits [half a kilometer], in the cleft be-
> tween the two pyramids at a depth of four cubits [two
> meters], the OEED.

It was there at Barot. It had been there while he set up
the cunning doings in Galilee, there while he interrogated the infiltrators, organized the intelligence missions,
scoured far and wide. There, under his nose; more accurately, under his feet. There all the time.

We looked at each other again. Agrot's nose seemed to
have become very pinched, and his mouth to have sucked
in on itself like the business end of a vacuum cleaner.

All this needed a bit of adjustment, of course.

5

"One moment, to see that I have it right," the Minister
said. There were four of us in his room, Agrot, myself
and the Head of the Department. "You're not able to
work out the position because you don't know whether
the distance should be taken from the middle of the tel or
the end, and anyway the term 'a thousand cubits' only
indicates a rough measurement."

"That's right," Agrot said.

"At the same time you believe the object is in ground at present being bulldozed by Mr. Teitleman."

"No," Agrot said. "He's already bulldozed it. That's the whole point. He's waiting to move in with his equipment the minute the standstill order runs out."

"So you're asking for an *additional* standstill order?"

"Yes."

"To excavate where?"

Agrot said heatedly, "As I'm trying to point out—"

The Head of the Department cut in swiftly. "The position, Minister, is that these pyramids—"

"Yes. I don't understand the pyramids. You say there aren't any pyramids."

"That is so, Minister. Mr. Teitleman has knocked down the pyramids. They would be pyramid-shaped structures of rock. Once the former position of the pyramids has been established the work of excavation can proceed very quickly. Unfortunately, we don't have drawings of the site as it was before it was cleared. Mr. Teitleman, of course, does have—"

"Yes. Gentlemen, I'm sorry to sound so obtuse. But would it not seem to be an idea to approach Mr. Teitleman first?"

"If Mr. Teitleman knows why we want the drawings," Agrot said, "then these are the first drawings to be lost."

There was a little pause.

"So what do you want of me?" the Minister said.

"Time," the Head of the Department said pleadingly. "Just a little time, Minister. If a point could be stretched —if the order could be extended, even for a week—"

"How? I must give grounds. You say if grounds are stated—"

"Minister!" the Head of the Department said intensely. "Don't state the grounds! It means political trouble, of course. We know this. But we'll *get* you the grounds—before he can make a song and dance. We have to get them. God will help us!"

"Quite," the Minister said. "On the other hand—"

"Minister! There is a time to take risks, for the things we believe in. Your interest in the Department—"

"Of course," the Minister said. "Of course. What I'd like you to do is leave this with me for the moment. I want to think all round it . . ."

"He's an immensely clever man. He'll do what he can," the Head of the Department said as we came out. "I know he will."

"M'hm," Agrot said.

I said, "So that's that, is it?"

Agrot looked at me. "Very far from it. The bastard naturally—I am presupposing this—has got to be made to give up the drawings. The question is, how?"

Lorries picked the work gangs up at dusk, and we watched them piling aboard. Teitleman hadn't been dragging his feet. The lagoon was now in full flood, and so was the mikveh. The lifts were in, the elegant flooring tiles were down in the foyer, and the enormous neon sign, its Hebrew letters stark against the unpolished marble, was in position: *Malon Kufra*, Hotel Camphire.

Teitleman's superintendent architect met us as we were admiring the tiles in the foyer. He shook hands without warmth.

"You asked to see me?"

"Wonderful progress you're making," Agrot said.

"Thank you. Can I be of some help?"

"Mr. Teitleman's not here, I suppose, at the moment?"

"No. He is today in his office. In Ashdod."

"Well," Agrot said more cheerfully, "in that case you can. We've lost some of our sketch plans of the old approach road to the tel. The Department would esteem it a favor if we could copy yours."

"Mr. Teitleman, of course," the architect said cautiously, "is always happy to help the Department."

"We'd be very grateful."

"When approached."

"Yes. The matter is actually so trivial, I thought we could quickly—"

"There is some question of time?" the man said.

"Not at all. No, no. It's simply—"

"Then it's not too small for Mr. Teitleman. He keeps all papers in Ashdod, at headquarters, in the drafting department."

"What I'd hoped," Agrot said, "is that there would be no need to bother—"

"From where they can be removed only on his signature. He remains in Ashdod all this week."

"I see," Agrot said.

We walked thoughtfully back in the dark.

"You know," he mused presently, "experience teaches that when such a bastard as this has you, even unknowingly, by the short and curlies, something seems to let him know. It's a sixth sense. We are going to need all our native wits."

I said, "Look, it is absolutely beyond the bounds of reason to explain—even to a man like Teitleman—the fantastic cultural—"

For the first time since all this started, Agrot seemed to

be enjoying a good laugh. "Caspar," he said, "stay in good health. Also, stay always as young as you are. Teitleman, of course, is very long on culture. But we'll see," he added.

Fourteen

A BASTARD IN ASHDOD

The pride of the Philistines.
—Zechariah 9:6

1

WE RAN DOWN first thing in the morning, and arrived
early; but not too early for Ashdod. In the old city of the
Philistines an enormous deep-water port is abuilding,
and most of Israel's Napoleons of industry have moved
in. On all sides, in the early-morning sun, their cheerful
hoardings flashed ambitious dreams of the future; and on
all sides from the sand dunes these dreams rose chaoti-
cally to fulfillment. An entire town was going up, all at
once: roads, docks, apartment blocks, shopping arcades,
office towers, hospitals, schools. Among the completed
buildings, Teitleman's was not hard to spot. It sat com-
mandingly on the corner of a large development—a
Teitleman development as each unit made clear—itself
bearing the simple but dignified legend BEIT TEITLEMAN:
The House of Teitleman. We shot up to the fourteenth
floor by express.

Teitleman's office was a big office, and there was a big
desk in it in front of a big picture window. None of this
seemed to interfere seriously with the smaller scale of

Teitleman himself. As I'd noticed before, the little bastard dominated his environment to an uncanny degree and managed to do so with the sparest of equipment. On the desk sat a single telephone, a diary and a pair of white cotton gloves. The diary was open and Teitleman was reading a scrap of paper in it as we were shown in.

"Good morning," he said. "I can give you three minutes. I have to go out."

"Well. It won't take half that," Agrot said amiably. "We've simply lost some sketches down at the tel and would like to copy yours. It's a trivial matter to bother you with—"

"So why are you?" Teitleman said unpleasantly.

Agrot took it in his stride. "We were passing," he said. "On the way to Tel Aviv. So I thought, apart from the courtesy, I would give myself the pleasure—"

"What are the sketches?"

"The lay of the land between the tel and the lagoon. That is, the way it used to be before you—" Agrot said, and checked himself slightly. "Before it was cleared," he said.

"All the land?" Teitleman said, looking down. "I thought only the old approach road." He was looking down at the scrap of paper. He had a pencil beside it in the diary. He'd jotted down our inquiry. Someone had been on the blower recently. I let out my breath very slowly.

Agrot's amiability became a shade more hard-working. "Well, that's what it is, basically," he said. "Perhaps we'll need an extra section or two here and there. I'm not sure what's missing. We'll work it out when we see yours."

Teitleman pondered for a moment. "All right. Why not?" he said. "I like to do good turns to the university.

Maybe one day it will occur to some of you to reciprocate. Let me have a note saying what you want, and we'll look it out."

"Today, perhaps?" Agrot said.

Teitleman's eyes narrowed slightly. "There's some hurry?" he said.

"Not for the information. We're packing the papers today. We leave the tel, as you know, in three days, but the paper work goes to the university this afternoon. I doubt if I'll see it again for three months, and these things drop out of mind unless attended to at once."

"Not out of mine," Teitleman said. "It's a matter of mental discipline. I can carry things in my mind for twenty years. I'm surprised you can't."

"You mean it won't be possible today?" Agrot said, his easy manner cracking slightly.

Teitleman closed the diary with a slight snap and stood up. "Today not. In a few days, perhaps. When we get on the tel," he said. "We've got work here too, you know."

Agrot's eye flickered. It flickered down to the diary. The slip of paper had moved in the draft as Teitleman closed it. It was now sticking out between the pages. He swallowed slightly.

He said, "Yes—yes, I've heard of your work here. You're doing big things, I understand."

"Big enough," Teitleman said. He picked up his gloves and moved out from behind the desk, doglike grin showing incipiently.

"To do with the harbor?" Agrot said, his eyes heavy with longing to turn the little bastard even momentarily in that direction.

"To do with the harbor," Teitleman said indulgently.

"So now I have to go. That's mine out there, the ship," he said, nodding negligently toward the window.

A solitary ship with a yellow funnel was clanking about some useful stationary task at the end of the mole.

"Which ship?" Agrot said desperately.

"Which ship? There's only one ship," Teitleman said, and turned to assure himself of the fact. "That bleddy ship."

"With the red funnel?" Agrot said hoarsely.

"Red funnel?" Teitleman said. "There's something the matter with your eyes. It's a yellow funnel—isn't it?" He turned a little longer.

Agrot palmed the paper. I watched him with stunned fascination.

"Of course yellow. I shouldn't know?" Teitleman said, turning back. "The thing cost a bleddy fortune. So. Put what you want in writing. It's the best way."

"Whatever you say," Agrot said, his hand now snugly round a specimen of Teitleman's very own.

We rode down the fourteen floors in silence together, and went out to the street. A limousine stood waiting there. Teitleman disappeared into it, without ceremony and without good-bys, in a flash of white gloves.

"Well," Agrot said, looking after the departing car, "God, after all, is good. Who else could make the bastard actually write it out for us? Come on."

We went rapidly back into Beit Teitleman.

2

An old clerk opened the inquiry window of the drafting office at Agrot's first buzz.

"Ken?"

"I want to see some plans from Barot." There was a slight huskiness in Agrot's voice. "I have a note from Mr. Teitleman."

The clerk looked at the note. "It's not signed," he said.

"Don't you know his writing?"

"I know his writing. It still isn't signed. Also this is irregular. There's a printed form for withdrawals."

"All right, call and tell him," Agrot said. "Tell him how irregular he's being. He was in a hurry. He's in his sweetest mood today."

The clerk looked at Agrot and then back at the paper. "You'd better come inside," he said.

He released the catch on the door and we went in. Several dozen men sat over drawing boards in the large room. The clerk went over to one of them with the paper. The man looked at us, rubbing his chin for a few moments, and then somewhat reluctantly picked up the phone. He looked much happier when he put it down. He came across.

"Mr. Teitleman is out," he said, "and his secretary knows nothing about this."

"Can't you just show me the files?"

"It's a difficulty," the man said cheerfully. "If you want, wait till he gets back. I can't turn over plans just like that."

Agrot's face didn't change much. He merely said, "All right. So if you wouldn't mind apologizing for me. Explain I couldn't wait and I'm very sorry. I know he's been trying to get me here for two weeks now, and he'll be upset. But, of course, rules are rules, I understand."

"Wait. Listen a minute. What rules?" the man said, the cheerfulness wiping off his face. "I'm simply thinking aloud. If he wants you so urgently, there's bound to be some way we can reason this out."

"I'm sure. If I had the time," Agrot said. "I haven't. I could only promise him a few minutes to look at his problems anyway."

"So give me a minute!" the man said indignantly. "Who's said anything yet? Are you saying you'd be looking at the plans here?"

"Where else?"

"So it's not a withdrawal. Idiot!" he said to the clerk. "There's always a reasonable solution if people will look for it," he said as, in a brace of shakes, we sat around a desk. "So what part of the project can I show you?"

We didn't speak much on the way back. Agrot's face was white and strained. But just as we ran into Jerusalem, he said levelly, "Caspar, I have dug in many places. I have dug in mountains, in valleys, in caves in the cliff and holes in the earth. I have never in my life dug through a brand-new mikveh."

"Do you think you'll be going to?"

"If necessary," Agrot said, "also through his hanging gardens, observatory, bowling alley, hydro, cinema, Turkish bath, synagogue, two ballrooms and four restaurants —and with my bare hands. But something tells me that what we need first," he said, turning sharply into Rabbi Kook Street, "is a bloody good rabbi."

3

"You have the yarmulke? Remember to put it on. Don't smoke unless somebody else does. Don't do anything unless you see somebody else doing it. And remember above all how I told you you should stay in there."

"Dumb," I said.

"Exactly. Stay dumb. If they want you to speak, they'll say so. I can't even guarantee they'll let a Gentile in."

His name was Bogeslavski. He had a white beard and a face of saintly calm, both of them masking one of the nimblest brains I'd ever encountered. He was finishing off a Russian cigarette as he spoke. He finished it off with short nervous drags, and a mere fraction of a second before the burning end could fall out of its tube onto his beard, wound down the window and flung it out.

There were six of us in the Plymouth: Bogeslavski, Agrot, myself, a lawyer, the Head of the Department, and a representative of the Ministry. A Ministry order, backed by a High Court injunction, had held Teitleman off for another week, and I'd had to postpone my own departure. Several hard-working sessions had been necessary before the present expert-bound state of affairs had come about. We were now bowling down King George V Avenue to a special meeting of the committee appointed by the Chief Rabbinate to investigate the matter of the Menorah.

The car pulled up outside Heikhal-Shelomo, the Supreme Religious Center, and we got out. I paused a moment to adjust the yarmulke on my head and looked up at the inscription over the entrance. "And they shall judge the people with righteous judgment," it said.

H'm. Well, their chance had come.

The committee was not yet in session; but Teitleman and a small pack of his advisers were. The little bastard's teeth and spectacles were flashing with some vivacity as we entered the room. His eye flickered at me, but he made no comment, and not long afterwards the committee members came in and the chairman declared the session open.

A small red-bearded man from Teitleman's ranks, evidently the rabbi to present his case, immediately objected to my presence. Bogeslavski got up and said his piece, and the committee of rabbis quietly conferred. The mild brown eyes of the chairman were on me as he listened, and he played with his beard. From it he said presently that the objection was overruled, and cited three precedents from the Talmud.

Bogeslavski showed no particular emotion. He merely got up and presented his opening case. He did it quietly and factually, and the only thing he underlined with any emphasis was the degree of reliability that could be placed in the scroll. The further copies of it had been found where they had been said to be. Blue marble was found where it had been said to be. And so had the so-called pyramids. If the scroll was right on all these matters, was it likely to be wrong on the most important of all?

"Nu," he murmured, blowing his nose as he sat down, "so we'll hear what they've got to say."

Teitleman's rabbi had plenty to say. He said he would first of all like to draw the committee's attention to the underhand, almost childish way in which this matter had been brought to light. It was typical of people who had nothing to lose to try to make trouble for those who had a great deal to lose. The latter class of people were always susceptible. In the land of Israel those who might with truth be called the Builders of Zion were peculiarly susceptible. Every inch of the land was holy. Every inch of the land bore traces of the holy past. Should the builder be stopped from building on this account? Certainly not. It was a duty, it was even a *religious* duty, to build up the land. So was it possible to reconcile the activities of those who built for the future with those whose task it was to look into the past?

Yes, the little red-bearded rabbi said, calmly answering his own question, such a reconciliation was possible. The legislators of the State of Israel had made it. In no country of the world had the archaeologist such encouragement, such protection as in Israel. Standstill orders without number had been issued at the request of the archaeologist. Mr. Teitleman himself—he was pleased to speak for Mr. Teitleman in this matter—had halted his work on many occasions to comply with such a request; and with the greatest willingness and interest. Mr. Teitleman—he did not have to tell the committee—was a religious Jew of the highest principles, to whom the welfare of Judaism, the Jewish people, and the State of Israel were the chief goals in life.

But what was the position when a standstill order came to an end? The position was that the archaeologist moved out and the builder moved in. And once in, nobody could stop him again. A moment's reflection would show the committee that this must necessarily be so. Enormous sums of capital had to be sunk in a modern building. If a builder were uncertain whether he might be asked to pause again, tomorrow, next week, next month, who would build at all? In any event, this was the law. It was all he really wished to say. There was no case to answer and nothing to be looked into.

However, in view of the circumstances, perhaps he would say a few things more, and the first was that he would totally agree with the revered Rabbi Bogeslavski that the scrolls were of profound interest. They were a part of Israel's heritage. They shed light on the past. Many other scrolls had been found that shed light on the past, some of them, even, "treasure scrolls." Many had mentioned geographical locations that could still be found—caves, hills, springs—exactly as they were. Why not? These things didn't move themselves. It was to be expected. But in no single case had any treasure been found. And this was to be expected, too. "Buried treasure," alas, did not long remain buried—it was childish to expect otherwise.

The second thing was about *this* piece of buried treasure. What was it? An OEED, they had heard. The members of the committee were wise men, but had they ever heard of an OEED? The claim was made that it was a piece of Temple property. And so it might be. Many of the items mentioned in other scrolls had been pieces of Temple property. All that could be said about this one was that if it still existed it could bear no resemblance to whatever it had once been.

His friend Mr. Teitleman, as a matter of academic interest, had supplied some figures relating to the weight of the building now on the spot. It ran to some hundreds of thousands of metric tonnes. If it were claimed—he understood it *was* claimed—that the article was of gold, it would now be a single sheet of gold leaf; a mixture of gold leaf and marble aggregate. As such it could no longer be considered to have the intrinsic properties of the original article, for it no longer was that article. Its value was in terms of gold leaf only. One would then have the unusual task of calculating whether it was worth tearing down a building that cost several million dollars to extract a few kilograms of gold leaf that might lie underneath it.

This amusing problem—he would like to stress this—was not indeed one for the committee. It was not even one for Mr. Teitleman. Mr. Teitleman, of course, was a very big businessman. But big businessmen did not own their businesses. If Mr. Teitleman should temporarily take leave of his senses—which God forbid!—and wish to indulge in such a harebrained scheme, he could not write out a note saying "Go and do it." Mr. Teitleman was responsible to his stockholders, many of them in America. He had heard some cloudy rumors that the government could be induced to pay. But Mr. Teitleman's unhappy experience was that the government rarely paid what it said it would pay and in any event had no conception of business expenses, loss of trade and so forth. Even in joke—and he must apologize for laughing now—did the committee think it advisable to consider jeopardizing the much-needed investments made by American citizens in Israel's economy?

He sat down still chuckling, and there was a rumble of appreciative laughter from his corner. Teitleman's own dog-like teeth were bared in a smile as he patted his little advocate's knee. He'd found, no doubt about it, a spry enough brain himself. I listened somewhat glumly as the evidence was called.

Agrot and I gave our views on the scroll and on the interpretation of the OEED. With regard to site identifications these had been very few and very ambiguous in the case of the only other actual treasure scroll. It wasn't so much that no treasure had ever been found as that it hadn't been found *yet*. And nearly all of the sites had been in highly populated areas.

Lionel Davidson

With regard to weights and pressures, the Menorah
had been covered by marble slabs, no doubt resting on
other rocks to protect the Menorah. So long as the building was properly constructed, there was no question of its
full weight falling on the one spot. Without knowing the
structure of the protecting slabs it was impossible to say
whether they would have cracked under pressure or
whether they would still be doing the job that the surrounding rocks were doing: safely supporting Teitleman's
building.

In any event it wouldn't be necessary to tear the building down. The mikveh, certainly, would have to come up,
since it appeared to be directly over the Menorah; but so
long as the building was properly constructed, little major
reinforcement would be required. And the question of
expense, however considerable—the lawyer frowned as
the Head of the Department mentioned this dangerous
point—was not one for this committee, which had simply
to consider the weight of the experts' case.

Then the evidence was over, and the opposing rabbis,
in reverse order, gave their closing addresses.

Teitleman's little advocate had been nodding humorously as the experts said their pieces, and he did some
handkerchief play at hiding a whimsical smile as he got to
his feet again.

He'd found it all absorbing, he said, deeply absorbing.
Who didn't love to hear scholars talk? It was a privilege
and God had to be thanked for sparing them to see in
one room so many learned men of Israel. But God in his
wisdom had given scholars scholars' brains. They should
use them for scholarship and not for political adventur-
ism or for meddling in business affairs. Scholars were
soon out of their depth in such matters.

They had been told that they should not consider expense. Of course! Scholars very rarely did. But why else were they here? If one wished to go and dig a hole in the middle of the Negev, would a council of rabbis need to sit and deliberate? What was being asked here was something more serious—and more farcical. What was being asked here was whether one could go and dig himself a hole under Mr. Teitleman's hotel—in the hopes of finding buried treasure!

Had Mr. Teitleman not been blessed with such a keen sense of humor he would be very indignant at this piece of tomfoolery. What!—it was being calmly asked whether it would be proper to rob the citizens of America to further some madcap scheme that had already led its proponents, with a disregard for frontiers and the safety of those who lived on frontiers, to endanger the security of the State itself? He didn't want to say too much about this—the committee would draw its own conclusions. But it was typical of the recklessness of the other side, of their lack of balance, their inability to see anything but their own narrow viewpoint.

As for the evidence, he had nothing serious to add except, he said, hiding his mouth again with the handkerchief, except perhaps just one thing: let one of these enthusiasts find himself some rocks, and upon the rocks place a marble slab, and under the slab place himself, and invite Mr. Teitleman to build—

He sat down, throwing himself helplessly about, with a number of small apologetic bobs to the committee for his inability to continue. The committee seemed to be surreptitiously sharing his amusement. He'd certainly given value, and with increasing gloom I saw Bogeslavski get to his feet. He hadn't smiled, he hadn't frowned, he'd simply looked more and more depressed as the confident little joker had kept flashing the bill. If he was going to do anything it was high time for him now to look lively. Bogeslavski didn't look lively. He looked simply confused and dispirited, and also a lot older than when he'd come in.

For a few moments he shuffled halfheartedly from one foot to the other without actually saying anything, and when he did get off, it was to a couple of false starts.

He said a bit desperately, "Of course, it's one thing to joke . . . I've produced *evidence*—these are not children—I must beg the committee to remember they are experts, scholars . . ."

I shifted in my seat, and felt Agrot shifting in his. It occurred to me to wonder if somebody hadn't been nobbling Bogeslavski. His little red-bearded opponent had just successfully made the point that experts and scholars *were* children, and now here he was . . . I looked at him sharply, and noticed that the committee were looking at him sharply, too. He was floundering about, patently trying to organize some kind of argument.

"If the rebbe would like a few minutes to collect himself," the chairman suggested mildly across the table.

"No. Thank you. That is," Bogeslavski said, licking his lips. "I have to confess I'm in a difficulty—"

He dropped his hands to his sides suddenly and stood there a bit helplessly. "I have sat here," he said simply, "and listened to this calculation, that calculation, engineering assessments, financial assessments, jokes, more jokes . . . What are we joking about? What is it we see fit to sit and joke about?"

He blinked a bit glazedly around the room. "When they came and told me that the possibility existed, that by some miracle of God's grace, the holy Menorah was still in Eretz Yisroel, I trembled. I said a *shechayanu* . . . If we here were Jews in the exile, a hundred, five hundred, a thousand years ago, living in the most dire poverty, in the most grinding oppression, and from out of the blackness this ray of light had appeared, a suspicion, just the suspicion . . . could anything have prevented us from selling, bartering, borrowing, begging—*everything*—everything that we had or might hope to have, to beseech the authorities . . ."

He got his handkerchief out and dazedly wiped his head. He said in a kind of quiet frenzy, "Gentlemen—God has made a greater miracle! He has brought us back. He has given to us our own again. Here we do not have to beseech. We do not have to beg. We can . . ."

His voice had been rising, and his eye, wandering about the room, suddenly fell on little Teitleman. " 'Give unto Him what is His,' " he said firmly. " 'Seeing that thou and what thou hast are His.' "

Then his eye fell on his red-bearded opponent, and he said, "Be exceedingly lowly of spirit since the hope of man is but the worm. And from the same source, the *Pirke Abot,*" he said, his glowing saintly face now on the committee, "we may read, 'It is not thy duty to complete the work, but neither art thou free to desist from it.' We are not free. We are never free. What does the blessed Akiba tell us? Rabbi Akiba says, 'Everything is given on a pledge, and a net is spread for all the living: the shop is open; and the dealer gives credit; and the ledger lies open; and the hand writes . . .' *And the hand writes,*" Bogeslavski repeated very softly, nodding to himself.

He could have repeated it a lot more softly still. He had the room's undivided attention as he stood there, raptly communing with himself. From out of his communion, he said with quiet intensity, "If on good authority I hear that in the earth of Israel the possibility exists that there might be a trace, an *atom of dust,* of the holy Menorah, and that it will cost me one million, a hundred million, a thousand million to get at it—*with my bare hands* —will a rabbi say something to stop me? Can there be enough money in the world? Is it possible—" he said, but didn't finish. He simply looked wonderingly around the room, and walked out of it, very slowly and very bent.

In the deathly silence that followed, a couple of the committee members cleared their throats. The chairman cleared his. He somewhat gruffly asked the red-bearded rabbi if he wished to say anything further. He said he didn't. The chairman said they would announce the result of their deliberations later, and in an awkward flutter the room began to clear. A couple of minutes later we were walking back to the Plymouth. Bogeslavski was sitting in it, smoking a Russian cigarette. Nobody congratulated him. Nobody said anything much. A seemly silence seemed indicated. We sat and waited in it for the lawyer, who'd popped over for a quick word with the other side.

He was back shortly, grinning, and showing none of our reserve in the matter of the rabbi's feelings. He patted him affectionately on the knee.

"Rebbe," he said, "promise me one thing. If I should ever God forbid find myself at the wrong side of the dock, you'll be there to plead for me."

"So what's the news?" Agrot said.

"They've had such a fright thrown in them they don't know whether they're coming or going. I think we're home," he said.

There was a general sort of sigh in the car; and in the

middle of it, a little squeak. It was the window being wound down. "Well," Bogeslavski said, tossing ash out of it, *"mann tracht, Gott lacht,"* which may be interpreted as "man proposes, God disposes." "We'll see," he said, as the car took off.

Fifteen

An End Is Come

> *Behold, it is come.*
> —Ezekiel 7:6

1

I COULDN'T BEAR to be at Barot, and Jerusalem wasn't much better. There was no living with Agrot at all, and he commuted between the two like a cat on hot bricks. I'd already overstayed my time by a week, but I couldn't tear myself away. And when I tried to think of all the things I should be doing elsewhere, I couldn't do that either.

The rabbinical meeting had been on a Monday, and on the Wednesday Uri turned up from London on a mission feverishly proposed by Agrot and approved by the Department. Uri brought with him a personal tape-recorded message from the Bogoritze Rebbe in London. The Bogoritze community, a small sect so intensely devout that they considered the British chief rabbinate a crypto-Gentile institution, was noted for its patronage of works concerning the mystical tradition in Judaism, and also for its comfortable financial position. The message from its rabbi was intended solely for the ear of the chairman of the rabbinical committee. We sat and listened to it a couple of times in the Rehavia flat. The piety came through very strong.

"He doesn't actually mention any money," Agrot said.

"Can't you hear the promise in his voice?"

"I suppose they've really got some?"

"You and I," Uri said, "should have what they've got. They've got half Stamford Hill. Unfortunately they haven't got it to hand—they're in deep at the moment with a big new yeshiva outside Epping. But who has to know? Play it again. I like that old bastard's tremolo."

We played it again. We played it several times, with varying degrees of hilarity and enthusiasm, while we had dinner and finished off the arrack. By the time I left with Uri, Agrot had worked himself into a state of total conviction in the Bogoritze Rebbe's powers of advocacy.

"So," Uri said, as we walked back to the King David, "you've had times here, eh? It was always my view we could make a man of you. When I've finished at the rabbinate tomorrow, take me to Barot. Maybe we'll still see your trousers keeping the flag flying in Jordan."

But I didn't go with him to Barot. I went to Tel Aviv. I'd not seen her for a week—she'd gone back to the military—but she'd phoned to say she was mortgaging some future leave to take a long weekend. Shimshon, unfortunately, also was having a weekend; but not till Friday. I went down on Thursday.

The bad-minded Mr. Benyamini was providentially elsewhere, so we slipped in unobserved, and spent the afternoon in Shimshon's bed, the eye of God prudently covered with a prayer shawl.

"I suppose this is wrong," she said.

"Do you think so, love?"

"But it doesn't *feel* wrong," she said curiously, drawing one silver-painted nail down my chest.

"That's all right, then."

"I mean, I'm not promiscuous. You know that."

"Of course I do."

"And it doesn't alter anything with Shimshon."

She was leaning studiously over me, au naturel, and mention of the absent behemoth seemed somehow improper in the circumstances.

"Do you know why Shimshon is coming?" she said with a secret little smile.

"No. Why?" They did seem to be letting him off rather a lot, I thought censoriously.

"We will be engaged, officially. I wanted it, suddenly."

"Well. I hope you'll be very happy."

"We will. I know it. I love him truly."

This line of talk didn't really seem to be getting us anywhere, so I put her lieutenant's cap on her head, and was roused by it suddenly to mad excesses. We retired for a while.

Uri was going back in the evening, so I rang him at the airport.

"Well, I honestly think everything is going well, love. They were impressed about the Bogoritze, and also by the fact that the Diplomatic were in some way involved. There were one or two snide comments about that."

"Is that bad?"

"No, it's good. There could be some small repercussions, but there are heaps of ways the Bogoritze could have heard, as well as from us. And I didn't have to be coming just for this. In the wider field, it's helpful. The more people who know, in a quiet way, the less danger there is of any little—you know."

"Did you get any idea when they're likely to decide?"

"Not before Shabat, anyway. Sunday would be the earliest. When are you coming back?"

"Well. They might want some further word from me," I said weakly.

"I understand. So, keep out of trouble. Shalom."

"Shalom."

She was waiting outside the telephone booth.

"We've won?" she said, seeing my face.

I hastily adjusted it. "Not yet," I said. It didn't do to court Providence, of course.

The old buffer didn't recognize me without the *shtreiml,* so I went next door and put it on.

"Hello, *bocher!*" he said delightedly. "So you made your studies with regard to the Mishmar Zin?"

"Yes, thanks," I said.

"Strangely enough, this week also we read of a mysterious place."

The weeks had rolled on. Four weeks after *Vayishlach,* and the Pentateuchal portion was *Vay'chi,* the forty-eighth chapter of Genesis to the end.

"In *Vay'chi* what do we find? Jacob is taking farewell of his sons. For Judah he prophesies everything. 'The scepter shall not depart from Judah,' he says, 'nor a lawgiver from between his feet, till men come to Shiloh.' *Ad kee-yavoh Shiloh.* What does it mean? The Christians, of course, read it 'Until Shiloh come,' and see a messianic reference. Rashi, Onkelos, Saadyeh, many others, also see such a reference. And the Targum, as we know, reads Shiloh as *Shaleh*—the poetical Peace. However, another school sees it as the actual physical place, Shiloh. So we must ask—"

"Idiot, leave off!" his wife said, coming into the room at that moment. "Excuse him. He lives only for the synagogue. So you're quite recovered now?" she said, smiling at me, and blinking only fractionally at the *shtreiml.*

"Yes, thanks."

"And you've heard the news with our Shana?"

"Yes. Yes. I was delighted."

"It's not unexpected, of course. He is a good man. He doesn't speak very much, maybe . . ."

"We won't be eating in tonight," Shoshana said, coming rapidly in. She'd been in the kitchen and the walls were thin.

"You won't—but, sweetheart, we looked forward—"

"The professor has studies in town and wishes me to assist him. We may have to say all night—"

"Stay studying *all night*?"

"Didn't you think, Professor?"

"Well. It's possible," I said. "That is; if it's not putting you—"

"Not at all. My parents understand. Study must come before pleasure."

"Study *is* pleasure," the old nut said, seizing on a familiar word.

"Of course," Shoshana said. "I'm ready now."

We went to the Sheraton, and studied all night.

2

The engagement party was on Friday night, so that Miriam and Avner could get pre-Shabat transport from Ein

Gedi. Shimshon had brought a friend, another strapping red-beret. The friend was very jolly, and Shimshon, now free of his smoldering tension, was much improved himself. He even cracked the odd joke about my drinking too much as the sacramental and later the celebratory champagne-type "President" wine went round the table. He sat with his arm round Shoshana and actually came up with a couple of well-chosen phrases from Proverbs in response to her brother's toast.

" 'A virtuous woman,' " Shimshon said, blushing slightly but giving her a squeeze, " 'who can find? For her price is far above rubies.' "

. "Hear hear," I said.

And Avner repeated it, raising his glass to cover a certain death-ray type glower beaming my way from Miriam.

The old man, excited by this reasonable talk that had sprung up, produced several more apt quotations himself, and as the festivity proceeded, and several simultaneous conversations with it, appeared to have found his way back to *Vay'chi.*

" 'A lawgiver from between his feet.' What can we read in this? Also 'The sceptre shall not depart from Judah.' Now Ibn Ezra takes the view . . ."

"So in the end, tell me, what happened? Did you do it through your embassy—the legal department?"

"We used to wonder—who is he writing to? He sits by himself for hours, writing, writing. And when the mail comes, who's there first? Now I see he wasn't wasting his time, the dog. These quiet ones . . ."

"Take a biscuit with the wine, Professor. Who can just drink without eating? Look at her—she's happy!"

"Similarly, if we regard it as a ruler's staff, some emblem of kingship, we're in the same difficulties. He's already mentioned the sceptre. So it is something mystical, some holy thing that Judah has between his feet . . ."

"All I can say, the fellow is very lucky. Myself, I wouldn't have rested. These swine with their big cars—I wouldn't have minded what it cost. I'd have got the biggest lawyer in town—Trouble, trouble, all right, it's trouble. For something like that I'd go to the trouble. I'm surprised your embassy didn't advise . . ."

"A long way from Ein Gedi! I say it's a long way—You haven't forgotten what it's like there? And the Cave of Shulamit—you remember that, eh? Eh? Ha-ha. Eh? Here's to the Cave of Shulamit. I say here's to—and you, of course. Your continuing good health. You should always have the strength . . ."

"So we have to ask ourselves, if not the Messiah, then some object, some holy object? And thus, if we take it in conjunction with Shiloh as *Shaleh*, Peace, we are left with the question—what is it that Judah will give up when Peace . . ."

It was a nice party, and nobody got drunk.

I slept by myself that night at the Sheraton.

Everybody left when Shabat was out on Saturday night, and Shoshana left, too. She came to stay with me at the Sheraton.

"Did you remember to telephone your unit?" I said.

"Yes, I did it."

"What did you tell them?"

"That I had to stay in bed."

"Quite right," I said. We were both there, with another

bottle of President. There was her new status to be celebrated.

Sunday was a terrible day. I tried to ring Agrot and couldn't get him, so I rang a few others instead, and finally got the lawyer. He said yes, he understood the decision was going to be given today. He was holding himself in readiness to go to Heikhal-Shelomo. No, he didn't think I could do any good. But he didn't think I would do any harm, either, so I went.

We took the *shtreiml* with us, and dropped it at the doctor's, in a big polythene bag, with many thanks. And then we tooled around and tried to find Agrot. We couldn't find him anywhere, and I couldn't get into Heikhal-Shelomo, so in the evening we went back to Tel Aviv, and walked into the Sheraton and found him there. He was sitting hunched over a glass of brandy and it only needed one look to see what the decision was.

He'd taken notes of it, and he unfolded them from his breast pocket and handed them over. There were two sheets, and the first read:

> The verdict is that the likelihood of anything of a sacred character—all that we are asked to determine—lying under the building works, now in an advanced stage of completion at Barot, must be considered to be remote. A minority opinion holds that the evidence is strong that a work of a sacred character was deposited there and that remains of it might still be found. The unanimous opinion is that these remains, if any, could not be considered to have the sacred character of the original work, and that such a sacred character could only attach to the work as a work and not to the material from which it was fabricated.

"Oh, Jesus Christ, I'm sorry."

"Turn over," Agrot said. "It's an insurance policy."

I turned over. The other sheet read:

> However, the committee thinks it proper to advise those responsible for the building works that a certificate of Kashrut for the catering will only be issued on the understanding that a certain mikveh in the premises is relocated, and it commends to the directors the suggestion that a proper use for the site might well be as a library for works of a devotional character or as a Bet ha-Midrash or study hall.

I'd been inhaling deeply and I let the smoke out.

"Teitleman, of course," I said, "will have a lot of use for a devotional library and a Bet ha-Midrash."

"You never know," Agrot said wearily. "I'd hazard the guess there might be a rabbinical element among the guests at the Camphire for some years to come. Special guests. Real guests. Also he's taking an increasing interest in religious affairs, is Teitleman. Another item came my way today—totally unrelated. It seems he's going to build a low-rent housing development for religious youths. A nonprofit-making development, to be administered by the rabbinate. He seems to think if he doesn't run into any unexpected expense he can raise the starting capital free of interest."

A bottle of President didn't seem indicated that night. There wasn't anything much to celebrate. I felt sad and I drank fruity Stock instead.

"Never mind. If it's there, nobody at least can take it now."

"True."

"And it's certainly been there a long time."

"Also true."

"Do you think it will ever be found?"

"Do you think there'll ever be a state of poetical peace?" I said.

"A state of what?"

"Poetical peace."

"I think," she said, moving the bottle farther from me, "we should change the subject. On our last night."

We changed the subject.

Afterwards she said, "I don't know what's the matter with me. I know this is terrible. But it just doesn't *seem* terrible." She was wonderingly tracing grooves with her silver fingernails again. "It doesn't seem to have anything to do with Shimshon. It doesn't seem to have anything to do with anybody, except you and me. It's—private, isn't it?"

"Well. Yes," I said.

"And you don't think it's wrong?"

I did. It seemed to me without any question wrong. But a lot of wrongness was in the air tonight. And Almogi didn't seem capable of the grosser kinds.

"Not terribly," I said.

"It's been nice, hasn't it?"

"Lovely."

"Will I see you again, Caspar?"

"Of course you will."

"But there can't be any more of this."

"Can't there?"

"Oh, no," she said, nodding seriously.

All of a sudden I was smiling at her, this gift of God. But I was thinking of something else. I was thinking that

Shimshon in the course of time would be thinking that somebody had short-changed him. I translated this one for her.

She said, "I don't think it's very nice to talk about this."

"All right."

"But if it worries you, there's judo."

"Judo?"

"Judo. It's energetic."

"Oh. Ah."

"What are you smiling at?"

"You."

"Because I'll marry Shimshon and you'll go away?" But she was smiling herself, a sad little smile.

"No. Because I love you."

"Do you think you do?"

"I think I do."

"Then I think I love you, too," she said. She was smiling at me from her pillow. I smiled at her from mine. "Now tell me what you truly think."

"I think we're sojourners, love."

"What does that mean?"

"It means we sojourn. We're transients. We're on the move. It's not to be taken seriously, most of it. But it can be nice."

"Nothing is serious?"

"Oh, yes. Sometimes in the rush somebody manages to leave a meaningful memento. Not very often, but sometimes."

"Aren't we talking about love?"

"We're talking about all sorts of things. We're talking a hell of a lot, aren't we?"

"Yes. Let's go to sleep now."

"In a bit," I said, adoring her again suddenly.

I said good-by to her in the morning. I paid the bill. I got a standby booking on a Caravelle to Brussels. Then, feeling more of a sojourner than ever, I got the hell out of it to Lod. I'd had a word with Agrot on the blower, and he was there at the airport. His wife was there, too. "Well, we'd better see if you're actually going," he said, after we'd made glum conversation for a while. He went off to look into it.

"So now you're off to quieter haunts," Tanya said.

"In a way."

"Of course! Your new appointment. I hear Silberstein got all the books for you."

"Yes." Uri had been full of tidings.

"Oh, every kind of good wish. It sounds wonderful, marvelous, a really stimulating challenge. I expect you're sorry you wasted your time here now. All the sound and fury and nothing came out of it."

"Well, I don't know," I said. "We know where it is. One day perhaps—"

"A long way ahead."

"It's always a long way to Shiloh."

"A long way to where?"

"All right. Come on. They can take you," Agrot said, hurrying back. "You'll have to be quick. Hurry now. Shalom. Shalom."

"Shalom," Tanya said, kissing me.

"Shalom."

"Shalom-Shalom."

And I was off; and an hour or so later, in that curious way of jet travel, in which the recent past slips away faster

297

even than the flowing geography below, could already feel it behind me, far far behind, in another time; with all the encapsulated figures in it still going about their evolutions: Himmelwasser and Teitleman and bad-minded Mr. Benyamini and red-eyed Shimshon . . .

I was already engaged with the future, that stimulating future spoken of in the long-ago by Tanya. There was the University of Beds. There was Lady Longlegs. There were challenges aplenty till Shiloh come. This satisfying thought was presently reinforced by another, which brought a warm and comforting glow as the Caravelle buzzed along. Shiloh, after all, might not be so far ahead. In a world of transience, the works of Teitleman were more transient than most.